A Step Too Far

A STEP TOO FAR

A novel by Will Cordes

iUniverse, Inc.

New York Lincoln Shanghai

A Step Too Far

iUniverse, Inc.

For information address:
iUniverse, Inc.
2021 Pine Lake Road, Suite 100
Lincoln, NE 68512
www.iuniverse.com

ISBN: 0-595-27871-X

Printed in the United States of America

"Life being what it is, one dreams of revenge."

—*Gauguin*

ACKNOWLEDGEMENT

The characters in *A Step Too Far* are entirely fictional, and any person who might pretend to identify with one of them is mistaken. I've never known—or even met—a character like Natalie Weinburg, and I'm not familiar with the workings of the Park County (Montana) Sheriff's Office or the Springfield (Massachusetts) Police Department. My experiences as an agent with the Montana Department of Justice are not reflected in this story, either, although certain procedural aspects of DOJ investigations—as defined by Montana law—are mentioned.

Global Support Group—or GSG, as it is called throughout the story—is a purely fictional entity, and it should not be compared to any legitimate enterprise engaged in the same types of endeavors.

The location of The Manor is fictitious, and I'm not aware of any property within the area described that might be confused with it. Although I've traveled through the valley there, I have no particular knowledge of any acreage beyond the pavement edges of U. S. Highway 89.

If I am guilty of taking liberties, it's with the first names of some of my characters, and I chose to use those of many of my friends and associates. Since no name was repeated unnecessarily, I guess my choices were workable.

As for the basic idea of the story—based upon almost three decades of law enforcement experience, I've found that the bonds formed between pets and their owners can be stronger than anyone might imagine. Todd's dog, Honey, bears the name of my first bulldog, and, although she lived a full life, her final resting place is far from my Montana home. I hope the dogwood tree I planted above her grave is flourishing.

CHAPTER 1

───────────── ▼ ─────────────

"You mean this was all over a dog?" Todd Milton asked incredulously.

The hospital emergency room in Missoula, Montana was never particularly busy on a weeknight—especially at 2 a.m., but Todd could see nurses struggling with three gurneys in the entrance bay, and he knew there were two more victims in the operating rooms. A busy night for both the hospital and state law enforcement.

As a resident agent with Montana's Criminal Investigation Bureau—or CIB, for short, Todd had been called to assist the local sheriff's office after one of their own had been wounded. The initial call had been reported as a neighbor dispute, but the incident had deteriorated quickly, and the responding deputy had found himself in the middle of a gun battle in progress as soon as he'd arrived.

Help calls had gone out. The sheriff's SWAT team had been notified. Two hours later, a man and his wife were dead, and five people—including the first responding deputy—were clinging to life. And it was all over a dog.

"That's what I said," Shirley O'Bryan replied. "Them Kinley kids let their dog loose again, and it got down inta our lambs. I told Sammy the dog wouldn't kill 'em, but he said they'd die a fright from runnin' from him. Two of 'em did, too, so I guess Sammy was right—for once in his fool life."

"Where's your husband, Mrs. O'Bryan?" Todd asked, noting that the bandage on her forearm was soaked with blood.

"Out with some whore at the truck stop, I s'pose," Shirley said with a sigh. "I guess he won't know his sister and brother-in-law are dead 'til he sobers up come Sunday."

"So, Sammy shot the dog, then?"

"I tried to tell him, but he was too pigheaded," said Shirley. "I know those Kinleys was fond a that dog. He wasn't a mean one, neither. Just a goofy kinda hound, I guess you'd say.

"Sammy got his shotgun, and he fired both barrels. Got the dog with the first shot, so I don't know why he shot twice. Hit one a the ewes with the second shot, the damn fool. I told Kate not to take up with him, but you know how young people can be."

"Did you see Kate and Sammy get shot?" asked Todd, waving at a nurse to get some attention for Shirley's arm.

"I guess I saw most all of it," Shirley said with a nod, taking a deep breath through her nostrils. "Sammy broke open his gun while them Kinley kids was runnin' up to the fence. The dog wasn't completely dead, just then, but you know how animals is. They don't really know when they're dead, themselves.

"Anyhow, the dog was yelpin' and kickin', and them kids ran down to our fence line. Pretty close to it, anyway. I never seen Abel Kinley, at first, their cabin bein' dark and all. Abel's an outfitter durin' the season, though, and I've seen him with guns quite a bit. I guess he's good with 'em. He's got lots a horns on his barn wall.

"When Abel came down to the fence, I seen him with a gun, so I went back in the trailer and called 9-1-1. The woman who answered was askin' all kinda questions, so I took the phone out to the front yard, so's I could see. I told her Abel was arguin' with Sammy, and I could see Kate tryin' to get Sammy to go back to their place—their doublewide's in the grove a cottonwoods right below us, y'know.

"I think Abel just wanted to get his dog back—dead or not. The kids was screamin' and leanin' on the fence, and the dog was lyin' down near the stock tank, but Sammy was cussin' like a sailor boy. He wasn't about to let them Kinleys on our place, even though he's really just a renter—*was* just a renter, I should say, damn him to hell."

"How long were you on the phone with the 9-1-1 operator?" Todd asked, trying to get Shirley back on track. A nurse had arrived to check her bandages, but the wounded woman paid the LPN no mind.

"I never did hang up, as I recall. That phone's still out in the grass somewheres, but I sure didn't hang it up. I guess the battery'll go dead, wouldn't you think?

"Anyway, I was still talkin' to the 9-1-1 girl when Sammy reached in his pocket an' tried to put some more shells in his shotgun, and that's when Abel Kinley drew down on him—ain't that how you say it? Drew down?"

"That's fine, Shirley, but do you remember what was said?"

"Abel told Sammy to put the gun down, 'cause Abel's kids was all right there at the fence, but Sammy wasn't listenin' to reason, right about then. Sammy just started cussin' without really sayin' anything but the cussin', if you know what I mean. Lots of 'fucks' an' 'sons a bitches' an' stuff like that.

"Sammy went to wavin' his shotgun, too, and I guess he kinda pointed it at Abel's kids, 'cause Abel shot him in the guts with his huntin' rifle."

"So, Abel shot Sammy?"

"Oh, yeah. Sammy kinda gave his guts a look-see, then he sorta twisted a bit, too."

"Did Abel shoot the deputy?"

"Heck, no," Shirley replied, shaking her head briskly and giving Todd an open-mouthed stare. "Charlie Cox went runnin' up there right when all the shoutin' was goin' on. He got shot when Sammy spun back around with a bullet in his belly. Sammy shot Charlie."

"So...who shot Kate?" Todd asked, checking his micro-recorder. Still plenty of tape left.

"Sammy," Shirley said matter-of-factly. "I think Charlie and Kate was shot with the same load."

"Then who shot you?" asked Todd, glancing over the nurse at Shirley's still bleeding arm.

"Sammy got me an' Marvin both," said Shirley, nodding toward her stepson, who was on the gurney next to her. "He had one more load in that gun a his, and he let loose while he was floppin' on the ground like a trout."

"So, how'd the two Kinley girls get hit?" Todd asked, rubbing at the stubble on his chin. The late night call-out hadn't given him time to shave.

"Charlie was shootin' in that direction. You'll have to ask him."

Todd took another look down the hallway toward the operating rooms. Charlie Cox was in one of them, with at least three buckshot pellets in his groin, and Nancy Kinley was in the other, paralyzed from the chest down with what would turn out to be a 9mm slug against her spine. Only Wanda Kinley was well enough to talk, and she had holes through both her legs.

"Sit tight, Shirley," said Todd. "I'll get back to you."

"I'll be here," Shirley replied, turning her attention to Marvin. "Unless they let me out for a smoke."

It took Todd a minute to get down the hall to Wanda Kinley's gurney, and another minute to wait for a nurse to check the girl's blood pressure. With no bullets to remove and no major arteries punctured, Wanda seemed to be in pretty good shape for a multiple gunshot victim.

"Wanda, I'm Todd Milton, the state agent here in Missoula," he said in way of an introduction.

"Yeah," the fourteen-year-old replied. "I seen you on TV a couple a times."

"How do your legs feel?"

"They hurt some, when I move 'em, but there's somethin' in that bottle for the pain," she replied, tilting her head back at the IV drip.

"Do you feel like talking with me for a few minutes?" Todd asked, pulling a chair close to the gurney.

"Sure."

"What do you remember about tonight?"

"It was Nancy who let the dog out," Wanda lied, betrayed by her averted gaze. "I tried to stop it, but the dog always goes down to Shirley's when the lambs is out. He done it last year, too, but he didn't bite none of 'em."

"Did you try to catch the dog?"

"I sure did, but he got through a hole under the fence. That's what got all them sheep to cryin'. Blue don't never bark, y'know."

"Did you see Mr. McGill shoot the dog?"

"I was right there," Wanda said with a nod. "I seen every bit of it. Sammy shot Blue without so much as a 'shoo dog' or nothin'. It was the meanest thing I ever did see."

"Did you see Mr. McGill get shot?" Todd asked, raising his eyebrows.

Wanda paused for a moment, and she pulled at the collar of her hospital gown. She let her tongue trace the edge of her dry upper lip, and she craned her head to look down the hallway. Only a male nurse at the emergency room station could be seen.

"They cut off my jeans—and my panties, too," Wanda said absently, without turning back to Todd. "I think that fella down there seen my privates when they put this here dress thing on me."

"He's a nurse, Wanda," Todd said, trying to sound reassuring. "It's part of his job."

"Is it his job to blab about my rose tattoo?" Wanda shot back with an angry stare. "It's right on top a my pussy. I had to shave the spot on purpose so the tattoo guy could put it there. You can't see the rose without seein' my pussy, too."

"Wanda, we really need to get back to what I was asking you about," Todd said with a sigh. "Did you see Mr. McGill get shot?"

"Daddy done it," Wanda replied dejectedly. "But he did tell Sammy to put his gun down first. That Sammy's crazy, y'know. An' he was really liquored up, too, like he is just about any night, I guess."

"Who shot you, Wanda?"

"I don't know," the girl replied, with a perplexed shrug. "After Blue got shot, I was cryin' an' I couldn't even see. I was holdin' on to Junior, and I turned away when Daddy shot Sammy. I was pushin' Junior up towards our place, when I felt my legs burnin', an' I fell down. I tried to get up, but it hurt too bad."

"Did you see Deputy Cox?"

"I didn't even know Charlie was there until my grandmomma told me. She told me not to talk to no cops, neither, but you bein' a agent is okay, I guess."

"Do you know who shot Nancy?"

"Nope, but she was the one who let Blue out," Wanda said with a firm nod.

"Do you think Junior would tell me the same thing?" Todd asked, fighting an urge to smirk.

"Hell," Wanda snorted, "that boy's a total retard. He don't even speak good, anyway. I bet he don't even know *my* real name."

"Thanks, Wanda," Todd said, rising to leave. "You hang in there."

"If you get a chance to speak with that fella," Wanda said, twisting her head for another look, "you go ahead an' ask him if he seen my pussy—at least the hairs."

Todd rolled his eyes, and he glanced across the room to a sheriff's deputy lounging in a vacant wheelchair. The man had a portable radio, and Todd needed some information. The deputy seemed half asleep, however, and he didn't notice Todd's approach.

"Have you guys got Abel Kinley booked in yet?" Todd asked, causing the nodding deputy to flinch.

"Uh, sure," the man said, wiping some drool from the corner of his mouth.

"Is Harry working the jail tonight?"

"No, but Jesse's there, as OIC. Harry's fishin' the Big Hole."

"Thanks," Todd said, turning to leave.

"Were you talkin' to that Wanda girl?" the deputy asked, before Todd could make good his escape.

"Yeah," Todd said slowly, looking back over his shoulder.

"How big's that tattoo?"

Todd smiled weakly and shook his head. Some people's priorities were hard to understand.

*   *   *   *

The old Missoula County Jail was on the upper level of the county court-house—a good idea at the time it was built, before overcrowding with no chance of expansion became a reality. To get in after hours, there was a rear sally port with an elevator. Since Todd didn't know who was watching the outside surveillance camera, he held up his badge case for proper identification.

"Yeah," came a crackle over the intercom next to the electric door.

"Todd Milton," said the agent. "CIB."

"Oh, yeah," the garbled voice said again. "I saw you on TV."

The door buzzed, and Todd pushed it open. The elevator was waiting on the ground floor, and it took him only a few seconds to reach the jail level. Once inside, he locked his unauthorized Smith & Wesson .357 revolver, two speed-loaders, and pocketknife in a vacant weapons locker, and he proceeded to the book-in area. The familiar smiling face of Jesse Pineup greeted him.

"Here to see the murderer, I guess," said Jesse, waving to Todd.

"Let's not jump to conclusions," said Todd. "Got an interview room I can use?"

"Pick any of the three," the deputy replied. "How's Charlie?"

"Still in the operating room, when I left. They weren't asking for blood donations, so I don't know how bad it is, but the groin's not a good place to get shot."

"Abel's in cell fourteen," Jesse said, still nodding at the thought of Charlie Cox under the knife. "Can you find your own way? I've got my other guys tied up with a waterline leak in the laundry."

Todd nodded, and he took the big cell door key from Jesse. Number fourteen was at the far end of a short corridor, and the agent found Abel Kinley sitting on the edge of his bunk—wearing only his underwear. The prisoner didn't look up as the lock began to rattle.

"Where are your clothes?" Todd asked, glancing about the confines of the narrow cell.

"Took 'em," Abel said with an awkward smile.

"Well, I'm Todd Milton, state agent, and I need to talk with you," said Todd, holding open the door. "Let's take a walk down the hall."

"Ain't we met?" asked Abel, rising from his bunk. "I seen you somewheres."

"Television?"

"That's it," Abel said with a nod.

Todd directed Abel to lead the way, and the agent guided the prisoner into one of the small interview rooms. There was a table inside, along with a stool on each side—all bolted to either the floor or the wall or both. Todd motioned for Abel to take the seat farthest from the door, and the agent produced a form for the inmate to read.

"This is our Miranda waiver form, Mr. Kinley," said Todd. "Do you know how to read the English language?"

"I only made it to the ninth grade," Abel replied, as though that was an answer.

"Well, you had to be able to read to get that far, so…can you?"

"I never did it much after I was out," the prisoner said, squinting up at the bright dome light on the ceiling. "Am I in trouble if I can't read?"

"I'd have to say that you *are* in trouble, Abel," Todd replied with a sigh, taking a seat across the table from the inmate. "But that's just the way I am, and it's too long a story to get into right here and now.

"If I read the form to you, do you think you'll understand what I've got to say?"

"Yeah, I guess so."

Todd went through the Miranda form, explaining as he went along. He even got Abel to initial and sign in the proper spaces, although the man's signature looked like that of a child. After tucking the completed form back into his notebook, Todd gave Abel a concerned stare.

"Abel," Todd said, the strain of the evening showing in his sagging shoulders. "I'm going to ask you some questions, and what I'm about to ask can put you in prison, so I want you to think about each answer long and hard. If you don't like the question, or you don't understand it, I want you to tell me so. Just because you've signed a waiver, doesn't mean you *have* to answer *any* of my questions, so think about your answers before you give them to me. Are we clear on that?"

Abel nodded, and he bit his lower lip. "Got a cigarette?"

"I don't smoke, and, anyway, this is a smoke-free jail, Abel," said Todd.

"I been meanin' to quit."

"Well, let's get to the big issue," said Todd. "Who'd you shoot, Abel?"

"Sammy," said Abel, with about as much emotion as he'd use to describe a gopher kill. "I thought he was gonna shoot my kids, so I shot him first."

"What kind of gun did you have?"

"I think them deputies have it. It's my .270—a Savage. I can't remember what model it is, but it's got a bolt action and a scope."

"Why'd you use a hunting rifle?"

"It was sittin' by the door. I keep it there in case...there's trouble."

"Abel," Todd said with a half grin. "This isn't about poaching. You shot a *man* tonight. I'm not worried about you killin' a deer outa season."

"I'm a landowner," Abel said defensively, sitting a little taller on his stool. "I gotta right to shoot deer when they come in the garden."

"Well, let's talk about Sammy, again. What happened?"

"He shot our dog. That's about it. I know Wanda let Blue outa the house, but that's no cause to shoot him. Blue's been in their sheep pens as much as any a their sheep, and he's never bit a one of 'em, neither. That Sammy-boy just gets crazy drunk sometimes. You can ask Kate. She'll tell ya."

"Kate's dead, Abel," Todd said solemnly. "We're still trying to figure out how she got shot, but she's not going to be telling us anything."

"Kate dead," Abel echoed, sinking lower in his seat. He let his elbows rest on the tabletop, and he rested his forehead in his hands.

"How many times did you shoot?" Todd asked, trying to regain the man's attention.

"Just the once," Abel replied. "The spent shell should still be in the gun. I never worked the bolt."

"Where'd you shoot Sammy?" asked Todd.

"In the stomach, I think."

"Did you aim at his stomach?"

"Hell, no," Abel said, finally looking up from the table. "He was only about five yards away. I don't need to aim when I'm that close up."

"Did you see Charlie Cox?"

"I saw a guy in a sheriff's suit. I don't know if it was Charlie or not. He was shootin' a lot after I shot Sammy, but he never shot down towards me none. I think he's the one who shot Wanda and Nancy, and they wasn't even doin' nothin'."

"Did you talk with Sammy before you shot him?"

"I listened to him a little bit, 'til I figured he was just gonna keep on cussin', then he started reloadin' that shotgun, an' I told him to put it down. He didn't listen to me at all. He just kept on diggin' for more shells in his pocket, and the things he done said. Little Abel's only just turned six, an' I don't allow that kinda talk in *my* house."

"Somebody said you asked if you could get the dog back, before the shooting started. Do you remember that?"

"I do. I *did* ask if we could get ol' Blue outa the pen. I remember, now. Sammy just gave me a wild look, as I recall."

"Was the dog already dead when you asked?" Todd asked.

"I…I think so."

"So, why was it so important to get him back, at that point?"

Abel Kinley canted his head, and his firm stare was as penetrating as any Todd had ever seen. It was as though the agent had asked the man the world's dumbest question, and, just maybe, it was.

"Ain't you ever loved a dog, Mr. Milton?" Abel asked, and the interview room faded away.

*   *   *   *

Vets' offices just don't smell like an MD's, but the aroma is distinctive enough to bring shivers of fear from their patients. Dogs and cats really don't know what treatment they're about to receive—a shot, an operation, or some less intrusive form of remedy. It's all the same to them, and they're always scared.

But not this time.

Honey was twelve years old. The oldest bulldog Todd had ever owned. His biggest male hadn't even made it to ten, but Honey had hung on past near blindness and stiff joints. Then she'd started throwing up her food, and her weight had begun to drop. A vet trip was the only answer.

Todd knew something was very wrong before he'd taken her, though. For an inactive dog, Honey had been doing her best to find a way out of his fenced yard. Something she'd never tried to do before.

Walking through the door of the clinic was the next clue. Honey didn't shiver, like she'd done for the countless visits in the past. She knew it was time, even if Todd didn't.

The examination table must've felt cold to her, but Honey never flinched. The vet had been patient and kind, telling him the dog had a strong heart but failed kidneys. She said the medication might take a few minutes to do its deed. Todd held his precious Honey close, looking into her clouded eyes and wondering when the last glimmer of life would be gone. As that failing spark passed on to whatever awaits good dogs, Todd felt the old girl's weight sag, and she exhaled for the last time.

*   *   *   *

"Are you okay, Mr. Milton?" it was Abel, tugging at Todd's sleeve.

"Huh?" Todd replied awkwardly, wiping at the corner of his eye. "Yeah. I'm okay."

CHAPTER 2

▼

"It's a strong case," said Finis Abernathy, the Missoula County Attorney. Finis's mother had picked his name out of the back of an old library book, and she'd had no idea what the word meant or even how to pronounce it. Consequently, most of the local pronunciations sounded like a quick *fine-ass*—except for those who preferred to call Finis *dumb-ass*.

"It's a total *mess*, and you know it," said Todd, patting the case file copy. "There's no way you'll convince a jury that Abel caused Charlie's death—or Kate's either. The lab reports on them show shotgun pellets in both bodies. Abel only shot once—with a rifle. Sammy's shotgun accounted for half of the injuries and two-thirds of the deaths."

"But," Finis said, holding up his finger in a pose he hoped to use in an opening address, "had Abel not fired, Sammy wouldn't've shot the others."

"I wouldn't even want to argue that, Finis," said Todd. "Sammy's blood alcohol level was .26. I'm surprised he could even hit the dog, and don't forget he shot one of his own sheep, too. Abel gave him a chance to drop the gun—even Shirley agrees on that count, and Abel only shot when he thought his kids were in danger—which they *were*, as it turned out."

"Your reconstruction of the shooting scene does disturb me," Finis said, flipping to his copy of the diagram.

"Imagine it wall-sized, with Abel's defense attorney identifying each projectile. Sammy's buckshot in the dog, in the sheep, in his own wife—"

"That's what I mean."

"And don't forget where Charlie's bullets went," Todd reminded him. "For a guy who was returning fire, he only managed to hit two unarmed girls. And what about the sight of Nancy in that wheelchair—complete with a noisy respirator? We'll be seeing her in courtrooms for years to come."

"Maybe Charlie's lucky that he died," Finis said absently.

"Charlie Cox was a lotta things, Finis," Todd said, rising from his chair, "but lucky wasn't one of 'em."

"You think I should let this slide?" asked Finis, pulling at his little button-nose.

"Make Abel a deal, Finis," said Todd, walking to the door. "This is definitely not the crime of the century, and I'm not even sure that it was a crime at all."

Finis started to speak, but he caught a reflection of himself in his office bay window, and he occupied himself with yet another pose. Todd was out the door without a word.

*   *   *   *

Missoula. The town had grown a lot since Todd was a kid. His folks had moved here from the eastern plains, when the timber industry was booming. Timber was still big business in western Montana, but it seemed like the town was much more than that, now. Heck, for a western Montana town, Missoula was, in some ways, more liberal than San Francisco. And to think Elmer Keith had once called Missoula home. Todd could only shake his head.

The days were getting longer, too. A good sign. The winter of '96—with its 100+inches of snowfall—had taken its toll on the souls of Missoula, and now the people were looking forward to the summer. The snowbirds were drifting back from Arizona, Nevada, and other points southwest. It wouldn't be long before the university closed its doors, too, and then the "party town" atmosphere would fade until the fall.

Todd watched the clouds drift over Lolo Peak. They were moving fast, for their light color. A storm? His yard sure needed it.

With his state car in the shop, Todd's personal pickup awaited him in the courthouse parking lot. At first, he thought there was a parking ticket on his windshield, but it was only a friendly note from a mischievous sheriff's detective. Cops can't resist an opportunity to mess with each other, after all.

The sun was still high, so Todd drove south, through town, and back into the Miller Creek drainage. The road grew rough, but it was dry, and he didn't feel the need to shift into four-wheel-drive. One logging road fed into another—some with fresh slash to hinder his progress. It took him half an hour to crest the ridge, and then he was there. He parked the truck on an up-slope, and he cut the wheels to keep it from rolling away.

A short distance from the road, there was a rock outcropping. Todd had found it when he was searching for stones to stock his many gardens. There'd been a small cave back then—not much more than a four-foot overhang, but it was now filled with stones, and no evidence of the opening remained. He took a seat beside it, and he rested his hand on a large flat stone that covered what had once been the entrance.

"I miss you," Todd said softly, his eyes filling with tears. "We had a lotta good times, Honey-dog, and I hope I'll see you again someday."

Taking his wallet from his back pocket, Todd flipped it open to a faded snapshot. Honey was not much more than a puppy then, her big smile covering most of her face. Where had the time gone, he had to ask himself. She'd had a litter of puppies in her early years, but he'd let them all get away. To good homes, he was sure, but they were still gone. If anything remained of her, it was beneath the pile of cold stones.

Todd rose and walked to edge of the rock outcropping. It fell away abruptly to the west, and he could see the white tip of Squaw Peak on the distant horizon. There was no breeze, but the air was much cooler at the high elevation, and his light jacket wasn't quite enough. Glancing about, he could see snow still clinging in the shaded areas of the ridge.

Filling his lungs, Todd shouted Honey's name into the vast emptiness of the forest below. It took a moment for the echo to return, and Todd took a few more minutes to appreciate the solitude.

"Yes, Abel," he said aloud in the windless dusk. "I've loved a dog."

CHAPTER 3

▼

For such a vivid dream, there was one critical element lacking. Todd couldn't make out the mystery woman's face. At first, he'd thought she was Alexandra Paul—just because of her lean muscular look, and the fact that Todd had almost memorized the tall actress's every detail. Todd was a *Baywatch* fan from way back.

Ever since his break-up with Leela, a master's student who was just a little too *bi*-curious for Todd's tastes, the intriguing dreams had been coming on a semi-regular basis—even though Leela had now been out of Todd's life for almost two years.

Tonight would be different, he told himself. His dream girl was starting to look over her shoulder. Just another second or two. If somebody would just get that damn telephone.

Phone?

The lighted dial on the clock told the tale. 2:18 a.m. on a Sunday morning! Officially, Todd knew a wrong number would be better than a right one.

"This is Todd," he answered in a dry, unused voice.

"I bet you were asleep," said the familiar voice of Andy Freund, the sheriff of Park County. He'd known Todd since the two of them had gone through the old state law enforcement academy in Bozeman.

"You're damn right I was asleep," said Todd, sitting up in bed. It was the kind of call that meant a return to sleep was not an option. "So, what's happening in Livingston?"

"Nothing, I hope," said Andy. "I'm down near Corwin Springs."

"Have I ever been there?"

"I don't know, but it's on the main highway, just north a Gardiner."

"I guess I've passed through, then. What's up?"

"A homicide."

"Just one?"

"Far as I can tell."

"Did you clear it through Helena?"

"Couldn't get 'em on the phone. Got the runaround from the highway patrol, too."

"It's a real stretch for me to go all the way to Park County, you know."

"Oh, I *do* know, Todd, but Dave don't answer in Bozeman, either, so you're actually my third choice."

"You really know how to hurt a guy."

"That's exactly why I said it," Andy replied with a chuckle.

"You're looking at…maybe a four-hour response time," Todd reminded him.

"That's the problem with Montana: sometimes there's just no quick way to get there," Andy lamented. "You're just gonna have to make that little Dodge purr a bit louder than normal."

"My Intrepid is in the shop, Andy," Todd said, breaking the bubble. "The state'll have to pay mileage on my Powerstroke, and it sure doesn't purr."

"Well," the sheriff said with a sigh. "It might take that one-ton Ford a yours just to get up to this place. I guess you ain't got a radio in that truck."

"Cell phone."

"Call me when you get to the Cenex, and I'll have my reserve come an' get you."

"Where's Willis?"

"Off fishin', an' my new deputy still has a week to go in Helena."

"I've got to run by the office to get my kit, then I'll be on the way."

"I'll be dancin' in a puddle a piss 'til you get here, partner," the sheriff said, before hanging up.

＊   ＊   ＊   ＊

To say the crime had taken place in Corwin Springs would be a mistake, but the little burg was the closest named place of any consequence near the homicide scene. As the eastern sky was beginning to brighten, Todd's Ford rolled into the Cenex service station, just in time for the yawning agent to get a fresh cup of coffee. Even though Todd made the call fifteen minutes before his arrival, Andy's reserve deputy still took nearly an hour to join up with him.

The drive back took Todd north on the main highway, then east on a freshly paved road—at least that's what Todd had taken it for. It turned out to be a private driveway.

When someone owns a hundred acres of anything, it's safe to refer to them as a landowner. Todd owned the city lot around his house, but he'd hardly qualify. The homicide crime scene, however, was located on a piece of land that included a hundred and four sections—each a square mile, and people who owned that much ground might best be regarded as heads of state.

The Manor—and that's how it was identified with an arch-covered gate—was a boldly situated, ten thousand square foot log structure, overlooking a steep stretch of rocky stream. There was a separate similarly constructed garage behind the main building, with bays for a dozen vehicles—two of the closed doors were tall enough to accept the largest of motor homes. The front entrance of the oversized residence was served by a large, circular driveway. That's where the pavement pretty much came to an end, too.

The sheriff's Bronco was nowhere to be seen, however, and Todd gave the reserve deputy a quizzical look, after the man had parked his cruiser in front of the house.

"We ain't there yet," the man said, walking over to the passenger side of Todd's F-350. "We'll need us this thing to get the rest of the way up there."

"Up where?" Todd asked.

"Eight miles in, or there abouts," said the reserve deputy, pointing to a gravel service road leading up from behind the garage. "Better drop 'er down in four-wheel-low."

Todd followed the man's directions, and the balance of the trip took them deep into the wilderness. The multi-section estate included plenty of high country, and much of the service road was covered in crusty snow. Todd could see the tracks left by Andy's Bronco, so he knew someone had preceded him.

For a remote area, however, the service road was properly constructed and well maintained, and there were sturdy bridges spanning the many mountain streams they had to cross. There was also a section of the road cut into the rocky face of a mountain, and Todd thought he could see sunlight reflecting off some of the tin roofs of Gardiner, far off to the south, as they crested the top of a rocky rise.

Then Todd saw their destination.

It was a smaller version of the big house. The same massive log construction, but on a not-quite-as-opulent scale. For its location, however, the high-country lodge was equally spectacular. Todd doubted if anyone within a hundred miles could see the sunset any later than the view afforded by the west-facing deck.

Sheriff Andy Freund was napping in a rocking chair on that deck.

"Wake up, old man!" Todd shouted, climbing down from behind the wheel.

"I'm awake," Andy replied, tilting his Stetson back to see. "I've been listenin' to that clatter-trap a yours comin' for the last ten minutes."

"So, what have we got?" Todd asked, noting the rubber gloves on Andy's hands. For a backwoods lawman, Andy was top-notch.

"Damnedest thing I ever saw," said Andy, motioning for Todd to join him on the porch. "I got a hold a Judge Mingle, and I dictated a pretty basic search warrant affidavit to him. You can clean it up when you get back down to his office.

"We found this place standin' wide open, though, so you need to see it like it is."

"Did you include the main house down below in the affidavit?"

"I kinda shotgunned it, listing all dwellings and structures found therein, or thereon, or somethin' like that."

"Even though it's remote, we should still get somebody to control access. Can we send your deputy back down to block the driveway at the highway?"

"Vince," Andy said with a nod, waving at the reserve deputy. "Take my rig back down to the house, then drive yours out to the highway and keep anybody without a good reason from comin' in here. If I need to, I can catch a ride back with Todd."

Without another word, the stumpy man jumped into the waiting Bronco—its keys still in the ignition, and he was off down the mountain.

"Now," Andy said with a wink, "come on in here an' tell me what you think."

Todd followed the sheriff through the open front door, and the agent could still feel the chill once he was within the lodge. That door had been open for a while, and whatever heat source that had once been available was now long gone. Frost had formed on the insides of the windows.

"He's still in good shape, considering," the sheriff said, canting his head toward a figure seated before the living room fireplace. "If the power *was* on, somebody's turned it off a while ago."

The victim appeared to be a middle-aged man—possibly older, dressed only in his boxers, and tied to an oak, ladder-back chair. The man's hands were tied behind his back, and a loop from his wrists was fastened to one of the cross braces on the back chair legs. The man's feet were tied to the front chair legs at his ankles, and there was a loop of rope cutting into his pudgy abdomen.

The most unusual aspect of the bondage was around the man's head. The victim's scalp was wrapped with silver duct tape, and a section of the tape was pulled back to the chair, forcing the man's head to tilt to the rear. The man's nostrils were stuffed with cotton, and there was a small metal funnel pushed into his mouth—also held in place with duct tape. Duct tape covered the man's eyes, as well.

On the floor beside the victim were two plastic antifreeze bottles.

"He's been dead for a while," said Andy, pointing to the discoloration in the victim's lower extremities. The victim's bare feet appeared to be badly bruised, as did the lower edge of his exposed legs and his fingers. "Rigor's come and gone."

"Care to give me an estimate?" Todd asked, knowing Andy to hold the county coroner's title along with his status as sheriff.

"No way in hell, right now. Not with the cool weather up here, and no one to confirm when he was last seen. It's been pretty clear all week, and I'll bet it was near zero up here last night."

"Let's go get a search warrant," Todd said, turning toward the door.

"Not so fast," Andy said, taking Todd by the arm. "You gotta see somethin' else."

The sheriff led Todd out the front door and back around to the rear of the lodge. The ground had been soft there at one point, and there were footprints leading both toward and away from the tree line behind the cabin. The footprints could also be seen on the snow-covered slope beyond.

"I made a couple a casts," Andy said. "Just to pass the time while I was waitin' for you. It's a Vibram sole pattern—you can see the logo real good—a little smaller than my gunboats. I'd bet it's a size eleven, D-width."

"Where does that go?" Todd asked, looking up into the shade of the trees.

"Miles an' miles a nowhere, buddy. There ain't much back there in the Absarokas but one mountain after another. Maybe twenty to twenty-five miles back that way, you might hit the gravel road runnin' south outa McLeod, but most of that's in Sweet Grass County," Andy replied with a shrug. "I figured we could hit it later on horseback, after you got done with the search."

"So, how in the heck did you find out about all this?" asked Todd, pointing from the footprints to the lodge below.

"An anonymous 9-1-1 call—I'm already gettin' the phone company workin' on it, though," Andy replied quickly. "We got it Saturday, around noon I think, but it took me a while to find this place. The phone company said the call came from a Big Timber exchange, so it shouldn't be too hard to run down."

"Have you got the call on tape?"

"Yeah, but it's just a guy's voice. No real accent. He said to look for the body in the house above The Manor, and this was the first spot we came to. It's the *last* spot we could come to, too."

Todd gave the sheriff an uneasy look. The footprints concerned him, and the way the call had come in was even more baffling.

"I know," Andy said, without a word from Todd. "You're worried about scene contamination—especially if someone can walk in here from the east. I'll stay put until you get back from seein' the judge in town. That porch rocker is pretty comfortable, anyway."

*   *   *   *

Judge Clarence Mingle had been an auto mechanic prior to the last election. A traffic fine disagreement with the previous judge had led Clarence to test the popularity of both, and the greasy-fingered—but absolutely honest—father of nine had come out the winner. Fortunately for the residents of Park County, their new judge had fostered an interest in the law even as he was rebuilding carburetors and regrinding brake drums. With two years of bench duty behind him now, Clarence could look back with the satisfaction that none of his decisions had been overturned by higher courts.

Todd found the judge in his Livingston garage, with the parts of an International tractor transmission spread before him. Consequently, Todd chose not to offer his hand.

"Got your laptop?" the judge asked, after an introductory nod.

"In my truck, your honor," said Todd.

"Disc's on the shop desk. You might wanna tweak it a little bit, but I think Andy's got the gist of it down pretty good.

"Get any ID off the victim?"

"He's in his underwear," Todd replied. "I didn't see any other clothes near the body. Do we know who the recorded owner of the place is?"

"The county clerk says it's corporate owned," said Clarence. "Some outfit called Global Support Group. Never heard of 'em."

"The next time you get a parts delivery from Billings," said Todd, "look at the fine print on the carrier. Global Support Group owns about half the trucks on I-90, I think."

"Yeah," the judge said slowly, almost wiping a stained hand through his thinning hair. "I *have* seen the GSG logo, now that you've mentioned it, but that doesn't really help us with the ID now, does it?"

"It gives us a place to start," said Todd, turning back toward his truck.

*   *   *   *

Vince Gilkey, the reserve deputy left guarding the main entrance driveway to the crime scene, was fighting a losing battle with sleep. He'd been up for almost twenty hours, and his last contact with a human had occurred two hours earlier, as Todd drove out on his way to meet the judge in Livingston.

Vince's county cruiser was just far enough off the main highway to prevent passing tourists from mistaking it for a speed trap. At least that was the indication he'd gotten from the CB radio traffic. There was only a report of some southbound speeders, but Vince knew his current assignment took priority over any traffic enforcement concerns.

Through the budding trees, Vince could see the highway, however, and, sure enough, he could also see the approach of a low-flying black Lincoln and an equally fast black Suburban. Vince guessed their speed at a "reasonable and prudent" one hundred and ten.

But then the two vehicles began to brake. Hard.

Vince sat up in his bucket seat, as both the Town Car and the GMC made squealing turns into the driveway he was blocking. Neither vehicle seemed to be slowing down while closing the distance, and the reserve deputy turned on his blue and red lights. He should've used his radio.

"Hold it right there!" Vince shouted, stepping from the door of his cruiser.

The car and the truck came to a halt side by side, and the driver of the Lincoln stepped out onto the pavement. Vince could see a badge case in the man's hand.

"A word with you, officer," the man said, in an accent unfamiliar to Vince.

*   *   *   *

"You know Ronelle's visiting her sister in Seattle," Judge Mingle told Todd. "Hell, I can't even remember which county attorney's office offered to cover while she's outa town. Her memo's still on my desk at the courthouse."

"This scene could be a week old, for all we know, judge," Todd said with a shrug. "I'll just take lots of pictures, and I can catch up with Ronelle when she gets back."

"She'll be in this Thursday, I think. I've got it on my desk calendar—the other one, at the courthouse, of course."

"Thanks, judge," Todd said, with a wave of the warrant. "I'll give you a heads-up call on the search warrant return."

"Be sure to call the house. One a the kids should know where to find me."

✳   ✳   ✳   ✳

The tracks in the snow had bothered Andy Freund to the point he just couldn't languish in the porch rocker any longer. He knew it would take Todd three to four hours to finish his paperwork in Livingston and make the return trip, so there was plenty of time to do a little follow-up of his own.

Trying to maintain a parallel course, Andy followed the tracks up into the trees, noting that the footprints had backtracked upon themselves. Whoever had made them, had come in and gone out almost exactly the same way.

The sheriff made himself a promise that he wouldn't leave sight of the lodge, but the tracks were intriguing, and he resisted the urge to look back. Anyway, the top of the ridge wasn't much farther than half a mile away.

At almost ten thousand feet, the mid-morning air was thin, but Andy Freund was used to this kind of walking. He was a sheep hunter, and the steep climb wasn't much more than a stroll to him. The snow was quite a bit deeper, though, and Andy found himself wallowing up to his waist in a shaded drift. He also took note that the man—Andy, of course, had assumed it was a man—who'd left the tracks hadn't suffered the same discomfort. The suspect was either taller or lighter than the sheriff—maybe both.

The top of the ridge afforded Andy an expansive view to the east, and, by using his compact binoculars, he was able to pick up the distant tracks in thinning sections of the forest below. The easterly course of the footprints didn't seem to deviate.

But where was there to go, Andy had to ask himself. There was nothing but mountains and wilderness for twenty hard miles or more, with the strong possibility of being injured or lost. Still, the tracks seemed to lead off in a purposeful direction, with no noticeable variation in the length of the strides. The sheriff didn't have a compass to confirm a particular bearing, however, so he tried to spot a landmark on the horizon to orient with his map. One snowcapped mountain peak looked pretty much like another, though, and there appeared to be hundreds of them.

From the top of the ridgeline, Andy turned back for a view of the lodge below, and he was surprised to be able to see the big house, as well. Through the binoculars, he could even make out what looked like a black van, parked near the side of the house. Freund wondered if Todd had been able to get some crime scene support from the Missoula lab.

As he began his descent, the sheriff could only hope so.

*   *   *   *

Todd knew something was wrong before he even left the highway. The county cruiser wasn't blocking the driveway, for starters. Then he saw the patrol car, nose down in the ditch beside the pavement. Todd pulled his truck onto the shoulder.

"*Vince*!?" Todd shouted, climbing down from the truck. There was no sign of the reserve deputy around the disabled car.

Making a quick but cautious approach, Todd found the cruiser empty, with wires from the onboard radio hanging out the open driver's side door. As he felt for the cell phone on his belt, Todd heard a noise from the other side of the driveway.

It sounded muffled, and it only took Todd a moment to discover why. Vince was handcuffed to a tree, with his jacket tied over his head. After several frantic seconds, Todd was able to free him.

"I don't know how many there was," Vince said excitedly. "He took my pistol to begin with, but then he put it back in the holster after he'd trussed me up. He used my own damn handcuffs."

"Where is he, Vince?" Todd asked, casting a worried glance up toward the main residence. He didn't like the idea of Andy being alone up on the mountain.

"They've come an' gone, Mr. Milton," Vince replied, rubbing his wrists. "I don't think they was up there more than fifteen—maybe twenty minutes. They been gone a hour or more, I'd wager."

"What're they drivin'?" Todd asked, dialing his cell phone. He hoped the highway patrol had a unit nearby.

"A big…Ford kinda car, I think, and maybe…a Tahoe, both of 'em shiny black," Vince answered haltingly, his forehead wrinkled in thought. "They came in from the north, an' I think they went back that way. I just couldn't see."

"Did you get any tag numbers?"

Vince could only offer a dejected shrug. "They was up on me too quick, Mr. Milton. I just didn't think to look at 'em too good, but I don't recall 'em havin' any front plates."

"That's okay, Vince, and stop this 'Mr. Milton' stuff. I'm Todd."

"Sure Mister, uh, I mean Todd."

"I can't seem to get a clear line," said Todd, snapping his cellular telephone closed. His attempt to make a quick 9-1-1 call had been met by the "system busy" tone. "Whoever said we don't have to pay for weekend minutes doesn't know squat."

"Even our sheriff's radios don't work too well in these deep valleys," Vince said mournfully.

"Hop in the truck, Vince," said the agent. "We need to find a real phone."

*   *   *   *

It had looked like a logical spot, and it was one. Andy Freund smiled to himself at his discovery. A clump of low evergreens had offered their suspect shelter from the wind, and the man had even left them a bodily fluid sample, in the form of yellow snow. Andy was now certain it was a man they were looking for, too. A woman would have to pee through a pretty long straw to leave a stain that far from her footprints.

*   *   *   *

Thick black smoke came into view long before Todd's truck rounded the last bend in the driveway to The Manor entrance gate. Both the house and the garage were well engulfed, and the garage fire was threatening a nearby stand of larch.

"Get in the Bronco," Todd told Vince, as he drew up next to the sheriff's 4X4. "Go back up the highway to that white house on the right. I saw people in the yard when I came by. They'll let you use their phone to call the volunteer fire department and the Forest Service, and get the highway patrol down here, too."

Vince bailed out of the truck, and he sprinted over to the other vehicle. Ignoring the damaged radio set in the sheriff's unit, he was relieved to find the ignition intact. The Bronco started with the first turn. Giving Todd a wave, Vince was off down the driveway with a squeal of rubber.

"Oh, man," was all Todd could think to say, as he watched a few million dollars disappearing before his eyes. Then he remembered Andy.

Paying no mind to the flames dancing from the garage roof to the tree line, Todd steered his truck onto the service road, and all four tires threw stones as he revved the diesel to the 3400-rpm level. He knew he was going too fast for the narrow roadbed, but his imagination kept adding unwanted details to the crime scene he'd already visited.

Curves that should've made Todd slow to ten miles an hour were negotiated at three times that speed, but it still took him twenty minutes to cross the last bridge, and he knew the lodge was another two miles up.

Then Todd saw a figure walking in the road ahead of him, and the agent let out a long sigh of relief. Andy Freund was coming down the slope to meet him.

"I guess things have gotten worse," Andy said, as he strode up to Todd's open window.

*   *   *   *

As a result of his earlier encounter, Vince Gilkey was much more cautious as a suspicious black sports car pulled up to his hastily prepared roadblock. He was easily half a mile up the driveway from the main highway, and no casual visitor should be in that far, he reasoned. The Porsche slowed in response to Vince's hand signal, and it stopped a few feet from the front of the sheriff's Bronco.

"Is something wrong?" an especially tiny woman asked, as she stepped from behind the wheel. Vince guessed her height to be about five feet—and she was wearing three-inch heels!

"Who're you?" the reserve deputy asked, in his most authoritative tone. He kept his hand on his pistol because he couldn't see through the dark tinted glass of the Porsche.

"I'm Natalie Weinberg," the woman replied. "I work for Mr. Draper."

"Who's he?" Vince demanded, as he worked his way up far enough to glance into the open door of the car. It was otherwise empty.

"He's the CEO of GSG."

"The...what of...what?" Vince stammered, looking her up and down. Without the shoes, she couldn't be much more than four-foot-nine.

"Matheson Draper. He's the man who owns this place," she replied, spreading her slender arms for emphasis. "At least...his business does."

"Look here, you," said Vince, taking a step forward. "If you've got something to do with this place, I think I'd better take you into custody—just for my safety and yours, you understand."

"Knock yourself out, cowboy," Natalie said with a palms-up shrug.

*   *   *   *

"I saw the smoke while I was ignoring your request to secure the crime scene," said Andy, as Todd's truck bounced down the mountain road. There were grab-handles on the dash and above the passenger door, and Andy had a hand on each. "I got interested in those footprints. Found where he took a piss."

"I hope you marked it well, so we can find it again. Maybe we can get some DNA, if we need it later on," said Todd.

"No need to mark it. It's still frozen. Yellow snow."

Todd nodded, and he was relieved to see the flashing lights of the volunteer fire vehicles through the still-billowing smoke. There was a welcomed black and blue highway patrol car on the scene, as well.

"Andy," Vince's voice crackled over the sheriff's portable radio. "You there?"

"What you got, Vince?" the sheriff called back.

"Got one in custody at the roadblock, boss," Vince replied.

Todd gave Andy an eyebrow-raising stare.

"We're on the way," said Andy.

∗   ∗   ∗   ∗

"We did not have time to locate the body, due to the presence of local law enforcement and the possibility of unexpected interference," a voice said over the speakerphone. "As a result, we spent minimal time on site, but the entire ground floor of the dwelling was soaked in fuel. Everything will be destroyed, I am sure. The one deputy we encountered was incapacitated before he could broadcast a proper warning. I am certain we were not positively identified or followed from the area."

"We can't have any slip-ups," said Yancey Fitzgerald, turning in his swivel chair. There were clouds forming on the western horizon, and he had a clear view of them from his fifty-fifth floor office suite. Rain? Atlanta could certainly use it.

∗   ∗   ∗   ∗

At first, Todd thought she was a child. She was seated in the passenger side of the Bronco, but she could just barely see over the dashboard.

"Says her name's Weinberg," said Vince, as he hung his chin on the open passenger window of Todd's truck. "Ain't that a Jewish name? That guy who took my gun had a funny accent. Maybe this is some kinda thing with the Jews."

"Does *she* have a funny accent?" Todd asked skeptically.

"Well...that is...no," Vince replied sheepishly.

"Why don't you bring her over and put her in the back seat with us?" Andy suggested. "We'll take it from here."

Vince nodded, and he returned to the Bronco. It took him a moment to retrieve his prisoner from the passenger seat, and both Todd and Andy were surprised to see she was handcuffed behind her back. Andy gave Todd a sideward glance and shook his head.

"Hey," said Todd, fighting a smile. "After this morning, I'm sure he's not taking any chances—no matter how harmless they might look."

Vince brought the woman to the rear passenger door of the crew-cab pickup, and he helped her into the seat behind Andy. Both Todd and the sheriff turned to get a view of the tiny woman.

"I don't think we really need the handcuffs," Todd said to Vince, after taking note of the prisoner's almost formal attire.

Aside from her black patent leather heels, she wore a glossy black skirt—that might make it to mid-thigh if she'd been standing—and an almost transparent long-sleeved white blouse. There was evidence of a frilly white bra beneath the blouse.

"I...don't think I can get 'em off, Mr. Milton...I mean, Todd," said Vince, hanging his head.

"What do you mean, you can't get 'em off?" asked Andy, glancing from Vince to the woman. "Don't you have a key?"

"It's not that, boss. Her wrists was so small, the cuffs...they just fell right off," Vince tried to explain. "So, then I put both wrists in one cuff, but I really screwed up when I had that empty cuff, 'cause I didn't want it just hangin' there, so I put it on both her wrists, too. Anyway, both keyholes are on the insides, now, and I can't get to 'em."

"Who the hell told you to put one cuff on *both* her wrists?" Andy growled.

"Well," Vince replied softly, his lower lip quivering. "She did."

Andy turned his attention back to the woman behind him, but all she could do was look at the headliner.

*   *   *   *

"Mr. Draper's private files were very brief and basic, sir," said the GSG data center technician standing before Yancey Fitzgerald's desk. "They were easily purged from his CPU, and his unit was not networked with the corporate server. He'd always insisted on a stand-alone, you know."

"Where is his CPU now?" Fitzgerald asked without looking up.

"I've removed the hard drive, as you requested, and the rest of the unit has been destroyed."

"And the hard drive?"

"It's here," the man replied, placing a sealed plastic box on Fitzgerald's desk.

"That'll be all."

*   *   *   *

"It's gonna take bolt cutters," Andy said through gritted teeth, as he knelt for a better view of the woman's handcuffed wrists.

"Got 'em behind the back seat," said Todd, as he opened the rear door on the driver's side. He always carried a long pair to cut cables and padlocks, but he'd never imagined using them for this purpose.

It took a little effort to position the cutters, but one snip removed half of the problem, and the other cuff was easily unlocked with a key. Natalie Weinberg checked her wrists, where both a gold Rolex and a heavy diamond tennis bracelet seemed to be relatively undisturbed.

"Let's take a ride," said Todd, taking the woman by her elbow. He helped her into the front passenger seat, as Andy hopped in the back seat behind them.

The drive back from the roadblock took a few minutes, but Natalie kept her eyes on the road and remained quiet. Only when the sight of what was left of The Manor came into view did she break her silence.

"This wasn't an accident, was it?" she asked, turning toward Todd.

"What do you know about that?" he asked in reply.

"Did they burn the mountain lodge, too?" her questions continued, as though she'd never heard his.

"Listen, lady," said Todd. "We've got a serious criminal investigation going on here. Why don't you get us off to a good start by telling us why you're here?"

"I'm here on…business," she replied, letting her narrow shoulders fall a notch. "I work for Matheson Draper, the CEO of GSG. I'm his…*private* secretary."

"Miss Weinberg, is it?" Andy asked, noting the absence of a wedding band on her slender fingers.

"Natalie Weinberg. You can call me Natalie, if you'd like."

"Is Mr. Draper supposed to be here, too?" Andy went on.

"Yes," she replied, glancing from Andy in the back seat to Todd beside her. "He almost always vacations here during this time of year. He likes the cool weather, and this retreat was one of his favorite locations. He could've gone abroad, I suppose, but he doesn't do well when it comes to foreign languages or the customs of other countries."

"What do you know about the mountain lodge?" asked Todd.

"I'm one of the few people who *does* know about the lodge," she replied, hanging her head. "It was my idea to build it. It offers more…privacy. Math preferred that aspect of it, too."

"Did he go by *Math?*" asked Andy.

Natalie didn't answer at first, letting the way he phrased the question sink in. She took a deep breath, and the tip of her tongue slid across her upper lip.

"He's dead, isn't he?" she asked lightly, the gold flecks in her hazel eyes almost twinkling.

"What can you tell us about that?" asked Todd.

"I'm…" she started to say, smiling at her own thoughts. "I'm just glad I wasn't in hell when that piece of fat hit the fire."

"I beg your pardon?" asked Todd, giving Andy a confused stare.

"You don't really know who Matheson Draper was, do you?" she went on. "He just might've been the most completely evil man on the face of the earth."

"Well, that's sure not gonna help with the suspect pool," Andy said with a laugh.

*   *   *   *

"I watched him very carefully, sir," said the broad-shouldered man standing before Yancey Fitzgerald's desk. "He only opened Mr. Draper's short list of file names, and he deleted all of them before he removed the hard drive. I disposed of the CPU in the ground floor compactor."

"Draper was not especially computer literate, to be sure," said Fitzgerald, frowning, "but he did have a personal laptop that's presently unaccounted for."

"My people took care of anything and everything within the structures. The house and garages were totally destroyed. Local radio traffic confirms it. Mr. Draper's Mercedes was in the garage bay, just where you'd told us, and it's a total loss. Any records of any kind that were in the house or the garage are now incinerated."

"Laptops are mostly plastic. It'll melt away to almost nothing in that kind of heat."

"I wish I could share your optimism," said Fitzgerald, rising from his chair. He strode to the full-wall window, and watched the clouds moving closer. "Have we been able to locate Miss Weinberg?"

"Not yet. The GPS satellite-locator in her vehicle must not be working. We've activated it remotely, but it's not broadcasting."

"Maybe she was with him," Fitzgerald said, mostly to himself. He took a photograph from his inside coat pocket and held it at arm's length. "What is that? Antifreeze?"

"That's what it looks like, sir."

"Whose people would use...such a sloppy method?" Fitzgerald asked, turning away from the window.

"Ethylene glycol. It's a common poison, even in small amounts," the man said with a shrug. "I've read about isolated uses—mostly on animals, but no...*group* that I'm aware of makes a habit of using it."

"Nothing on the envelope?"

"Hand delivered to the security desk downstairs, but the camera only got a view of the attire. The...subject was wearing a broad-brimmed hat. We don't even know race, since gloves can be clearly seen in the video."

"And the weekend guard didn't notice him?"

"The guard was away from the desk making rounds—but we can't say for sure the person who delivered it was even a *man*. The subject came through the delivery entrance, and we're checking with the other vendors who signed in during the same time period."

"I'm sure your efforts in Montana will...hamper any investigation," said Fitzgerald, returning the photo to his coat pocket, "but certain liberties must be taken for the good of the company, after all."

"And Miss Weinberg?" the burly man asked.

"I'm sure a little slut like that might be missed in the ashes of such a big structural fire, but do try to locate her, nonetheless. She has no family?"

"That was always one of Mr. Draper's requisites, I believe."

"Yes, I suppose so. If nothing else, the man was surprisingly thorough."

"Are you...sorry to see him gone, sir?" the man asked, watching Fitzgerald intently.

"I'm only sorry we don't know more," Fitzgerald replied, rubbing his soft hands together. "I'd like to know if this...*retaliation*...was enough to satisfy...them."

"Satisfy whom, sir?"

"That *is* the question, I suppose."

"And should we succeed in locating Miss Weinberg elsewhere?"

"A person without family is easily disposed of without much fuss. She's been with Draper for...over ten years now, as I recall. I'm sure he couldn't keep her completely in the dark, in regard to particular...business decisions. As a matter of fact, I'm equally certain a careful analysis of those deleted files would reveal a definite element of *her* computer skills. So, you can well appreciate our dilemma."

The big man nodded, but his blank expression never wavered.

*   *   *   *

With Andy supervising the arson scene and Vince still on guard at the roadblock, Todd found himself alone with Natalie Weinberg, in the front seat of his truck. Her eyes seemed to follow the drifting smoke, as they drove past the remains of the buildings, but she faced front when they began their ascent on the road to the lodge. The sun was now high, and she rummaged through her purse for a pair of designer sunglasses.

"I'm still not used to Big Sky Country," she said, as she put on the shades.

"I'm sorry to have to do this," said Todd, "but I'm sure you're the only person around who might be able to identify him."

"The description you gave couldn't be anyone else," said Natalie, shaking her head.

"How would he have gotten up there?"

"He had some four-wheelers in the garage, and he liked to let them 'do the walking,' if you know what I mean. Did you find one up at the lodge?"

"We really didn't have time to look around."

"He would've parked it in a covered shed, uphill behind the main building. I think the well pump and the air conditioning unit are in the shed, too."

"I'll check on it when we get there. He didn't have horses?"

"Math was scared of animals," she said with a laugh. "I think it was a childhood phobia. He even made me give away my cat."

"How long did you work for him?"

"Directly for him," Natalie replied, biting her lower lip, "about a lifetime, but I guess you're asking about dates. It'll be eleven years this fall. But I've worked for GSG for almost twelve years, total. It's the only job I've ever had, actually. I was hired fresh out of college."

"Where'd you go to school?"

"Georgia State, downtown Atlanta. You?"

"MSU."

"What is that, Mississippi State—"

"*Montana* State. Remember where you are."

"Oh, yeah," she said, putting her hand to her cheek.

"Do you still live in Atlanta, then?" Todd asked, slowing for a wet spot in the road.

"For the last eleven years, I've had to...travel...for the company. I've got a corporate townhouse assigned to me there, but it's not mine."

"Did they give you that car, too?"

"No, the Porsche does belong to me. But I guess working for GSG *did* pay for it."

"Pretty fancy ride. Did you drive it all the way out here from Georgia?"

"No way. GSG airfreights it wherever I need to go. I drove over from Bozeman."

"That's where MSU is, by the way."

"Oh...well now I can relate. You're a little out of your neighborhood, too, then."

"I'm way out of my neighborhood, since I now live in Missoula, but I'm the agent who got the call, and the Criminal Investigation Bureau never turns down a request on a homicide."

"You mean you don't work with that nice man who arrested me."

"No, ma'am. He's just a reserve deputy—who happened to have the hell scared out of him earlier this morning."

"Well, you can see how threatening *I* am."

"I was gonna ask you," said Todd, slowing for a switchback, "just how tall are you?"

"Mr. Milton," said Natalie, leaning forward to look over the top of her dark lenses, "I'm not *tall* at all. If you'd care to know how *short* I am, however, I'm four feet ten inches without the heels, and I weigh seventy-four pounds. Black hair, hazel eyes, and I'll be thirty-four this Halloween."

"I...think that just about covers everything for the moment, Miss Weinberg—and it is *Miss* Weinberg, as I recall, isn't it?"

"Yes," Natalie said with a sigh, turning back to look out the windshield. "That was another company requirement for my...position. But if you wanted to be a little less formal and call me Natalie, I wouldn't mind."

"Only if you'll call me Todd."

"I guess I'm not a murder suspect, then," she said hopefully.

"I...don't think so," said Todd, rubbing at his now day-old beard, "but I think you might be a material witness for the time being, so you'd better plan on staying in my custody for a little while."

"You mean...like...*jail?*"

"I think we can do better than that, but you might have to stay at the sheriff's place. He's got a very nice guest cabin, though."

"Why can't I stay at the lodge? I've spent as much time there as Math has."

"But it's a crime scene—"

"The whole place?"

"We'll see," said Todd, dropping the stick shift down a gear.

*   *   *   *

"Got a call for you, sheriff," the highway patrolman said, offering Andy his cellular telephone.

"This is Sheriff Freund," Andy said.

"This is Yancey Fitzgerald in Atlanta, Georgia, sheriff," a man's voice said through some ringing static. "I'm executive vice president with GSG. Our alarm company out there has reported a fire alarm at our property in your jurisdiction. Is something wrong?"

"I'd have to say yes, Mr. Fitzgerald. You've had yourself a fire out here, sir," Andy replied, moving his head in an effort to get better reception. "This place of yours is a total loss. Looks like a case of arson, too. We've got the state fire marshal on the way. Who's got the insurance on this place?"

"GSG is a self-insured corporation, Sheriff Freund," said Fitzgerald. "We've been trying to reach Mr. Draper, our company CEO. Is he out there with you?"

"He's not with me," said Andy, giving the patrolman a frown. "Is he supposed to be around here somewhere?"

"His vacation itinerary shows him at The Manor for the entire month. He probably got there before the weekend. Is his car in the garage?"

"The garage is gone, too, sir, but it looks like we've got a couple of burned out vehicles in there. What kinda car does he drive?"

"It's...uh...a Mercedes V-12 sedan, I believe. I'm not absolutely sure of the model. Black in color. All of the GSG vehicles are black, you know. There should be a Porsche Turbo there, as well—also black."

"Yeah," Andy said guardedly. "I can see the outline of the big Mercedes, and that sports car is here, too."

"Well, then. Mr. Draper should be...in the vicinity, and a Miss Weinberg, too. She drives the Porsche. She's a very tiny woman. Have you seen them?"

"I've called one of the Montana CIB agents in on this, Mr. Fitzgerald," Andy replied. "Have you got a number where he can give you a call back?"

"Certainly, sir. If you'll just stay on the line, I'll have my answering service give you our toll-free number."

Andy nodded, and he turned his attention to the eastern mountains.

*   *   *   *

"That's him," Natalie said, fighting off a shiver. She made no effort to look away, however, but she did flash a quick smile of gratitude when Todd slipped a work coat over her shoulders. His 44 regular Carhart covered her to mid-calf.

"Do you know his full name?" Todd asked quietly, flipping open his notepad.

"Hugh Matheson Draper—the *Fourth*, if you can believe it. The family's originally from Charleston…that's in South Carolina, for the benefit of you Westerners. They were plantation owners from before the Revolutionary War. *Very* old money and lots of it.

"He was sixty-one on February 2nd—I know it's hard to tell from the face-lifts and tummy-tucks. For his birthday celebration, half the world sent reps to pay homage at our Atlanta offices. Princess Diana was there. So was Elton John."

She paused for a moment to wrap the coat more tightly around her, but she still stared icicles at the lifeless shape in the chair.

"It was…quite an event," Natalie went on. "A day…like so many hundreds of others I'll never be able to forget."

"Are you okay?" Todd asked, looking up from his note pad.

"Yeah," she replied slowly, still not willing to divide her attention.

"Did you have…feelings for him?"

She turned quickly, causing Todd to take a step back.

"Contempt is a feeling, isn't it?" she asked pointedly, bringing a hesitant nod from Todd. "Well, that's how I felt about both of us."

*   *   *   *

"The presence of the two cars in the burned garage building is significant," said Yancey Fitzgerald, a frown pasted beneath his otherwise blank stare toward the south. It appeared as though the hoped-for rainstorm would miss the downtown area. "The sheriff out there didn't tell me much more, however, and that's a bother.

"But, perhaps they haven't gone to the trouble to search for any human remains in the building, as yet. I may be getting ahead of myself."

"Those embers will remain hot until the evening, sir," said the broad-shouldered man. "I doubt they were able to assemble the proper equipment to put out such a fire. As for recovering the bodies…their efforts might not yield results until tomorrow."

"Will the fire destroy the…evidence in the photo?"

"Completely, sir. The accelerant used would produce a very hot fire."

"If they do an autopsy," said Fitzgerald, turning away from the window, "can the presence of this…antifreeze be identified?"

"They'd have to know to look for it, sir. Off hand, I'd have to say no. Heavily charred remains make for a difficult forensic examination."

"I just wonder how Miss Weinberg was disposed of."

"There may be a problem with her, sir," the man said, glancing behind him to make sure they were alone. "Her corporate fuel card was used in Livingston this morning, at a little after ten a.m. Mountain Time."

"Is that before or after the fire?"

"That's just about when it was set, sir."

"But the sheriff said her Porsche had been located."

"There's always the possibility that the card was stolen."

"And used on the same day and time that The Manor was torched? I seriously doubt the coincidence," Fitzgerald scoffed.

"Maybe there was another vehicle in the garage that was mistaken for the Porsche," the man suggested, canting his size-8½ head.

"I think we need to send someone else out there," said Fitzgerald. "Someone with the right *connections*. You know the type."

"I'll get right on it, sir."

✳   ✳   ✳   ✳

"Since you're the closest thing we've got to an owner," said Todd, unfolding a legal-sized document, "I'll go ahead and serve you with a copy of our search warrant."

"If this is a murder investigation," said Natalie, taking the paper from him, "why do you even *need* a search warrant?"

"Any time you've got a suspicious homicide—and I'd have to say this *is* one of those times," Todd replied, removing a 35mm camera from his evidence kit, "it always helps to follow all the rules of evidence. In this case, the suspect or suspects might be related to the company somehow, and they might even be in a position to refuse a consent search somewhere down the line. I just like to cover all the bases."

"What are you looking for?"

"Evidence of someone who didn't belong here," said Todd. "Who else knew about this place?"

"I guess...the contractors who built it," Natalie replied, taking a seat in a rocker. "I'll have to check the records, but it was a local firm...out of Livingston."

"What other people might've been up here?"

"Nobody but...us," said Natalie, nodding toward the body of her boss.

"Did you have any housekeeping staff?" asked Todd.

"Not up here," Natalie replied, glancing about. "The place isn't really all that big. Two upstairs bedrooms and baths, and a half bath downstairs. The kitchen. Not a whole lot to get messy. I'd always clean up just before we'd leave."

"Look," said Todd, gnawing at his lower lip. "I don't know another way to ask you this, and I don't mean to pry, but...what did the two of you *do* up here?"

"Since I was on salary," Natalie replied, again staring intently at the corpse, "I guess I was his...*whore*...to a certain degree, anyway. Does *that* answer your question?"

"You weren't...like...his girlfriend?"

"No," she said sharply. "I am a girl, true enough, but there was no *friendship* to it. Matheson Draper used me like his personal sex toy, Mr. State Agent, and I suppose that makes me a suspect again, doesn't it?"

Todd licked his lips, but he didn't know how to reply.

*   *   *   *

Andy Freund had his back to the west, but he could see a shadow moving across the narrow valley floor. He turned to see a rapidly moving front, and he glanced back up the mountain toward the lodge. The clouds were traveling quickly, and the temperatures were dropping perceptibly.

"Looks like snow, sheriff," one of the volunteer firemen said.

"Not what we need right now," said Andy, his thoughts still high in the east. "It'll help with the fire, though."

*   *   *   *

Todd had given some thought to making Natalie remain in the truck, but he'd left her in the lodge, instead, as he'd gone about the business of collecting the outside evidence. He'd found a four-wheeler in the shed, just as Natalie had told him, and he'd also collected a sample of the "yellow snow" and the casts Andy had made of the intruder's right and left boot treads.

Like Andy, the trail of footprints had intrigued Todd, and he followed it to the top of the rise and down to the other edge of the snowline—a distance of over a mile. Farther east, the terrain became rocky, and he knew there was no sense in continuing. Tracking dogs might work, he reasoned, but it would take a while to make the arrangements.

As he turned back toward the lodge, he could see the dark clouds moving overhead, and the snow was falling heavily before he was halfway back. Even in June, a deep snowfall wasn't out of the question, and only the lights of the lodge were visible by the time he regained the ridge top. The tracks of the suspect—and even his own much fresher tracks—were now covered in a thick blanket of white, and there was no end to it in sight.

Todd found half a foot of fresh powder on the deck at the lodge, and he shook off his damp shirt and hair as he entered the building foyer. It was warm inside, however, and he found Natalie dressed in a flannel shirt and jeans.

"I don't think we'll be going anywhere any time soon, cowboy," she said, offering him a cup of hot cocoa. "Hope you found what you were looking for out there."

"Just about," said Todd, taking the cup with a grateful nod. "Anything else will have to wait for the summer thaw."

"That'll be August," Natalie said with a tight grin. "You might as well get your *inside* work done."

"I might be able to get us out of here, if we hit it right now," Todd offered. "I've got a full set of tire chains in the truck."

"You're willing to abandon your crime scene?" she asked.

"I don't think anybody else will be able to make it up here to disturb the place."

"I still say there's no way we're gonna get out of here, Mr. State Agent," Natalie said, shaking her head. Her hair was a little damp, as though from a shower. "That snowstorm came in fast from the west. Whatever's getting dumped on us right now has already been dumped on the road down below, and it's still coming down. There are a couple of spots on the road where the loose snow will slide your truck right off the mountainside—even with those chains on it."

"Listen," said Todd, dragging the toe of his boot on the floorboards. "I've got a body bag in the truck. I need to do something with Draper's body before the heat in the house starts making things...a little ripe in here."

"Like I said. You might as well get your *inside* work done, while I see what I can find for us to eat around here."

Todd nodded slowly, before turning back to the door.

*   *   *   *

"What about Mr. Milton?" Vince Gilkey asked Andy.

"If he didn't see this coming," said Andy, turning in the front seat of the Bronco to see if there was a break in the clouds to the west—no such luck, "he's stuck up on the mountain. He'd be a fool to try coming back down with the weather like it is. I guess he'll have to stay up there until this stuff calls it quits."

"That little woman's with him, too, boss," said Vince, raising his eyebrows. "He took her up there to ID the body."

"Todd knows how to take care a things. That's why I called him."

"I thought you called the other CIB offices first."

"Shit, no," Andy said with a laugh. "I just told Todd that to piss him off."

*   *   *   *

"He's out on the deck," said Todd, brushing snow from the shoulders of his coat. His boots had left wet spots on the hardwood floor. "I don't think he's going to deteriorate too much in the snow. It'll keep him preserved better than the morgue cooler."

"I...uh...went upstairs earlier to...take a shower and change—after you'd left the first time," said Natalie. "It didn't look like anything had been disturbed in the upstairs bedrooms. Math's pants and shirt are still lying on the bed, if you want to check them. His watch and jewelry are up there, too, but I guess you really didn't figure this thing to be some kinda robbery, did you?"

"No...at least not after what you told me. The problem will arise just like Andy said, since you make the suspect pool sound like the Pacific."

"Math was a total cutthroat businessman," Natalie said, motioning for him to follow her to the kitchen. She had bowls of steaming soup waiting on the kitchen table. "He's caused the financial ruin of over a hundred competitors since I've been with the company. Some of those now-defunct businesses had over a thousand employees. He knew how to make money, but he never once made a friend."

Todd waited for Natalie to take a seat before joining her at the table. The barley soup had an inviting aroma, and he stirred in some black pepper while he waited for his bowl to cool down a bit.

"From the looks of things," Todd said, glancing up from his soup, "Draper was in the living room when the intruder came in. I found some videotapes on the coffee table, and there's a towel tossed on the floor in front of the leather couch. I think he was watching some movies—dressed...or...*un*dressed just like Andy first found him."

Natalie remained silent as Todd spoke, and she seemed to be fascinated by the steaming bowl before her.

"Lucky for you, you weren't here when it happened," Todd went on. "Whoever did this probably would've viewed you as a potential witness—one he could do without."

"I wasn't supposed to be here," Natalie admitted absently. "As a matter of fact, for the last month I've been busy with employee interviews, desperately trying to find my replacement. When I took the job—that is...the job I have now, the understanding was that I'd keep it no later than my thirtieth birthday, but, as you can see, that wasn't to be.

"For one reason or another, Math kept putting off my...*retirement*, much to my dismay—"

"If you couldn't stand the guy," Todd broke in, "why'd you stay with him?"

"Because he paid me two hundred thousand dollars a year," Natalie replied, giving him a stare that might've frozen the soup in his bowl. "I've got a piddling little degree in communications, Mr. State Agent. Where else could I make that kind of money?"

"What's with all this 'Mr. State Agent' nonsense?" Todd asked, his tone a bit lower. "I thought we were going to be...a little less formal."

"I'm still not so sure I'm not a suspect," Natalie replied. "You haven't exactly been too...relaxed around me, you know."

"My fault," Todd apologized. "I'll admit to being a little awkward and nervous around any pretty woman I've just met. I'll try to do better...Natalie."

"That is...better."

"So, where were you—I mean, before you showed up here?"

"I was in Tokyo, earlier in the month. I interviewed three girls in our branch office there. Math had a thing for...little women, and the Japanese girls would've easily met his...particular standards.

"When I got back to LA, I interviewed a young Mexican girl in one of our shipping offices there. The girl had strong religious convictions, however, so I knew from the beginning she'd be a difficult one to convince. She was very attractive, though, and I think she might've been swayed by the salary. It's…all immaterial now."

"Forgive me for saying so, Natalie, but this whole thing sounds pretty weird."

"I thought so, too…once," she said, dipping her spoon into the soup. "When I was first hired in Atlanta, I'd applied for a job with their media relations office.

"With all the print and broadcast media in Atlanta, I didn't expect to do much but sit behind a desk in an out-of-the-way cubicle, but after four or five months I was brought…*upstairs*, for an interview with Math's staff assistant. She told me I might be able to advance within the company, and she had me fill out a more detailed background form. The form included a lot of personal questions—including my exact clothing and shoe sizes. I thought *that* was weird, and I told the woman so. She just blew it off, saying that company employees might have to travel on very short notice. She said the company would provide employees with clothing at the intended destination, under those circumstances. It sounded believable enough to a kid fresh out of college."

"But it wasn't true," said Todd, taking a spoonful of soup.

"No…of course not," Natalie replied with a sigh. She, too, spooned up some soup. "Math was always on the lookout for…a particular *kind* of young woman. Since I've managed to hold the position the longest, I guess…*my* kind of woman.

"He has—that is, he *had*…certain interests, when it came to female companionship. I was young, I weighed the pros and cons as best I could, and I found the salary…tempting…"

"Look, Natalie," said Todd. "I'm not trying to be judgmental here, but you've got to admit that a woman who was about to lose her two-hundred-grand-a-year job sure would make a good suspect."

"I was the one who resigned, though…Todd," she replied, nodding. "There's a record of my resignation in GSG's Atlanta personnel office, dated in February.

"His little birthday celebration sort of…pushed me over the edge."

"You make Draper sound like a real degenerate," said Todd, leaning back from the table and wiping his mouth with a cloth napkin.

"If you do a *thorough* investigation," she said, raising another spoonful of soup, "you might just decide to call this a justifiable homicide."

*   *   *   *

Andy Freund fidgeted in the front seat of his Bronco, while members of the local search and rescue squad set up a large tent and portable kitchen in the paved parking area near the front of the burned out garage. The state fire marshal had yet to arrive, and the worsening weather promised to keep him away. At least the volunteer fire crew had managed to pull Vince's patrol car out of the ditch, using their all-wheel-drive pumper.

Still, there were plenty of other details to be addressed, and Andy didn't feel comfortable leaving the scene to someone else. As sheriff, he'd be the one answering the questions and taking the heat if something went awry.

"After they've got the tent set up," Andy told Vince, as they watched the other men at work, "I want you to run down to your place and pick us up some sleeping bags—and some pillows, if you've got 'em to spare. The search and rescue boys'll have folding cots for us, I think.

"Have your wife call down to Gardiner to see if she can find a place that rents portable toilets, too. They may have to bring 'em down from Livingston, though, if she can't find 'em closer. Until then, we'll use that stand a trees just this side of the creek."

"Do I get paid overtime for this, Andy?" Vince asked, rubbing his hands together in front of the heater vent.

"Don't get all fuzzed up over it. I'll cover whatever hours you get," Andy replied with a nod. "Even when you're sleepin'."

*   *   *   *

"I've got just about everything around the fireplace bagged and tagged," said Todd, as he returned from the living room. "Since there's nothing to indicate that the killer went upstairs, I think you can go wherever you want in the lodge."

"Did you find any fingerprints?" Natalie asked from the kitchen sink.

"Nothing on the bottles or the chair," Todd replied. "I doubt we'll find any on the duct tape, either. I found a little piece of Latex stuck to the tape. It's not a fingertip as best I can tell, but I'll bet it came from a rubber glove."

"The killer was careful," said Natalie, mostly to herself.

"I'd have to say so, except for the boot prints—but, hell, it's a pretty common size, and the sole pattern is used on most of the popular brands."

"I put Math's billfold and watch in the jewelry box on the dresser in the master bedroom," Natalie said, turning away from the sink with a towel in her hands. If not for the known circumstances, she might've been mistaken for a housewife—albeit a tiny one. "His shirt, pants, shoes, and socks are still upstairs. I guess you'll want all that stuff, too."

"Yeah," said Todd, pulling out his notepad once again. "I'll give you a receipt for everything, once it's all collected. Can I go get his things now?"

"Sure," Natalie replied with a shrug. "Take a left at the top of the stairs. The door's still open."

Todd nodded, and he watched to see if she'd follow him upstairs. Natalie returned to the stove, however, where a teapot was on the verge of a boil.

The stairs were polished wood, and they were a little too slippery to take two at a time. Todd climbed them quickly, though, and he found the bedroom lighted for him.

Using three large paper bags, Todd collected the clothes, shoes, and jewelry box. He counted out only fifty-seven dollars in cash from the victim's wallet, but there were plenty of credit cards in the billfold to cover any and all needs. Oddly enough, Draper had a New York driver's license, although it had expired the previous year. The watch was a diamond-encrusted gold Rolex, heavy in the hand, and there was also a class ring from The Citadel.

Todd took note that the bed had not been disturbed, with the exception of the now collected pants and shirt. Unless Draper was in the habit of making his own, the bed might not have been slept in.

Todd took a seat on the edge of the dresser, as he completed the evidence tags for the bags. He also added the more recently collected property to the search warrant inventory sheet. The waiting bags were on the bed, and he checked the contents of each before sealing them and attaching the proper tag.

He was about to gather up the bags and return downstairs when something metallic drew his attention. There was a silver eyebolt attached to the left side bedpost near the headboard. He'd caught the glow in the lights from the dresser. A further check revealed another on the opposite side of the headboard, but when he turned back toward the footboard he found himself staring into Natalie's eyes. She was standing in the open doorway, watching him intently.

"Looking for something?" she asked in an innocent tone.

"I just…uh…"

"To be honest with you," Natalie said, looking down at her bare feet, "I wouldn't really know how to answer that question either…if I were you.

"I guess the easiest way to explain it is to say, sure, I was a…willing…*participant*, when it came to bedroom games, but that wasn't always enough for…"

"Hey," said Todd, ending the awkward pause. "You don't need to get into all that if you don't want to. That is…unless he hurt you."

"Nothing…physical," Natalie said with a sigh. "I'm sure a few dozen sessions of weekly psychotherapy, and I'll be just as good as new."

"We really need to talk, Natalie," Todd said firmly, as he gathered up the evidence bags, "but first, I think I'd better read you your rights."

*   *   *   *

"Got a weather report, Andy," said Vince, having returned in a roundabout way from the designated temporary latrine area. "Heavy snow until early tomorrow morning, then it'll turn clear."

"Will it warm up?" Andy asked, his pen still busy with his report.

"Some…I think."

"I wonder if Todd knows. Do you think he's got his cell phone on?"

*   *   *   *

Todd and Natalie were seated across from each other at the kitchen table when his cellular telephone began to ring. Todd winced at the interruption, before digging it out of his coat pocket.

"Now you know how Tiger Woods feels," said Natalie, concealing her grin with a dainty hand.

"You got me," Todd answered, giving Natalie a stern stare.

"Hey, CIB man," said Andy Freund. "Are you folks gettin' cozy up there?"

"We're making do, sheriff," Todd replied. "What's going on down below?"

"Snow and more snow. Not much different until tomorrow morning. We've got almost a foot down here, so I know you're lookin' at twice that much up top."

"Maybe more than that," said Todd, turning toward the picture window overlooking the deck. There was no sign of Draper's body bag beneath the snow.

"I've got my search and rescue crew set up down here," Andy went on. "We've got snowmobiles ready whenever this weather breaks. Just sit tight, and we'll come up there for you in the morning. No sense in tryin' to drive down in this mess."

"Thanks, Andy."

"Don't mention it," said the sheriff. "Sleep tight."

Todd hung up the phone, and he turned back to Natalie, catching her in mid-nod.

"Sorry," she said, fighting to keep her eyes open. "I guess the soup made me a little sleepy. I've been up for almost twenty-four hours."

"Look," said Todd, returning his tape recorder to his gear bag. "Why don't you get some rest? We can do this in the morning."

"Are you sure you don't mind? You were looking pretty darned determined before you got that phone call."

"I'll be just as determined come morning," Todd replied with a slow nod. "And, besides, I've still got some things to do down here, and I can catch some sleep on one of the couches whenever the urge hits me."

He thought she gave him a quick wink, but it might've been his own tired eyes playing tricks. At any rate, she rose from the table and wandered off in the direction of the stairs. Todd made it a point not to watch her go, but he did listen for the upstairs bedroom door to close. After several more minutes without a sound, though, he went on about his business.

*   *   *   *

"I've located a competent individual near our Spokane office. I've already got him on the move, sir," the broad-shouldered man told Yancey Fitzgerald. "I believe he can take care of whatever's needed out there."

"To include what?" Fitzgerald asked, supporting his chin with the fingertips of both hands. The old man's itchy nose was in desperate need of a picking, but he didn't want to be crude. Not just yet.

"He'll see what he can find out about Miss Weinberg, and he'll make an official inquiry about the investigation. He's been issued company officer credentials, so there shouldn't be a question about his interest or authority."

"I dislike using too many people on this," Fitzgerald started to say.

"I'm doing my best, sir," the big man said defensively. "Mr. Draper had his own…contractor, but I was never given access to that person."

"Hopefully, any incriminating information about Mr. Draper's associates will be lost with the burned laptop."

"That was the idea all along, sir."

*   *   *   *

The heavy snow brought an early darkness to the otherwise bright western Montana mountains. By nine o'clock, a blackness had enveloped the lodge, and Todd found comfort by the burning logs in the fireplace.

It took him an hour to review his notes and make sure his search warrant inventory and return documents were in order, and he took another half hour to prepare an evidence list and photograph log. For some reason, though, his eye-straining efforts still couldn't bring about a much-needed sleep.

The combination television/VCR caught his attention, and he reached for one of the unmarked tapes Draper might've been watching.

*   *   *   *

Vince Gilkey was stretched out on a cot, snoring like an out-of-tune chainsaw. Andy Freund could only shake his head, as he, too, tried to find solace in sleep.

The state fire marshal had sent word he was holed up in a Livingston hotel until morning, and there was no sign of the portable toilets, but the rest of the ground operation was pretty much under control. And, still, Andy couldn't sleep.

His thoughts were with Todd, high up the mountain, and he wondered if his favorite CIB agent was making any headway. Andy couldn't make himself stop thinking about the evidence. Had Todd recovered all that was possible? Something he should've asked during their earlier phone call, but it was too late to trouble the agent now.

Andy gave his snoring associate a poke in the ribs, and the snorts came to a brief halt. The sheriff silently hoped there'd be enough quiet time for him to fall asleep during the momentary lull.

*   *   *   *

"It looks like the inclement weather has the location effectively isolated, sir," said the broad-shouldered man, passing a satellite photograph across Yancey Fitzgerald's desk. "Our man from Spokane probably won't make it beyond Missoula. They've got sections of I-90 closed down around Butte, so there's no sense in proceeding until the morning."

"I suppose we might as well head home, too," Fitzgerald said with a sigh. "Did you see my driver in the outer office?"

"Yes, sir. He's waiting for you."

"If something should break, will you be notified?"

"Yes, sir," the man replied with a nod, "and you'll be notified immediately thereafter."

"That'll be fine," said Fitzgerald, removing the photograph from his pocket for yet another look. "Do you think those union people might've done this?"

"Mr. Draper broke the union over two years ago," the big man said, shaking his head. "If they're behind this, the method is…confusing."

"How about any of the…remnants of what was once Worldwide? We, that is…he…settled that issue in January, but there's always the possibility…"

"The few remaining Worldwide beneficiaries were relatively happy with the eventual outcome, as far as our sources could tell. The insurance settlements alone were in the eight-figure range. The one surviving member of the Klaus family is now a delighted little drunken gambler. His after-tax inheritance was substantially more money than he'd ever dreamed of, although I've heard he's already gone through about thirty percent of it."

"Trans-Pacific?" Fitzgerald asked with a feeble squint.

"There are just too many possibilities, sir, and Mr. Draper didn't keep my division totally informed. There's even a chance this might be something involving a foreign government. From what I understand, he really angered some of the Saudis by…flaunting Miss Weinberg in their faces. You know how the Arabs have a different…perspective, when it comes to the value of women."

"I'd almost forgotten about Draper's silly teasing," said Fitzgerald, returning the photo to his pocket. "His little Jewish prize. Didn't one of the Saudis want to *buy* her?"

"I think the offer came from one of the royal family in Kuwait."

"It was an obscene amount of money, as I recall."

"Mr. Draper turned down five million dollars."

"How ridiculous. What woman could be worth that much?"

"Since he didn't take the offer, sir, it would appear that Mr. Draper thought Miss Weinberg was worth even more."

"Oh, whatever," Fitzgerald said, with a toss of his hand. "I'm sure she had her…merits—but only to Draper. If we do determine she's still alive, perhaps we should consider the offer from the Arabs. Five million is nothing to sneeze at, and that's one way to make sure she'll never be heard from again."

The broad-shouldered man let his eyes drift, but he remained silent.

＊   ＊   ＊   ＊

There was no sound, and Todd took a moment to fiddle with the remote in a fruitless effort to correct the problem. Then he realized there was no sound for a reason.

He recognized the man as Draper—several years younger, as was obvious from the not-quite-so-absent hair, now hidden by his expensive toupee. The elevated camera angle gave a good view of the top of the man's head and the large bathtub he was seated beside.

Draper seemed to be involved in some sort of preparation, although he was fully dressed in what appeared to be black silk pajamas and leather slippers. He was seated beside the tub on a low stool with a cushioned seat, and there were shampoo bottles and a lathered washcloth resting on the edge of the tub.

The girl's entrance took Todd by surprise. She arrived a full three minutes into the film, and Todd was close to nodding off when she made her sudden appearance. She drew his immediate attention, however, and sleep was suddenly and absolutely out of the question. Todd found himself rewinding the tape, just in case he'd missed an earlier detail.

She was blonde—with pigtails. The downward camera angle and her down-turned forehead were just enough to keep her facial features obscured, but she was clearly nude. She stood with her knees pressed tightly together, and her hands covered her chest and pubic area. Draper could be seen looking her up and down, and the fingers of his still-visible right hand seemed to flex uncontrollably.

Todd felt uncomfortably hot on the back of his neck, and he turned away from the screen to glance back at the stairway. He let out a protracted sigh, still uneasy with the scene being played out on the tape. His eyes snapped back to the screen.

She was in the tub, now. Todd thought about rewinding the tape to see how she'd gotten there, but he couldn't make his hands move. She seated herself on the edge of the tub with her feet in the water, and Draper slid his hands inside her thighs to force her legs apart.

Taking the washcloth in his still shaking right hand, Draper proceeded to apply it strategically, as though only selected areas were in need of cleansing. The camera angle now allowed Todd an unobstructed view, and the revelation brought an unfamiliar tightness to his chest. His heartbeats pounded in his ears.

She was a little girl—not more than ten or eleven from the evidence on the screen. Todd swallowed hard, but he continued to watch Draper's right hand move over her.

"I couldn't sleep either," Natalie said from just behind him, causing Todd's heart to take a momentary pause.

*   *   *   *

Yancey Fitzgerald's limousine was a stretch Lincoln Town Car, easily identifiable by its GSG-2 license plate. There was no GSG-1 license plate, but Matheson Draper had always made it clear who was Number Two in the organization, and Fitzgerald resented it. No doubt, a problem already rectified.

But for the present, the stranger's binoculars followed the vehicle with its distinctive plate, as it cleared the company garage.

"Late night," the stranger said to himself, as he dropped the rental car into gear.

*   *   *   *

"I didn't mean to scare you," Natalie said, scampering around to Todd's side of the couch. He was still blinking from the shock, and he took a long deep breath of fresh air.

"I'll...I'll be okay," he managed to finally say.

"I suppose I should've told you something about those tapes," said Natalie, taking a seat beside him. She was dressed in a Dallas Cowboys football jersey, with Emmitt Smith's name and number on it. It covered her beyond mid-calf, and it gave him cause to wonder if she was wearing anything underneath. "Math was not much of a...*movie* fan. In fact, he couldn't even follow the storyline of your typical half-hour network television program. I think he had some kind of an attention span disorder.

"But he did like his...home movies. That one was filmed in his mansion in Vinings, a pretty ritzy area north of Atlanta."

"How can you talk about him so...casually?" Todd asked incredulously, fumbling with the remote to turn off the all-too-revealing image before them. "He's nothing but a goddamned child molester."

"I know it looks that way," said Natalie, her eyes on the now blank television screen, "and, if he'd really had the guts, you'd probably be right. But remember what I told you about his silly fears. On top of being the most evil man I've ever known, Matheson Draper was also the most cowardly man I've ever met."

"But the evidence—" Todd tried to say, pointing at the television.

"The evidence is deceiving, agent man," said Natalie, reaching for the remote.

Todd made a feeble attempt to keep it from her, but he finally allowed her to pull it from his sweaty fingers. She pressed the necessary buttons, and the image reappeared. Rather than watch, Natalie rose and stood beside the display on the screen.

"I'll bet I know something you don't know when it comes to official law enforcement responsibilities," she said matter-of-factly, not waiting for his reply. "There's a branch of federal law enforcement that reviews tapes just like this one, to determine if they're genuine—or fake—kiddie-porn.

"I'm sure that's hard for you to imagine, but it's absolutely true. This tape has been scrutinized by cops who are carefully trained experts in the field. I'll bet there was no end to the whining when those assignments were made, too. 'Gee, chief, I don't want to go to porno-film training. Can't somebody else go in my place?'

"But I stray from the point. Do you have any idea how those very detail-conscious officers make their determinations?"

Todd kept his eyes on her, but he could only offer a shrug.

"From their thorough review of this tape—based upon what I'm certain was a previous careful scrutiny of *hundreds* of others like it," Natalie went on, "those dedicated keepers of the public trust were able to identify the age of the depicted female by the development of her...genitalia."

Todd thought he'd heard her right, but he was still only able to offer a confused expression. Natalie could see the need to elaborate.

"Even with the miracle of electrolysis," said Natalie, walking across the screen to stand on the opposite side of the television, "the truth was still there—staring them in the face, so to speak.

"I once thought breast size might throw them off, too, but those crafty G-men have received training in that particular anatomical area, as well. It would appear—at least to *them*—that nipples, too, have a way of showing their age. No telling how many thousands of little bullet-nips they had to go through for that assessment. And lo and behold they were able to discover yet another positive indicator of a woman's maturity."

"Give it a rest," said Todd, waving his hands. "You've got to get to the point, 'cause I don't know what the heck you're talking about. Are you telling me this videotape has gotten somebody's...stamp of approval?"

"Exactly," Natalie replied with a tired but satisfied smile, draping her arm across the top of the television.

"But...why?"

"Because Matheson Draper was a chicken shit," Natalie said, gritting her teeth. "Haven't you been listening to me? He was afraid somebody would catch him with this stuff and *think* it was kiddie-porn. There's a form letter around here somewhere with an official seal on it. He never took the tapes anywhere without it."

"But I know what I saw—*see*," Todd said, pointing to the screen. "I mean, I'm no expert on preteen girls, but that's a...*little* girl."

Natalie tightly closed her eyes and exhaled loudly at his reaction, and she started pacing back and forth in front of the flickering images on the screen. The little blonde was standing in the tub, now, with one foot resting on the edge, and Draper was using a continental showerhead on her overly exposed privates.

"I don't doubt that you're a competent cop—I mean I saw the way you handled the other evidence around here," she began again, still pacing, "but I'm still willing to bet this is something entirely new to you."

"You're right, if you're talking about child pornography."

"What I'm talking about is a man with more money than the Rockefellers but fewer guts than your average night crawler. A man who wanted so desperately to fuel his fantasy that he *bought* the means...to legally realize the sick dream."

"Are you telling me...the little girl I think I'm looking at is...an adult...*actress*?" asked Todd, his eyes now fixed on Draper's wandering right hand.

"What I'm telling you, Mr. State Agent," Natalie said, pulling the jersey over her head to reveal what he'd only suspected, "is that the 'little girl' you see on the screen before you is...*me*."

*   *   *   *

Yancey Fitzgerald lived in the suburban Smokerise area, near Stone Mountain Park. A relatively short commute compared to most of Atlanta's workforce, and a quick one due to the late hour. His driver only remained long enough for the bony sixty-year-old to make an awkward departure, and the limo's passing headlights briefly illuminated the stranger's rented Taurus parked across the street. The driver paid the idle car no mind, however, as he made his way out of the subdivision toward his own waiting home.

On the Fitzgerald mailbox, there was a sticker for an alarm company, and the stranger didn't doubt its validity. Some of the other homes in the area had electronic gates, but Fitzgerald's was nothing more than a big house on a large residential lot. No fence. No wall. But lots of trees. Mostly pines, some oak, and a scattering of dogwoods. Azalea bushes flourished along the front wall of the house.

The stranger checked his watch, and he took note of each interior light as it was turned off. Fitzgerald and whatever company might reside with him were in bed within half an hour of his arrival home. There wouldn't be any new activity until morning.

The stranger reached for the ignition key.

*   *   *   *

"All right," Todd said, hanging his head and averting his eyes. "I can...*see* it's...you. Now, I'd appreciate it if you'd turn the thing off, so I can tag the tape as evidence."

Natalie pressed the stop button, and she handed him the remote. She took a seat on the opposite end of the couch, and she waited for him to lock eyes with her.

Todd rose from the couch, and he removed the tape from the VCR. He placed the videocassette in an evidence envelope and sealed it with red tape. He stood with his back toward the couch as he wrote the necessary case information on the evidence tag. After a couple of minutes, he stooped to lift the Dallas jersey from the floor in front of the television.

"Is this really one of Emmitt's jerseys?" he asked without turning around.

"It's not just *any* old Emmitt Smith jersey," Natalie replied lazily, leaning back into the soft leather. "It's the one he wore in Super Bowl XXVIII, in Atlanta in '94, when he was named MVP."

"Would you...like to put it back on?"

"Sure," she said lightly. "Would you be so kind to bring it to me?"

Todd finally looked her in the eyes, as he handed her the billowy shirt, and he didn't take his eyes off her as she slipped it over her head.

"It was a wig," said Natalie, as she pulled her hair through the collar.

"Huh?" Todd asked in confusion.

"Those blonde pigtails," she replied, waving at the television. "I was wearing a wig. I wore my hair much shorter back then, and it was easy for me to tuck it under the wig. The film doesn't show enough of my face, but you can still see my black eyebrows from time to time. That tape is nine years old, by the way.

"One of the other tapes is pretty much the same, except I'm a Raggedy Ann redhead and the camera angle is much...lower. He was going through an equally demented but disgustingly different phase back then, and he liked to...put his—"

"I'll take your word for it," Todd said quickly, gathering up the remaining tapes.

Natalie rose from the couch, and she stood at his side, watching him complete a second evidence tag. She hardly came up to his armpit, but he *was* wearing boots.

"I guess I was a little out of line," she said softly, bringing a pause to his writing. "I suppose I could've...*explained* the tapes...a little less provocatively. I had no intention of embarrassing you, agent man. I suppose I've grown insensitive about certain issues over the years, but now...well...I'm sorry."

Todd remained silent, but he did turn to look down at her. She couldn't get a read on his expression, however.

"Hey," said Natalie, holding out her empty palms. "I'm just trying to apologize here. If I screwed up, I didn't mean to. I've gotten cynical in my old age. Give me a break. Come on. Say something...please."

"In the last half hour," Todd said with a hint of a grin, "you've stopped my heart *and* restarted it.

"If *you're* sorry, I can accept that, but don't you even begin to think *I'm* sorry."

"Now I'm the one who's confused," Natalie said, squinting and shaking her head.

"Well...I guess it's your turn."

*   *   *   *

A heavy gust of wind made the canvass wall tent strain against its wooden frame, but it didn't rouse Andy Freund. He was already awake.

He glanced at his watch: almost 1 a.m.

Vince Gilkey had rolled onto his stomach, so there was no snoring coming from his cot, but two of the search and rescue volunteers were trying to outdo themselves at the other end of the tent. Andy rolled his tired eyes and unzipped his sleeping bag.

The snow was still falling, but the flakes were smaller. Beyond the edge of the overhanging tarp—serving as an awning at the door of the tent, the snow was now nearly 18 inches deep. Andy was sure there'd be three feet of the stuff to contend with up top. The morning snowmobile ride wouldn't be a quick one.

Turning back to the stove near the tent door, Andy used a leather mitt to manipulate the handle and add some much needed wood. He then made a slow return to his cot, where he hoped the night sounds and snoring company wouldn't continue to keep him awake.

*   *   *   *

"The other two tapes were made more recently," said Natalie, as Todd marked the evidence tag on the one they'd been able to identify as the *redhead* tape. "It's hard to say which is which, but they're both what you might call…bondage-oriented."

"As in…the hardware on the bedposts in the master bedroom?" Todd asked without looking up from the tag.

"Well…yes and no," Natalie replied awkwardly, finally distracting him from his paperwork. "I mean, he never filmed here, but…yes, that's what the eyebolts were for."

"But why?" asked Todd, placing the pen and evidence tag aside. "It's not like he had to…rape you. Did he…expect you to resist?"

Natalie rose from the couch once again, and she took a seat on the coffee table in front of him. She let one bare foot rest atop the other, and she rubbed her palms together nervously. Even with a troubled look on her face, she was still strikingly beautiful.

"There's something I need to tell you, and it's going to be hard for you to believe, but you need to understand," she said, her eyes turned somewhere near her feet. "Matheson Draper never raped me. He never even had what you could call…normal sexual intercourse with me."

Todd reached out and lifted her chin until their eyes finally met.

"I'm still a…virgin," she said almost apologetically.

"Was that part of your…contract?" Todd asked, raising his eyebrows. "Did you know it was going to be that way all along?"

"I might've not known it in the beginning," she tried to explain, "and I guess that's why I think of myself as his…whore. I was prepared to trade sex for security—and I suppose that's exactly what I've been doing all these years. It just took me a while to learn what *his* idea of sex happened to be—and even that changed over the years. And my role changed, too, from…molested child to…humiliated submissive, but only my self-esteem got lost along the way. Much more so, near the end, as those last two videotapes will clearly illustrate."

"Do you not want me to look at them?"

"They're...evidence, aren't they?"

"If you'll just tell me what's on them, I can tag 'em, and we'll be done with it," he offered.

"As much as I'd like to do that," she said softly, picking up one of the tapes, "in *your* eyes, I'd be a lot more of a suspect if I discouraged you from watching them."

Without another word, Natalie rose and put the tape in the VCR. She used the remote to start the film, and she returned to the couch.

"At least I picked the right order," she said, as images began to fill the screen. "This one was filmed in the GSG company compound in Jubayl...Saudi Arabia. It was made back in January of 1996."

The setting was a huge banquet hall, brightly lighted, although there only appeared to be a dozen men in the cavernous room. All of the men were dressed in the traditional flowing garb and colorful headgear of Arab royalty. Some even wore jewel encrusted scimitars and daggers. For the first couple of minutes, there was no evidence of another culture present.

Then Natalie's image filled the screen. This time there was no mistaking her. No wig for a disguise—nothing at all. She was absolutely nude, with her hands hidden behind her. She made no effort to cover her nakedness, as she looked directly—and defiantly—into the camera, and then Todd was able to see why.

Draper followed closely behind her, and he held the end of a narrow leather leash. Dressed in a tuxedo with glossy black lapels, he smiled broadly into the camera lens before walking across the expanse of carpet to greet his companions. The camera shifted from Draper to Natalie, and Todd could see both her wrists bound in a single handcuff.

"So, that's how you knew to tell Vince about both hands in one cuff," Todd said, giving her a sideward glance, but she remained silent, her eyes fixed on the screen.

Todd took the remote from her without a protest, and he stopped the tape and hit the eject button.

"Don't you think you ought to see more of it?" she asked, covering her eyes with her hands. "It's almost two hours long."

"I think we know which tape is which, now," he replied.

"He let them...touch—hell, they *examined* me," she went on, "reminiscent of an old fashioned Middle Eastern slave auction, although I do believe some Arab countries still keep slaves in this day and age. Just before we walked in, he told me about…their Arab customs. He taunted me with their—"

"Enough, Natalie," Todd said firmly. "Just give me…an overview of the other one, so I can fill out the evidence tag. I'll need a date and a place. That is, if the…substance is the same."

"The substance," she echoed, looking up with tears in her eyes. She wore a wounded smile, though. "Yeah. It's pretty much the same, except it was filmed earlier this year in the GSG Atlanta office. We were in the penthouse ballroom. It was right after his gala birthday celebration. Fewer people. Three other men…and a woman. All of them *pillars* of our American business community. Math liked watching the woman go down on me, but she was more than a little rough, and that's what brought about my resignation.

"It's one thing to be humiliated for a living, and quite another to be abused."

"That would've been in February of this year?" Todd asked, trying to sound official with his pen busy on the evidence tag.

"It was well after midnight," Natalie replied, "so I guess it would've been the third."

"From the sound of things, you picked a good time to resign. If Draper was becoming more…aggressive in his behavior toward you…"

"It wasn't so much…him. It was how he'd started…sharing me. The way his tastes were evolving. Did you ever read *The Story of O*?"

"Huh?" he asked, putting his pen back in his pocket.

"Well, Math didn't read it either—books confused him," she went on, "but he was able to grasp enough of the *movie* to start exploring new perversions. He even consulted the corporate surgeon about having me…*pierced*, but he didn't have the patience to wait out the required healing process, so he gave up on the idea.

"It was things like that. I don't know. Maybe he *was* getting worse, but it's hardly important now. At the moment, I guess he's trying his best to negotiate with the Devil. Who knows? By the time I get there, Math could very well be the one in charge."

"Hey, look," Todd said lightly, finally able to distract her from her momentary funk. "Whatever *had* happened between the two of you is past history, now. Don't sell yourself out as a lost cause. You're still in one piece—*unpierced*. You're young enough to make a fresh start at something else. Heck, I'd be satisfied with my lot just to drive your *car*."

Natalie wiped at her eyes with one of the floppy jersey sleeves, and she pulled her hair back behind her shoulders. She wanted to check herself in a mirror, but none was available. It took a moment, but her smile returned, even more fatigued than before, however, but gorgeous, nonetheless.

"Are you trying to cheer me up, agent man?" she asked.

"I'm just trying keep us focused, that's all. It would be a big help—especially for you, if you could give me some kind of an idea of who might want Draper dead. I mean, who would've wanted it the most? And who the heck would've done it...like that?"

Natalie nodded, and she rose from the couch. Her stretch was almost feline, but she appeared to be revitalized by it. She turned to Todd with eyes wide and clear.

"For most of 1996," she began, returning to the couch and sitting cross-legged, "GSG was doing its best to absorb the assets of an outfit called Worldwide. GSG bought up an awful lot of Worldwide stock, but Math still didn't have a controlling interest.

"The catch was that Worldwide had developed a better product tracking system than GSG, and Worldwide's market share was growing in an area otherwise dominated by GSG. It was only a drop in the bucket to a company like GSG, but Math felt it like a...thorn in his butt, and he talked about it constantly—even to me.

"During the last quarter of '96, the hostile takeover of Worldwide dominated the company board meetings, but then everything changed abruptly when the Worldwide corporate jet disappeared in flight."

"I remember seeing that on the news," said Todd. "Didn't it happen during the Christmas holidays?"

"Just after New Year's," said Natalie. "They were making their way back from Hong Kong. The speculation was that the plane went down somewhere in the South China Sea. They had scheduled stops in Brunei and the Philippines, but the exact route was never determined, and no wreckage was ever located.

"The real kicker was that the whole Klaus family was on board, along with most of the corporate officers. Almost every brain in their outfit conveniently out of the way. I think the only Klaus family survivor was an outcast grandson who happened to be sweating it out in drug rehab at the time."

"But that was some kind of...terrorist attack, wasn't it?" Todd asked.

"It was the most popular guess at the time, anyway. One of the tabloids ran an alien abduction story, but nobody believes that crap. Except for the fact that GSG bought up the remaining Worldwide assets within the month, I'd be willing to accept the terrorist theory, too. Somebody's always mad at the good ol' USA, after all."

"Did Draper ever say anything?"

"That's just it," said Natalie, her eyelids starting to droop a bit with fatigue. "With the exception of a few self-congratulating grins in the mirror, he never made mention of it—even when he was signing the final buyout checks."

"There were over forty people on that plane—"

"Fifty-eight, with the crew. It was a full-sized Boeing airliner. Sixteen children were onboard."

"And you really think Draper was behind that?"

"I don't know," she said softly, glancing down at her hands in her lap. "I'd like to think he wasn't, but his behavior was so…inappropriate. While the rest of the country was either in shock or in mourning, Math was almost…jovial. The only time I ever saw him like that was when he was…well, you know…busy with me.

"But there was this other time, too…"

"I guess Andy did have you pegged right," said Todd, flipping open his note pad, "but at least you've given me somewhere to start. So, what's this about another time?"

"Do you remember an outfit called Lonnie Axtell Trucking?"

"Wasn't he a baseball player?"

"Catcher for the Dodgers. I can't remember when exactly, but I think he retired in the late seventies or early eighties. He was no Hall of Famer, by any stretch, but he did pretty well as a broadcaster for a couple of seasons.

"Anyway, he started a truck line down in Texas, and he underbid GSG on some rail shipping business. In less than three years, he had GSG edged out of west Texas, and he was working on the rest of the state."

"Don't tell me Draper was behind the Axtell kid's kidnapping," Todd scoffed.

"*Déjà vu*, agent man. Except I guess it really can't be déjà vu since it happened before the Worldwide crash, but you get my point. And it wasn't Axtell's kid; it was his grandson. I'm pretty sure the boy had a different last name."

"Yeah, it's a funny kinda name, too. It'll come to me, but…that's still an open case. They run a notice on the back page of our regional intelligence bulletins every month."

"Then you know Axtell paid the ransom. They've never said how much, but it ate up a big chunk of his personal liquid assets."

"And all this happened in the middle of another GSG buyout?"

"No," said Natalie, slowly sliding onto her side on the couch. "But Math hit Axtell with the buyout offer the day after the ransom demand arrived—and *before* the kidnapping story hit the news. You might say it was an opportune business moment, but I still think it stinks to high heaven."

Todd continued to take notes, but he couldn't resist keeping an eye on Natalie, as often as he could. She was making a valiant effort to stay up with him, but the hours without sleep were taking their toll on the tiny woman.

"You know there's a difference between unethical business practices and criminal behavior," he said, scanning his notes.

"I guess you don't want to hear about Trans-Pacific, then," Natalie whispered, before burying her face in her crossed arms.

"That's a new one on me," said Todd, sitting a little straighter.

"The *Kahili Maru*? It was an older style oil tanker," she continued, her voice muffled by her reclined position, "but the investigation following the wreck and the spill never turned up anything mechanically wrong with the ship."

"Isn't that the Oregon coast thing?" Todd asked, nodding even though she wasn't looking.

"It goes back a ways, but 1989 isn't really so long ago," she replied. "There *was* a crew member unaccounted for on the manifest. The Merchant Marine records were forged, but they never were able to identify the guy. The photo they found in the file and used in the broadcast was nothing but a blurry smudge. It could've been O. J. Simpson, for all the picture showed."

"Did Draper buy them out for a song, too?" asked Todd, his pen busier than ever.

"He didn't have to," she replied, raising her head to rest her chin on her crossed wrists. "He already had a much more modern fleet of tankers. The real problem was that he had to charge more to pay for the ships. After the spill, though, he just picked up the Trans-Pacific contracts while they went under fighting the lawsuits. There was no other competition in the area."

"You make him sound like Attila the Hun," Todd said almost absently.

"Well, at least nobody died when the tanker went aground. That is, unless you count all the thousands of fish, birds, and seals."

Todd flipped his note pad closed, and he turned to look down at her. Her eyes might've been tired, but they never wavered.

"How do *you* know about all those things?" asked Todd. "Did Draper run his mouth that much? Was he a braggart?"

"Not enough to draw attention to himself," she replied, squinting in thought. "Most of the stuff I just told you is public knowledge—it came from magazines and newspapers, but the corporate reaction to those disasters was…generally disgusting.

"I may not have much when it comes to character, but I *do* resent those who revel at the misfortunes of others."

Natalie's openness made Todd take a momentary pause, but he reminded himself there was still work to do.

"How in the heck am I gonna verify any of this, Natalie?" he asked. "I mean, nobody's just gonna come prancing forward and say, 'yeah, he had me do this and that.'"

"Think about it this way, agent man. All those things had to cost money—lots of it," Natalie replied, raising her chin just high enough for him to catch a glimpse down the front of her jersey. "That kinda monetary outlay can't be completely hidden."

"Y'know something," Todd said, unable to resist the temptation. "Those G-men were wrong. Your nipples really don't look thirty-three years old—speaking of things that aren't completely hidden."

"Oh," she said, quickly pulling the collar up to her neck. "Sorry."

"You were talking about money," he said, biting his lip to keep from smiling.

"Yeah," she said with a nod, letting the collar fall open again so she could prop her chin up with her hands. This time, Todd kept his mouth shut. "Math really wasn't a very smart guy. In fact, in lots of ways he was downright stupid."

"Now, wait just a minute. I found his college ring upstairs. I've got it in one of the evidence bags. If he went to college, he couldn't be that stupid."

"Oh, that. He just *bought* the ring. Even with his family's pull, he got booted out of The Citadel after only a couple of days. His prep school grades were forgeries. He couldn't spell. He couldn't even do simple arithmetic. Numbers gave him fits. He had…*billions* of dollars, but he couldn't tell you how many zeros were in a billion. He didn't even know where to put commas or decimal points. He had an accounting staff to pay all his bills and prepare every one of his checks."

"What are you getting at?"

"I know he kept his own private set of records. His office in Atlanta had a stand-alone computer. He kept it locked in a walk-in vault, since he couldn't memorize passwords. I showed him how to set up and save documents, but that's as much as I know. He didn't trust the other GSG corporate officers or anybody else.

"Not even a woman whose nipples don't look thirty-three."

Todd gave his forehead a smack, and he turned away. She'd known he was looking all along, and she'd stung him but good.

"Don't feel bad," she said, her hand on his sleeve. She was up on her knees, right next to him on the couch. Todd could feel his neck warming up.

"It's…kinda nice to be stared at by a guy who blushes so easily. It's been so long. Why…I don't even know if I *can* blush anymore."

"I…I knew better," he stammered, still unwilling to look in her direction. "I'm sorry."

"Maybe I just got the wrong signals," she said. "When you mentioned it the first time, you didn't seem too disappointed, so I…"

"Can we get back to the office computer…please?" Todd asked, turning just enough to catch her out of the corner of his eye. She was pretty well covered by number 22.

"I'm not the only one who knows about it," she said, releasing his sleeve. "Chances are, Fitzgerald or one of his flunkies has already drilled through the vault door to get at it."

"How do you know about drilling vault doors?"

"Right after he had the vault installed," Natalie replied, her eyes twinkling at the memory, "Math forgot the combination, and he had to have the door drilled. I was there. It was no easy task. Lots of noise, smoke, and the smell of burning oil. It took over an hour.

"After that, he had a keypad lock installed, and he programmed it with a simpler combination. I once heard Fitzgerald say that the new combination was probably Math's birth date, but I doubt he could even keep those numbers straight. It wouldn't surprise me if it turned out to be 1-2-3-4—and that's just because it's the same as the combination on all his luggage."

"If somebody else in the company drills the vault door, there won't be anything left on Draper's office computer for me to find, will there?" Todd asked.

"I guess that depends on how far they go. If the CPU itself isn't destroyed, a real computer whiz can retrieve the information even after it's been manually deleted. At least it's worth a shot—and there's still another possibility. Did you happen to see a laptop computer around here?"

"No," said Todd, leaning forward on the couch, "but I didn't really bother to look too hard, either."

"I didn't see it in the master bedroom closets," Natalie said with a shrug, "and I don't think he'd even bring it up…I mean all the way up here. When he traveled, he usually kept it in the trunk of his car, since it'd be out of sight but still easily accessible."

"That's no good. His car got cooked with the rest of the garage. I think the gas tank blew when I was making the drive up to get Andy."

"Well," she said lazily, sinking back into the couch cushions, "I guess you're going to have to make a trip to the Old South."

"Oh, yeah. Like my boss is gonna approve funding for *that*."

"Look, agent man," said Natalie, making no effort to open her eyes. "We're going to have to resume this in the morning. Right now, I'm so tired I don't think I'll be able to climb those stairs."

Without another word, Todd rose from the couch, and he scooped up all seventy-four pounds of Natalie Weinberg with an easy fluid motion. He was careful to keep his hands away from anything personal, but the bend of her knees and her narrow back felt pretty firm to his touch. For a tiny woman, she had good muscle tone, but the closest she came to stirring was when she rested her head against his shoulder.

He took the stairs more carefully, and he carried her to the still-made bed in the master bedroom. She was so manageable, he was able to pull back the covers while still holding her in his arms, and he placed her gently on the silk sheets. After pulling the covers up to her chin, he took a moment to stare down at her in the dim light coming from the outside hallway.

There was a rustling beneath the covers, and then the jersey came up over her head.

"Silk sheets are best experienced in the nude, agent man," she whispered, still without opening her eyes. If she had opened them, though, she'd have seen the hasty departure of a blushing man shaking his head.

CHAPTER 4

▼

The new day greeted Vince Gilkey in the form of a coffee cup held out by Andy Freund. The aroma was inviting.

"What time is it?" Vince asked with a dry voice.

"Not quite daytime," Andy replied, staring out at the gray sky, "but the snow's stopped. You better get yourself moving. There'll be work to do."

"No breakfast," Vince said mournfully.

"The eggs are on right now," Andy said with a broad smile. "They've got potatoes and bacon goin', too. I think there might even be some sausage. I wouldn't send you out on an empty stomach, but they don't feed deputies in their skivvies—even reserves."

*   *   *   *

Yancey Fitzgerald's cellular telephone began to ring, as he was collecting the morning newspaper from his front lawn. Like his driver only a few hours earlier, he didn't notice the maroon Ford Taurus parked just one door down from his driveway.

"Yes," he said, after placing the newspaper beneath his arm.

"The interstate's open again, sir. Our man in Montana is on the move," came the curt reply.

"Thank you," Fitzgerald said before terminating the connection.

*   *   *   *

Judge Clarence Mingle rubbed at his tired eyes, while counting heads at the morning breakfast table. One of the twins was missing, and he gave his harried wife a one-eyed frown.

"I know, I know," the woman said nervously. "He's still in the tub. We're running a little behind, that's all."

"It's his turn to shovel the driveway," said Clarence. "That damn highway department plow has pushed a four foot wall a snow right across it. I can't even see our stinkin' mailbox. If I could catch that sum-bitch, I'd have him in court this mornin'."

"I'll get the boy going," was all she could think to offer.

Taking the rotund woman by the shoulders, Clarence held her close. She could see the corners of his mouth twitch, and he felt the tension pass from her.

"I just haven't heard spit from the boys down the road, honey," he said in way of an apology. "I'm sure the foul weather's to blame, but I hate not knowin', just the same."

"You want your sourdough toast?" she asked softly, bringing a broader smile to his chapped lips.

*   *   *   *

At first, Todd thought a waterline had sprung a leak, but then he realized it was a shower running in one of the upstairs bathrooms. He rubbed at his now two-day-old beard, and he wondered what might be available in the way of a razor. From the looks of things, Draper didn't use a suitcase, so there had to be a selection of toiletries in the house.

The shower stopped, and he sat up on the couch to see what the new day might bring. There was no snow falling, but what had fallen was up to the top of the deck railing. The sky was clear, though, just as Andy had promised.

Evidence bags and envelopes cluttered the floor around the couch, and Todd busied himself with his report forms. He gave some thought to a real shower, but he figured a sink scrubbing in the downstairs half-bath might have to do.

"The best I can manage for breakfast is instant oatmeal," Natalie offered from the living room doorway. She was wearing one of Draper's dress shirts, and it was almost transparent in the growing glow of the morning sun.

"Didn't he keep any of *your* clothes up here?" Todd had to ask, but a raised pair of carefully plucked eyebrows was the only answer he got.

"How about…socks…underwear?" he asked, following her toward the kitchen.

"The only underwear I had," she said, turning so quickly he almost walked over her, "was the *thong* I was wearing when I got here. Have you ever worn a thong, agent man?"

Todd had to smile at the thought, and he shook his head in silence.

"Well, it's not the kind of thing you want to wear two days in a row," she went on, turning back toward the kitchen. "As for socks, I guess I could wear a pair of his, if my feet get cold, but I'm used to going barefoot."

"How do you keep this place so warm, way up here?" Todd asked, making sure not to follow her quite so closely.

"Electric heat," she replied with a shrug.

"Way up here?"

"They ran the lines when they cut the road. I can't remember how many miles of cable Math said there was, but it's all buried."

"But what about in the wintertime? Does somebody come up to flush out the waterlines and winterize the place?" he persisted.

"The power is *always* on," she said, standing on a stool to return the instant cereal box to a cabinet shelf. "So is the heat. There's a programmed thermostat under the stairway. This place is always sixty-eight degrees. When it gets too warm, the AC unit comes on. It's in the same shed where you found the four-wheeler."

"Always on," said Todd, mostly to himself. "That must cost a fortune."

"Matheson Draper *has* a fortune. That is…he had one, anyway."

"But why didn't the fire in the big house cut the connection?"

"Search me," she replied, turning to face him. "This place was completed last July, but The Manor's been here since the early eighties. It was here when I started with the company. Maybe the newer construction is on a separate power line."

"Man," Todd said with a sigh. "I guess it's just hard to fathom that kind of money. Hell, my gross pay is only about thirty-five grand a year. I can't even imagine bringing home *your* salary. Do you realize you make over twice as much as the governor of Montana?"

"Is your governor a man or a woman?"

"A man."

"Then I'm sure you can take my word for it," she said, holding up two bowls of piping hot oatmeal. "If the governor of Montana had to parade around naked just to titillate a bunch of horny Arabs, *he'd* be asking for a lot more than two hundred thousand dollars a year."

"Thanks for *that* image," Todd said with a smile, happy to accept a bowl of hot cereal.

"You're welcome," said Natalie, returning the grin. "And thanks for not taking me up on my offer."

"How's that?" he asked absently, stirring his oatmeal with a spoon.

"That offer to search me," Natalie replied, watching him closely. "You were right about the underwear thing. I'll see what I can do about the clothing situation."

"What about the jeans and shirt you had on yesterday?"

"Those were the only things I had up here—and Math didn't even know about them, but I screwed up last night. I threw them in the laundry chute without thinking. They're probably down in the basement in a pile of dust."

"You mean you've got a washer and dryer up here?" Todd asked hopefully.

"In the basement."

"Well, I'm going upstairs to try on some of your boss's clothes, and then we'll do us some laundry. I kinda liked the looks of you in those jeans you were wearing yesterday."

"Do we have time?" she asked, turning toward the morning sunshine.

"Have you ever ridden a snowmobile?"

"Never."

"It's not really all riding, you see. There's lots more lifting, dragging, and cussing. Mostly cussing, when Andy's involved. It'll be noon before they get here, and they'll probably clear enough of the road for me to drive the truck back down. Anyway, Andy'll give us a call on the cell phone before he starts up this way. I'm sure we've got plenty of time for a load of wash."

*   *   *   *

One of the snowmobiles wouldn't start. Andy Freund watched over the shoulder of the search and rescue volunteer, as the man fiddled with the intricacies of the two-stroke motor. Andy knew better than to offer help, though. The only thing he knew about snowmobiles was where to put the key and where to put the gas.

"Andy," Vince Gilkey called out, almost out of breath. He seemed to be leading another man toward the makeshift garage.

The sheriff squinted into the rays reflecting off the snow, and he headed toward his lumbering deputy.

"This guy's from Spokane," said Vince, motioning toward the newcomer. "He works for the outfit what owns this place."

"Baxter Carlton," the man said, extending a gloved hand. Andy took it, but only briefly. "I was hoping to talk with the state agent in charge here. Isn't that what you told our home office in Atlanta?"

"As you can see," said Andy, motioning toward the fresh snowfall, "we've had some setbacks. The snow helped with the fire, but now it's covered up everything else. I don't want anybody tramping through the debris here until this stuff melts off, and that probably won't happen until this afternoon—or even tomorrow."

"What does the state agent have to say about that?" Carlton asked.

"He left me in charge," Andy replied firmly, giving the man another look up and down. "As the county sheriff and chief law enforcement officer around here, I can override him, anyway."

"Oh, don't get me wrong, sheriff," the man said in an obvious condescending tone. "I'm not about to question your authority. We're all friends here. I'm retired law enforcement myself."

"What outfit?" Andy asked abruptly.

"Overseas," Carlton replied, his eyes well hidden behind a pair of dark glasses. "Contract work. I'm sure you understand."

"And if I don't?"

"Sheriff," said Carlton, taking a step closer and lowering his voice. "This is a multi-million dollar property. You can well imagine the GSG interest here. The home office informed you of our two missing persons. Mr. Draper is the CEO of Global. He's a multi-*billionaire*—the most important man in the company. Miss Weinberg is his private secretary, and she was most probably with him. If they were in The Manor when it burned…well, you can certainly appreciate the concern."

"If they *are* in there, they won't be any deader when we find 'em," said Andy, hoping his unbrushed teeth had made a lasting impression.

"Are you telling me I can't remain on site while your investigation progresses? I do have every right to be here. In fact, you'll need to show me a search warrant before *you* can proceed."

"The CIB agent has got the search warrant with him, but I'm aware of its existence, and that satisfies the legal requirement, as far as I'm concerned."

"Where is this agent now?"

"He's on the way."

"May I be permitted to wait for him?"

"You got a car?"

"The black Range Rover," Carlton replied, nodding toward the vehicle parked on the edge of a plowed path nearby.

"Stay in it," Andy said, turning back toward the snowmobiles. "I don't want to catch you wanderin' around, either, and there aren't any portable toilets out here, so you'd better be careful where you go."

Carlton tried to remain expressionless, but it didn't matter. Andy had taken Vince by the sleeve, and the two of them never looked back. They disappeared into a large tent.

"Keep an eye on that guy, and don't tell him *anything*," Andy hissed through clenched teeth.

"What about Todd?" Vince asked, a worried look in his eyes.

"Don't tell him about Todd. Don't tell him about the girl. Don't even tell the bastard your first name. Do you understand me?" Andy growled. "There's somethin' mighty fishy about all this, and I think this guy knows more than he lets on. That Fitzgerald guy told me all of the GSG company vehicles are black. Those guys who got the drop on you and torched The Manor were drivin' black cars, and so is this suck-up asshole. I don't trust any of 'em."

Vince nodded, and he gave his gun belt an upward tug. Andy watched Vince's back as he left the tent, then he checked the charge on his cellular telephone.

*   *   *   *

"If you should get a call, sir," said the broad-shouldered man, dressed as neatly as the evening before but now wearing a different suit, "he's using the name Baxter Carlton. It's one of our standard aliases. He has sufficient supporting corporate ID."

"Not to worry," said Yancey Fitzgerald. "All the executive office staff personnel know to play dumb. Any inquiries will be routed directly to me."

"What's he been able to learn?"

"He's on site, and he's confirmed the total destruction of The Manor and the garage building. He's certain anything within the structures that might've been of evidentiary value has been destroyed. No effort has been made to inspect the damage due to the heavy snow, but the heat from the structures has melted much of the snow above it, and he can plainly see the extent of the damage. He also said he saw the burned out hulks of at least two vehicles in the garage debris."

"What instructions have you given him?"

"He told me the sheriff there had denied him access to the actual structures until the snow melts and the fire marshal arrives. I suppose they're hoping to find evidence of our crew from yesterday, but those men do an exceptional job, and I'm sure there's nothing left to tie them to the scene."

"Where are those people now?" Fitzgerald asked, again fiddling with the photograph he dared not let out of his grasp.

"Their flight landed in La Paz earlier this morning—"

"Why on earth there?" Fitzgerald asked.

"We have...other work there, sir," the man replied hesitantly.

"Oh...of course. I'd forgotten. Please continue."

"I've given...Carlton instructions to remain close. I think he can make better progress with the state law enforcement there. Sometimes the local cops can be difficult. It's our understanding that the Montana Criminal Investigation Bureau has been called in. Once Carlton contacts the agent on site or, perhaps, the fire marshal, we should know more about the evidence situation.

"He also checked at the service station in Livingston where Miss Weinberg's corporate card was used. The clerk on duty didn't recall either a black Porsche or Miss Weinberg's distinctive description, so the card might've been used to fuel another vehicle, although fuel payments can be made at the pump. The only real concern is that her unique personal code number was entered to access the account."

"Ah, the stupid little bitch probably wrote the code on the back of the card," Fitzgerald snarled in disgust.

"I thought you gave her credit for more sense than that, sir," said the big man, perhaps taking too much of a liberty. Fitzgerald paused to regard his subordinate, his eyes narrow slits.

"You don't know her like I do," Fitzgerald finally replied.

"Yes, sir. I've only seen her in person a few times...and I was allowed to view the videotape Mr. Draper had made at the Saudi compound."

"Draper and his tapes," Fitzgerald said, drifting off on a tangent. "What a strange man, indeed. So powerful in some respects; so insecure in others. Both publicly and privately corrupt, of course. A total package of degeneracy.

"Did you know the man had an atrophied penis? And only one testicle, too."

The big man could only shrug uncomfortably.

"I've got his medical and dental records right here. With any luck, the Montana agent should be calling for them soon, and we can bring an end to this silly game of ours."

"And what about Miss Weinberg?" the big man asked, breaking his silence.

"Her records are here, too," Fitzgerald replied, tapping his finger on a large manila envelope. "There are even some interesting photographs of her. Graphic, you might say. Draper had them taken a couple of years ago. Quite a *unique* woman, I must admit. Like an adult in miniature. What a fascinating concept. Now I know why so many people fawn over those tiny dogs.

"Of course, when the time arrives we won't share *these* photos with our Montana friends. Did you ever actually meet her—I mean, as opposed to just…seeing her?"

"At your house, six years ago. It was the reception after your daughter's wedding."

"I couldn't believe he brought her along," said Fitzgerald, shaking his head. "My wife was furious. Did you know the little slut wasn't wearing any panties? Draper told me later, but I'm surprised I didn't notice. Her skirt was so short, but, then again, so was she. Draper thought it was so funny, the perverted bastard."

"I was also with them in the Mediterranean after the Barcelona Olympics. I was there with *you* for two days, on the corporate yacht."

"Then you *did* have the pleasure of…seeing her at her best. I'm sure next to you she must've looked especially small. As far as I know, that's the only time Draper ever spent his summer vacation away from his Montana hideaway."

"She wasn't having her period, was she? I can't seem to remember, now, but I've seen her much more often than you, after all."

"I beg your pardon, sir," the big man said, standing a bit taller—if that was at all possible.

"Was she wearing that…*g-string* affair?" the old man asked impatiently.

"Oh, no, sir. She wasn't wearing anything."

"Then she wasn't having her period. Draper only let her cover her privates during the *red tide*. The rest of the time she was more naked than Eve. He once told me he'd kept her nude for twenty-two days straight. He thought it had to be some kind of record, as if they'd keep records like that. There were times he regarded her as a real show piece, like that bit of distraction with the Arabs."

"Still, with all due respect, sir, I never saw anything in her behavior to indicate she was stupid."

"I can't believe you," Fitzgerald said, rising from his chair. He opened the envelope and withdrew and 8X10 glossy of Natalie Weinberg bound to the corners of a four-poster bed. "What kind of *intelligent* woman would allow herself to be portrayed like that? I'm beginning to wonder if stupidity might be infectious around here."

The big man remained at rigid attention, in tight-lipped silence. Fitzgerald couldn't be sure that his subordinate even took a glance at the photo on his desk.

"You...talked to her," the old man said softly, a sly smile forming on his face. It was not a natural expression for Fitzgerald, and he didn't wear it well.

Still, the big man maintained his silence.

"I remember it all, now. You knew talking with her wasn't permitted," Fitzgerald went on. "*You* broke one of Draper's strictest rules. It's all coming back to me, that sticky summer on the bounding main, but what bothered me then—and still bothers me now—is that *you* never told me. I had to get the word from Draper himself.

"Why that's almost...disloyal. I don't know if I should continue to trust you."

"Have I ever failed you before, sir?" the big man asked.

"We'll see, my fine friend. This may be your true test."

Again, the big man remained silent.

✳   ✳   ✳   ✳

"Are you folks awake?" Andy asked, before Todd could even say hello.

"We're waiting on laundry to come out of the dryer," said Todd.

"Oh, yeah," Andy said lightly. "So what have you got on in the meantime?"

"A pair of Draper's pants—the waist is too big, and the legs are too short, but I'm not about to enter any footraces in 'em, either. The man did know how to shop for underwear, though. I've never been a fan of boxers, but these are pretty darn comfy."

"What's the little lady doin' while you're playin' the Chinaman?"

"She's sitting right across from me. We're both watching the timer."

"And...what's she got on?" Andy asked, almost at a whisper.

"I'll never tell—"

"God damn it!" Andy shouted, loud enough for the men outside the tent to hear.

"Okay, okay," Todd said with a laugh. "She, too, is wearing a pair of Draper's boxers, although, if she hadn't found some safety pins to cinch up the waist, she'd be hanging on to 'em like a barrel."

"Does she have a shirt on?" asked Andy, his voice lower once again.

"One of Draper's, as a matter of fact, and it's so big on her I can't really see the boxers, but she swears she's wearing the boxers, just the same."

"Are you two doin' okay up there?"

"It was a long night, Andy," Todd replied with a sigh, "but I don't think she's got anything to do with this—*whatever* it turns out to be, and I think she can be a big help to us, if we let her."

"Can you put her on the phone?" asked Andy.

"Sure," said Todd, passing the phone across to Natalie. "It's Andy—the sheriff, that is. He wants to talk to you."

"Hi, sheriff," said Natalie, giving Todd a quizzical stare.

"I hate to be so short, Miss Weinberg, but I gotta ask you some quick questions," said Andy, "and I think my phone battery isn't gonna last too much longer."

"I can empathize, sheriff," she replied. "I hate being short, too."

Her response made Andy take a breath, but he had to grin once he realized that he'd heard her right.

"There's some guy down here from GSG," Andy went on. "Says his name's Carlton. He's from the Spokane office, but his car's got California plates on it."

"I don't recognize the name, sheriff."

"Well, I may be wrong, but this guy's actin' like Draper's not the only one dead."

"Are you saying he thinks I'm dead up here, too?"

"That's another thing. I don't think he even knows there's an 'up here,' if you catch my drift. He's been lookin' over the burned buildings with binoculars, and he seems pretty anxious to crawl through the ashes."

"If he sees my car down there, he'll know it wasn't burned in the garage."

"Hell, honey, your little pavement-pounder is covered in snow. You can't tell your car from one a the piles the plows pushed up."

"I just don't know what to tell you then," said Natalie. "The company does have a big office in Spokane, but it's just a distribution center. There aren't any company administrators there. Is he in a company vehicle?"

"It's a shiny black Range Rover. I think one of those network newsmen has one on his place near Gardiner, so I'm kinda familiar with the brand."

"All the company vehicles are glossy black," said Natalie. "Will he be down there when we get back? I might recognize him."

"If he thinks you're dead, it might be best if we didn't let him know different. I know you won't have any trouble hidin' in Todd's truck, so let's keep a low profile, and I'll be up with the snowmobiles before you can get your clothes outa the dryer."

"We were sort of hoping you wouldn't be quite so quick."

"Why's that?" Andy asked with a giggle. "Are you two tryin' to elope on me or somethin'?"

"What…makes you say that, sheriff?" Natalie asked. Now she was the one lowering her voice.

"Well, they say desperate conditions call for desperate measures. I just figured you folks might've had to share a blanket or two to survive the night. I mean, it's not like you're doin' somethin' *illegal*. You're both single and old enough to know better."

"He *is*?" she asked, barely above a whisper. Now Todd was the one with the quizzical stare. "He doesn't act it."

"What? Single? Sure he is. He's just the shy type. Why ol' Todd there gets red in the face when I make him ride my mare. I think women scare him a little bit, that's all."

"Oh, I don't know what I'm thinking," said Natalie, shaking her head. "In a few hours, I'll be gone, and I'll probably never see Montana again. Just forget I asked, okay?"

The phone connection was too scratchy for Andy to hear, and he pressed the off button to see if the battery might build a little more charge.

"I think I lost him," Natalie said, passing the phone back to Todd.

"I think you lost me, too," Todd said, rubbing his still stubbly beard.

$$* \qquad * \qquad * \qquad *$$

Judge Clarence Mingle gave the northbound snowplow driver a stern frown, as the mechanic-cum-jurist continued south toward the address Todd had listed on the search warrant. The roads were still partially covered in snow, but the warm morning sunshine was already turning the remnants of the white flakes into gray slush.

The judge's pickup truck was a monument to his ability as a mechanic, but Clarence was still pretty careful about where he parked it, lest it be impounded as abandoned. For a 1959 International, though, it ran like Joan Benoit, but outwardly it more closely resembled something being chased down a sewer pipe by a wad of toilet paper.

After making the proper turn, Clarence found himself negotiating a narrow path plowed by less ambitious snow removal equipment. There was just enough

room for two vehicles to pass in opposite directions, but only if they were oper-
ated in creep mode. After a few minutes of cautious driving, the judge found
Vince Gilkey's patrol car blocking the driveway.

"Where's Todd?" Clarence asked before Vince had time to say hello.

"Still up on the mountain," Vince replied, glancing around to make sure he
wasn't overheard. The nervous reserve deputy had taken Andy's words to heart.

"Why would he be up on the mountain?"

"That's...where the dead guy is."

"I thought he was in the house," said the judge, trying to look beyond Vince
through the trees. "Is that smoke?"

"It's pretty much out," said Vince, turning to look in the same direction.

"What's out?"

"Didn't you hear the fire call?"

"Hell, no. When was that?"

"Yesterday...maybe noon."

"I was in the shop. I musta had the country music station turned up too loud.
What got burned?"

"The big house. The place they called The Manor. And the garage, too."

"Did you get the body out before it burned?"

"No...well that is—"

"*No!*" Clarence shouted. "What do you *mean*?! *No!* Did you lose all the frig-
gin' evidence, you knuckleheads?"

"Calm down, Clarence," Vince said in a soft voice, hoping the judge would
follow his lead. "There's a guy around here snoopin', and Andy thinks he might
be workin' with the same guys who started the fire."

"What the fuck kind of a case *is* this?" asked Clarence. "The house got burned
after the guy got dead?"

"It's complicated—"

"Oh, I can bet it is, Vince, but I'm still not clear why Todd's up the mountain
if the fire's down here."

"The dead guy's up the mountain with Todd."

"What the...did Todd *take* the dead guy up there to get him away from the
fire?" Clarence asked weakly.

"I think the dead guy's name is Draper," said Vince.

"Just get the fuck outa my way, Vince, and point me toward Andy," the judge
growled.

"Sure, Clarence," said Vince. "He's just a little further on down the road. Just
let me move my car back a skosh."

After Vince had cleared his path, Clarence let out the clutch and inched his way around the front bumper of the patrol car. Vince was out of the vehicle and running toward the truck before the judge could completely pass by, however.

"Remember what I said about the snooper, Clarence," said Vince.

"What's he look like?" the judge asked, pressing in the clutch to let the truck idle.

"Tan overcoat. He's drivin' the black SUV."

"Speakin' of," said Clarence, his eyes narrowing. "You still owe me two hundred for the engine swap I did on Martha's Trooper."

"Sure, Clarence," said Vince. "This call-out oughta pay for that, don't you think?"

The judge nodded, and he fishtailed his way up the driveway. He saw the black Range Rover parked across from the search and rescue vehicles, and he parked his truck near the field kitchen. Before he had the engine switched off, Clarence could see Andy Freund walking toward him.

"What a mess," Andy said, as the judge tried to find his footing in the slippery slush.

"I figured you were up to here in it," said Clarence, taking Andy's hand, "but I was worried about you boys, so I thought I'd come down for a look."

"Sheriff," a man's voice called out from behind them. It was the snooper Vince had warned Clarence about. "I thought your deputy was controlling access to the property. What's this piece of junk doing in here?"

"Who the *fuck* are you?" Clarence snarled, taking a step toward the well-dressed man.

"Name's Carlton, judge," said Andy. "His outfit owns this place."

"Listen here, Carlton," Clarence shot back, before the other man could stutter an apology. "If you don't get your prissy ass outa my face, I'm gonna have this man plant your carcass in the county jail. You got that?"

"Sir, uh, yes, sir," said Carlton, glancing from the judge to Andy, who made no effort to hide his smile.

Both the judge and the sheriff watched Carlton's retreat with equal satisfaction.

"Vince told me somethin' about him back at the roadblock," said Clarence, turning his nostrils toward the field kitchen. "I guess that took care of him for now. Do I smell bratwurst?"

*   *   *   *

"Didn't you ever come up here when there was snow on the ground?" Todd called out from deep in the master bedroom closet.

"Sometimes there'd be snow," said Natalie, sitting on the edge of the bed, "but Math was never…an outdoor person."

"Why did he build something like this—in the Great Outdoors—if he wasn't an outdoor person?"

"Actually, building this place was my idea. I figured a smaller place meant fewer people, if you know what I mean."

"Well, there's nothing in here," Todd said, shaking his head. He stood at the closet door empty handed. "No boots. Not even any high-top shoes."

"He didn't regard the lodge as a boots-and-high-top-shoes kind of place."

"Well, you don't want to wear your high heels down the mountain, do you?"

"If that's all I've got, they'll have to do. Haven't you ever seen girls in jeans and heels before?"

"In that snow out there, your feet'll freeze."

"Then what do you suggest?" she asked, sticking her legs out straight and wiggling her tiny toes.

"How about three or four pairs of his socks?"

"They'll get wet."

"Not if I cover 'em with plastic evidence bags."

"Won't that be too slippery for walking?"

"Then I'll *carry* you," said Todd, shaking his head in frustration.

Her laughter had a calming quality, and he walked over to the edge of the bed and sat beside her.

"You do blush a lot," she said, falling back onto the bed.

"I think you're mistaking anger for embarrassment this time," he said, turning to look down at her.

"I'll tell you a secret," she said, her eyes squinting with mischief. "As little as I am, I've never had a man pick me up and carry me until last night."

"It was nothing," he said with a shrug.

"That's what you think, cowboy."

✳   ✳   ✳   ✳

"At the moment, they seem to have gotten some kind of judge involved," said the broad-shouldered man. "Apparently our man made a poor initial impression. I've instructed him to remedy the situation using whatever means are necessary."

"Here we go again," Yancey Fitzgerald said with a light sigh. "Checkbook diplomacy. The proven solution. Did you give him any restrictions?"

"The account is…substantial, sir."

"Whatever it takes," Fitzgerald said absently. "At any rate, we seem to have another type of crisis to occupy our time. It's down in Bogotá. There's talk of the Columbian government nationalizing our gold mines. It's only in the rumor stage at the moment, but the company stock has already taken a downturn. How I hate those banana republics."

"In regard to Mr. Draper's personal documents, sir," the big man began, causing Fitzgerald's stooped spine to stiffen, "we've found an unusual…modification…in his last will and testament."

"What the devil are you talking about?" Fitzgerald asked through gritted teeth.

"Apparently, the last review and modification took place in April of 1996. His personal assets are…enormous, as you can well imagine, and the change in monetary distribution involves only a small fraction of his total worth—"

"Will you *please* stop toying with me," the old man whined.

"He named Miss Weinberg as a beneficiary in his will," the big man replied.

"Preposterous! Our company legal staff will quash that with ease."

"I initially thought so, too, sir, but I've already had the document reviewed by our corporate counsel. Mr. Draper had the proper witnesses, and we've interviewed the secretary who'd drafted the change. It's all…perfectly legitimate."

"How much money are we talking about?" asked Fitzgerald, sinking lower in his padded leather chair.

"As I said, sir, compared to Mr. Draper's total worth, it's…relatively minor— only the name of the new beneficiary sent up warning flags, but the asset transfer into her name has already begun."

"And what *fool* authorized that?" Fitzgerald snapped.

"You did, sir," the big man replied, stone-faced. "When you initiated the automated portion of the corporate officer restructuring plan, you had Mr. Draper's status changed to 'deceased' in the company mainframe. By making that change, you started the distribution of assets automatically. In fact, the transfer has already been completed at this end."

"Fucking idiot," Fitzgerald muttered.

"You shouldn't take it so hard, sir—"

"I wasn't referring to *me!*" the old man shouted. "That damned Draper. *I* wrote his goddamned will *for* him. Do you think the fool could even *read* a document 212 pages in length? How *dare* he!"

"It's his money, sir," the big man said softly.

"Not anymore."

"The change does raise another question, though, sir."

"I'm listening," said Fitzgerald, taking a deep breath to calm his nerves.

"If she knew about this, Miss Weinberg might've had a motive."

"What?" Fitzgerald scoffed. "*Her*...kill Draper? We should be so fortunate."

"The photograph you have, sir. His fascination with...restraints."

"*He* was never the one bound. It was always *her*...tethered to the bedposts—or anywhere else his warped mind could imagine."

"Precisely my point, sir. If she did do it, don't you think she'd pick an intentionally demeaning method? You're the only one who's gotten a good look at the photo, sir, but, from your description of it...well, would *you* want to be found like that?"

Fitzgerald leaned forward in his chair, and he stared up into his subordinate's eyes. The man was almost too tall for the office doorways, and Fitzgerald despised having to look up at him.

"Is there some way we can pass this information along to the proper authorities?" the old man asked.

"If all evidence was destroyed in the fire, sir, you'd have to give them that photograph—and come up with an explanation of how it came to GSG."

"Well, that certainly wasn't Miss Weinberg on the lobby surveillance tape."

"An accomplice, perhaps?" the big man said with a shrug.

"But who says we need to share the surveillance tape with the authorities, either?" said Fitzgerald, thinking as he went. "Let your Montana man know about this development—the particular details are hardly important. It might complicate matters, but perhaps we should also instruct him to...eliminate Miss Weinberg, should she unexpectedly reappear."

"I believe...such a decisive order should come directly from you, sir," replied the big man, giving Fitzgerald a cold stare.

"It has," the old man said curtly.

*   *   *   *

"We got the snowmobiles runnin'," Andy Freund said, as Todd answered his cellular phone. "We won't be quick, but we're on the way."

"Who's coming up with you?" asked Todd.

"Oh, it's the guy…I know you know him. He does the rentals in Gardiner," said Andy. "I can never remember his name."

"I think it's Fischer," said Todd, "but don't quote me on that."

"Oh, you're a big help."

"See if you guys can make your tracks about the width of my truck tires. I'm gonna chain up and try to make it down behind you. The stuff's melting up here, but it's still pretty deep. With chains, I should be able to get enough traction—especially if you pack down the snow coming up and going back."

"I've left Clarence down here mindin' the fort," said Andy, giving the judge a thumbs-up. "He's keepin' an eye on this Carlton fella, too."

"Sounds good, Andy," said Todd. "We'll be ready when you get here."

"As deep as this stuff looks, you probably got time to get your clothes dirty and wash 'em again. I'm bringin' you folks some food, too."

"Good. Everything we've got up here has to be mixed with water."

"I got brat sandwiches, but they might be cold by the time we get there."

"No problem. We've got a microwave."

Andy flipped his phone shut, and he pulled on his full-face helmet. After making a motion toward the service road, the sheriff roared off, with the other snowmobiler in pursuit.

Judge Mingle turned his attention toward the black Range Rover, and he saw Carlton following Andy's progress with a pair of 50mm binoculars.

*   *   *   *

There was a pair of rubber boots in the shed with the four-wheeler. Natalie had to shovel her way up there, but she remembered them from her trip the previous summer. Draper had worn the boots during a rain shower, and they still showed evidence of very dried mud. Slipping off her heels, she pulled on the ugly green footwear. The tops almost came up to her knees, and her bare feet had enough room to turn around in them, but they were better than nothing. To walk in the boots, though, she had to slide her feet to keep from tripping right out of them.

"Very fashionable," Todd said, when she reached the back door.

"I think if I stuff them with towels, I can make them fit," said Natalie, wiggling her feet on the inside—with no evidence of same on the outside.

"They make you look like a circus clown."

"I just want to help, if I can," she said with a shrug. "Aren't you gonna go out and put the tire chains on your truck?"

"The snow is higher than the tops of those boots. You'll get soaked."

"Well, I'll start by shoveling a path for you. I think I can do that without getting snow in the boots."

"You don't have a coat."

"There are some of Math's sweaters in the dresser upstairs."

"You don't have gloves."

"I can use a pair of his socks for mittens."

"You win," said Todd, stepping aside to let her in the door. "Just watch out for the body bag on the deck when you start shoveling."

Natalie gave him a satisfied nod as she stepped out of the boots. Todd watched her carry them into the house, and then he paused to scold himself for admiring her from behind. He had no idea what size her jeans were, but she did fill them out well.

∗   ∗   ∗   ∗

"Something wrong?" Yancey Fitzgerald asked, as the broad-shouldered man made a quick entrance. For such a big man, he was light on his feet.

"I'm not sure, sir, but…Carlton reports some suspicious activity at the scene of the fire."

"What kind of activity?"

"Carlton says the snow is melting fast, due to the warmer weather," the big man replied. "But there's a man there who keeps shoveling snow onto a pile near the edge of the circular driveway. It's as though they're trying to keep something hidden.

"I think it's Miss Weinberg's car, sir."

"The sheriff did say it was there," Fitzgerald said uneasily, "but I don't recall him confirming it was burned.

"But that still doesn't mean she *wasn't* in the house. We may be worrying about nothing."

"Except for the timing of the fuel card use," the big man reminded him. "She may have arrived right after the fire, and she may be talking to the police right now."

"It's been...what...over twenty-four hours? I'm sure we'd've heard something by now. She wouldn't know what to do in a situation like this. She'd've called the corporate headquarters for instructions."

"I don't think so, sir. Her corporate affiliation was entirely with Mr. Draper. She has no other responsibility to the company. She was pretty much an independent...*vendor*, you might say. She might just pack up and go home."

"You forget she has no home," Fitzgerald growled. "The high-rise town house suite she uses when she's here in Atlanta is owned by GSG."

"Well...not according to Mr. Draper's amended will, sir."

"That's immaterial under the present circumstances," the old man snapped. "Did you relay my...that is, *the* instructions to your Mr. Carlton?"

"Yes, sir."

"Call him back, and tell him carry them out at first contact."

"That may be difficult for him with so much ancillary activity on site," the big man said cautiously.

"Remind him about the checkbook he's carrying. Tell him he can decide what his services are worth," Fitzgerald said smugly.

The broad-shouldered man nodded, and his eyes remained down-turned as he retraced his steps.

$*$ $*$ $*$ $*$

Vince Gilkey was thankful there was so little activity at the checkpoint, but he was even more dismayed that the portable toilets had yet to arrive. Along with a mild bratwurst, he'd made the mistake of eating a much more spicy Polish sausage, and his guts were paying the price. Not being a full-time deputy—and lacking any associated thoughts of officer safety, he returned to the front seat of his unlocked cruiser with his gun hand occupied with a roll of toilet paper.

"Where did the sheriff go?" asked Carlton, as he pressed the barrel of a submachine gun into Vince's still-unsettled stomach.

While Vince's lower lip quivered, his determined adversary removed the deputy's duty pistol, and Carlton used the muzzle of his own weapon to push Vince back out of the vehicle.

"He...he's up the mountain," Vince finally managed to answer, as Carlton slid across the front seat of the patrol car. "He's gone to get Todd."

"Who's Todd?"

"The…state agent. He's the guy who's doin' the investigation."

"Why is he up on the mountain?" Carlton asked, turning Vince toward the tents.

"He was collectin' evidence. He got caught in the blizzard."

"Get moving," said Carlton, giving the frightened deputy another prod, "and keep your mouth shut."

*   *   *   *

"That wasn't as tough as I thought it was going to be," said Natalie, as Todd fastened the last of the tire chains. Dressed in two large sweaters—with her sock-mittens pulled up to her elbows, her tiny figure was almost unrecognizable.

"Hear that sound?" asked Todd, brushing the snow from his gloves. "That's at least two snowmobiles."

"Sounds like a chainsaw."

"When it snows this late—after the trees have leafed out, the weight of the snow will pull the trees over or break off limbs," said Todd. "They might have to use saws just to get up here, but I've got one in the truck box if they haven't cleared enough of a path for us."

"I don't think you'll have to worry about downed trees," said Natalie, pulling the socks off her hands. "The guys who cut the road up here cleared anything that was close enough to fall on it."

"Well, I've got Draper in the truck bed, and the evidence bags are in the back seat. Is there anything else you want to take back down?" asked Todd.

"My purse is in the truck," she replied, giving the lodge another look. "I guess this is it. I should have a suitcase with fresh clothes in the trunk of my car."

"Aren't those the clothes you had in LA?"

"No," Natalie replied, kicking the snow off one of her rubber boots. "I didn't have my car in LA. It was shipped straight to Bozeman, and that's where I picked it up yesterday. My Tokyo/LA clothes were shipped back on the same plane."

"What happens to the stuff you sent back?"

"It gets cleaned and sent to my place in Atlanta."

"I'm surprised you even know how to do laundry," Todd said with a laugh.

"I do just enough to stay in practice, agent man," said Natalie. "The machines in the room downstairs aren't exactly foreign to me, you know.

"So, what happens next?"

"For now, all we have to do is wait," said Todd, his eyes on the road below.

*　　*　　*　　*

"What the hell's wrong with you?" Judge Mingle whispered to Vince Gilkey. The hapless pair was back-to-back on the floor of the wall tent, hog-tied together with several pairs of flexible handcuffs. The two other search and rescue volunteers were bound in a similar manner in the field kitchen tent.

"You better be quiet, Clarence," Vince whispered back. "You know what he said."

"But why are you squirmin' like that?" the judge persisted. "He's gonna hear you."

"I got a bad case a the screamin' shits," Vince said weakly.

"You got the *what*?!"

"Cla-rence," Vince whined through gritted teeth. "He's right outside."

"Like hell he is. I heard him fuckin' around with my truck. The hood springs need some oil, and I heard 'em creakin'."

"What do you think he's up to?"

"Hell if I know, but you'd better not shit all over yourself while I'm tied to you."

"I think it was that Polish sausage—"

"Just quit talkin' about it, and maybe the feelin' will pass."

"That's what I'm afraid of," said Vince, tasting some of his breakfast with a welcomed belch.

*　　*　　*　　*

"Anybody hungry?" Andy Freund shouted, as he opened the unlocked front door of the lodge. He almost paused to knock before entering, but the idea seemed silly under the circumstances.

"Starved," said Natalie from the kitchen doorway. "Come on in and have a seat at the counter. I've got hot water for instant coffee or hot cocoa."

"Where's your partner?" Todd asked, making his way across the foyer from the living room.

"Outside with the machines," Andy replied. "One of 'em won't run at full throttle."

"Is he going to eat?" Natalie asked, holding up cocoa packets in one hand and a jar of instant coffee in the other.

"He tanked up down below," said Andy, "but he might need to hit your out-house. We had a couple a quick stops on the way up. Greasy camp food, you know.

"But I'll take some a that coffee, if you've got any sugar and creamer."

"Plenty of both," said Natalie, "and tell your buddy there's a fresh roll of toilet paper in the bathroom under the stairs."

"Buddy!" Todd and Andy said in unison, pointing at each other.

"Excuse me," Natalie said softly. "Is that some kind of Montana greeting?"

"Oh, no," Todd said with a laugh. "We just couldn't remember the guy's name who rode up with Andy. That is, until you said 'buddy.' His name is Buddy Fischer."

"Always trying to be helpful," said Natalie, placing some mugs on the kitchen countertop. "Do you think *Buddy* might like some coffee, too?"

"Yeah," said Andy, "but he likes his black."

"Like his women?" Natalie asked with a sly grin.

"Huh?" Andy had to ask, and Todd shared the sheriff's confused look.

"Sorry," she replied. "I guess that's an East Coast joke. You know. He likes his coffee like he likes his women: hot and black."

Both Andy and Todd shared a smile, but otherwise they remained silent.

"It's a little funnier on the East Coast, too," said Natalie, thankful to hear the kettle boiling. Her rubber boots made a squeaking sound as she headed for the stove.

Andy motioned for Todd to lean closer, while the tiny woman busied herself in the kitchen. The sheriff took another look, before giving Todd a clap on the shoulder.

"How come I don't remember her feet bein' that big?" asked Andy.

*   *   *   *

"We should know something shortly, sir," said the broad-shouldered man, as soon as the door to Yancey Fitzgerald's private office had closed behind him. "Carlton has had to…take control of the scene. For some reason, the sheriff and the state agent are away from The Manor. Carlton said the state agent was caught up on one of the nearby mountains when the storm hit. He was apparently gath-ering some kind of evidence, although just what the evidence is has not been determined. I've instructed Carlton to find out more, but he may have to act quickly if the sheriff and the state agent return."

"He hasn't had to…eliminate anyone?" asked Fitzgerald.

"I didn't ask him, but you did give tacit authorization."

"How will we explain this? His company credentials and whatnot?"

"He's not on any employee record," said the big man. "His credentials are false, and they don't actually resemble the true GSG corporate identification. The account is drawn from an independent cost center, not otherwise associated with the company, and the money in the account cannot be traced. The vehicle is leased to a post office box in Sacramento—"

"Very well, very well. I think you've covered everything. What success have you had with the photograph I gave you?"

"Another problem, sir. You should've shown me the photo earlier."

"What now?" asked Fitzgerald, rummaging through his desk for an antacid tablet.

"The location where Mr. Draper was murdered was *not* The Manor," the big man replied.

"But that's where he was," Fitzgerald said, his voice a little too high-pitched. "The police were there even before your people arrived. Of course it's The Manor."

"There's a fireplace in the background of the photograph," the big man started to explain.

"There's a fireplace at The Manor. I distinctly remember it," the old man said firmly.

"The one in The Manor is big enough to park a car in, sir, and it was the only fireplace in the structure. The guest rooms all had freestanding stoves," the big man went on. "The fireplace in the picture is much too small, and that means Mr. Draper did not die in The Manor, as you'd led me to believe. The real question at the moment is *where* did he die, and I'm also concerned about the law enforcement presence prior to our arrival.

"Do we know how the police were notified?"

"No," Fitzgerald replied in a tone almost too low to hear.

"Do you want me to make an official inquiry to the Criminal Investigation Bureau headquarters in Helena?"

"Since I made the initial inquiry to that tight-lipped sheriff out there," said Fitzgerald, watching the traffic build so many floors beneath him, "I think I should be the one to call the state agency, as well."

"As you wish, sir. I'll get you their number."

"What time is it out there, anyway?"

"They're two hours earlier."

"A little after their lunchtime," Fitzgerald said, shooing the big man away with a flick of his wrist.

*   *   *   *

"Are you sure you don't want to ride behind Andy?" asked Todd, as the two snow machines idled in front of the big Ford truck. "He didn't have much trouble coming up, and the trip down'll be a snap. There's plenty of room on the seat behind him."

"I think I'd rather ride with you," Natalie said. "I like the idea of having a roof, doors, and a seat belt, and I'm still pissed that he thought these were *my* boots. Besides, you've got heat, and it doesn't look like those things keep the wind off you."

Todd gave her a shy smile, and he helped her into the front passenger seat. Before joining her, though, he ran down to Andy and Buddy.

"The lady's made her decision," said Todd, canting his head toward the truck. "I might take it a little slower, but I think I can stay in your tracks."

"There's a little band a bighorns about a mile down," Andy shouted over the chatter of his snowmobile. "One a those rams has got more than a full curl. Think your girlfriend might know how I can get permission to hunt up here?"

"I'll ask her on the way down," Todd replied, giving the pair a wave, "and try not to get too far ahead of me."

Both the snowmobilers gave Todd several nods, and they eased off together. He let them get down the road a bit, before turning back to the truck.

"We're movin' out," he said, climbing behind the wheel.

"You make it sound like a cattle drive," Natalie said with a laugh.

"It'll be just about as slow," said Todd, dropping the Ford into four-wheel-low.

*   *   *   *

"Montana Department of Justice," the young woman answered the phone pleasantly.

"This is Yancey Fitzgerald," the old man said in the most friendly tone he could muster. "I'd like to speak to the…bureau chief of the Criminal Investigation Bureau."

"I'm sorry, sir," said the young woman. "Mr. Meacham isn't in the office this week. Would you like to speak to the agent who's acting for him?"

"That would be fine. What is his name, ma'am?"

"He's Rudolph Rosser, and his office is right here in Helena. If you'll hold the line, I'll transfer you."

"Thank you," said Fitzgerald, as music filled the empty airspace.

Rudolph Rosser was one of the most senior agents in the Criminal Investigation Bureau, as he was quick to remind anyone who might listen. In his case, however, he'd mistaken years of service for experience, and most of the local law enforcement agencies in the state hated to work with him. Whenever he was left in charge, Rudy—as he was most often called—was usually faced with a drop in investigative requests, since many sheriffs and police chiefs didn't even want to talk to him on the telephone.

"Agent Rosser," he answered, after leaving Fitzgerald on hold for an unnecessary couple of minutes.

"Yes, Agent Rosser," Fitzgerald said soothingly. "This is Yancey Fitzgerald in Atlanta, Georgia. How are you this fine day?"

"I'm okay," Rosser replied stiffly. "How's it goin' with you?"

"Very good here, sir, but we seem to have a problem out your way."

"How's that?"

"It's the investigation down in…Park County, I think it is. One of your CIB agents is working on it, as we speak."

"That's a new one on me. I'm not aware of anybody assigned to a case down there."

"Well, I…don't know what else to say. Uh, I've spoken to the sheriff there, a man named Freud—"

"It's *Freund*. Andrew Freund, but I haven't heard anything from him, either. When did they call it in?"

"I believe the investigation was started yesterday."

"I was home all weekend, and nobody called me on Sunday. If CIB does have an agent over there, I didn't send him."

"You mean an agent wouldn't just go to Park County on his own?" Fitzgerald asked.

"We don't work that way, mister. Somebody has to ask us officially. We can't just work on our own. It's the law."

"What if the sheriff did ask him?"

"Ask who?"

"The agent who's there. I don't know his name, but I believe Sheriff Freund said he'd turned things over to a state agent. Sheriff Freund must've asked your agent for help."

"He's gotta ask me. He can't just call any old agent. Requests come to Helena, and they're always in the form of an official letter, unless it's an emergency. I wrote that policy back in 1982, and CIB has been followin' it ever since."

"And I'm sure it's a fine policy, too, Agent Rosser, but this may have been viewed as an emergency. It seems an expensive building owned by GSG was burned, and we also have one—or maybe even two—missing employees."

"What's GSG?" asked Rosser, still resisting any thought to take notes.

"Global Support Group," Fitzgerald replied, "although we've been using the initials for so long, most everybody knows us as GSG. I'm sure you've seen our commercials. The black trucks and airplanes?"

"Oh, yeah. You deliver out here."

"We deliver *everywhere*, Agent Rosser. I've been told we employ more people than the Russian Army," said Fitzgerald, faking a laugh.

"So, what are you callin' me for?"

"Information, Agent Rosser. According to Sheriff Freund, one of your state agents is in charge of an investigation on our property in Park County. Wouldn't you agree we have some right to know what's going on?"

"Let me get your number," said Rosser, finally uncapping his pen, "and I'll give you a call back after I do some checkin' around."

"That would be fine," said Fitzgerald, rolling his eyes in frustration. "If you'll wait a moment, I'll get my secretary to give you our toll-free number."

*   *   *   *

"Listen," Clarence Mingle whispered, as Vince Gilkey tried to suppress a moan.

"I'm strainin' way too hard to hear much of anything, Clarence," Vince groaned.

"I think it's the snowmobiles."

"Oh, shit—"

"What do you mean? He's only one guy, and Andy and Todd have got guns."

"That's not what I meant, Clarence. I think my last fart had a lump in it," Vince replied woefully.

*   *   *   *

The man calling himself Carlton cursed his luck, as the high-pitched sounds of the snowmobile motors grew closer. He pocketed an extra thermite grenade—

the one he'd intended to use on the still-snow-covered Porsche, and he checked his inside overcoat pockets for spare magazines. He had three 30-rounders—plenty for what he needed to do.

Around him, the other grenades were taking their toll on the engine blocks of the parked vehicles—all except the sheriff's cruiser. He planned to use the patrol car to drive out to the highway, where his Range Rover was waiting.

✷   ✷   ✷   ✷

"Do you smell somethin'?" Clarence Mingle asked Vince Gilkey.

"Sure I do," Vince replied defensively. "I told you I crapped in my pants."

"Not *that*!" Clarence growled. "It smells like somethin's burnin'."

"Maybe there's still food on the stove."

"Nah. It's like…a metallic smell."

"Yeah," said Vince, trying to shift his weight. "I *do* smell that."

"Quit your squirmin'. I don't want none a your shit on me."

"Sorry, Clarence," Vince said dejectedly.

✷   ✷   ✷   ✷

Buddy's snowmobile began to sputter, and Andy slowed to stay back with him. They were just one switchback from the last stretch of the service road, just above the burned buildings, and Andy motioned for Todd to pull around the snowmobiles. There was barely enough room in the sweeping curve, but the snow there was almost gone, thanks to the early afternoon sun. Todd pulled up next to Andy's ride.

"If I was you," said Andy, leaning in the truck window, "I'd just keep her rollin' right on through. You can take the little lady straight to my place, if you're not followed, and, if you *are* followed, pour the coals on all the way to the court-house."

"Will do, Andy, and thanks," said Todd, giving the two men a farewell wave.

"I'll wait with Buddy until he gets the choke unstuck," Andy said with a nod, stepping back from the truck.

Todd eased off the clutch, and he shifted into four-wheel-high. He figured he might need some speed, just to hamper the suspicious GSG-man's view into the truck.

"You'd better keep your head down," he said to Natalie, as they began the long incline down to The Manor. Ahead, he could see a lot of smoke in the area around the tents, but there were no people in sight.

"In this thing, I don't have to try too hard to stay low," said Natalie, crouching down on the passenger side floorboard. "Even when I'm sitting in the seat I can't see out the windshield."

"Stay real low, sugar," Todd said absently. "Something's not right down here."

And then the first rounds hit the windshield.

"*Shit!*" said Todd, as shards of glass showered the inside of the Ford. He felt a piece of glass cut his cheek, but he was more concerned about the source of the machine gun fire. "Hang on, darlin'. I think I got a flat tire—maybe two."

Todd cut the wheel to the right, exposing the left side of the truck, and a second stream of bullets punched through the sheet metal. A bullet grazed his right forearm, as he fought the sluggish steering wheel, but the remainder of the shots put holes through the rear passenger door and the bed.

As the truck slid to a stop—with steam rising from the perforated radiator, Todd pushed his way across the seat, and he took Natalie by the arm.

"Keep your head down, baby," he shouted, as another burst of shots began. "I'm gonna get us outa here."

Pausing only long enough to grab a carbine from floor of the truck, Todd threw open the passenger door, and he scooped up Natalie in his arms. The over-sized boots slipped from her feet, as he lifted her out of the truck. There was a stand of trees about seventy-five yards away, and the closely bunched timber appeared thick enough to offer cover. The only problem was getting there.

But, complicating matters, Todd couldn't see where the shooting was coming from. The only consolation seemed to be that his truck was still taking the brunt of the attack, and he wasted no time to wonder why.

Fifty yards. Thirty. Ten. And suddenly the shooting had stopped, and Todd was kneeling beside a tree. He turned Natalie with her back to the trunk, in a position offering her the most cover, then he did a quick peek back at his wounded Ford. Someone's legs were just visible beneath the jacked-up undercarriage.

"Cover your ears, honey," said Todd, as he took careful aim with his Marlin .357.

Even so, Natalie felt the concussion, and she couldn't resist turning to look.

"I think I got the son-of-a-bitch," said Todd. "He took off toward the tents."

There was the roar of a motor, and then a moment of silence, followed by the sound of a snowmobile motor revved well beyond redline. It was Andy, and he had his revolver drawn.

"Over *here*!" Todd shouted, as Andy slowed on approach. The sheriff knew better than to barge in on a gunfight. "I think he's headed out to the road."

Andy parked his snowmobile behind the truck, and he motioned for Todd to join him. The truck would offer them cover if it was needed.

"Stay put, sweetheart," said Todd. "I don't think he saw you, so you should be safe here. Just wait for me to come back for you."

Todd started to turn away, but Natalie managed to grab the sleeve of his coat. When he looked back at her, her expression was a combination of fear and wonder.

"I've got to know something, cowboy," she said, unable to release her white-knuckled grip. "What's with all this 'sugar,' 'darlin',' 'baby,' 'honey,' and 'sweetheart' talk?"

"Oh," he said, blushing in the middle of a battlefield, "I get kinda brave when things turn sour. I guess it makes me express myself a little differently, too."

She released his sleeve and took his lapels with both hands. She had to stand to kiss him, even though he was still kneeling, and she thought she felt a shiver run through him. They held the kiss for about fifteen seconds, though. When she let herself move back a step, she felt his hands behind her back.

He lifted her easily, and returned her kiss for at least twice as long. As he gently returned her stocking feet to the ground, she could see he wasn't blushing anymore.

"Thanks," she whispered, unable to take her eyes off him. "Now, go do whatever it is you're supposed to do, but *please* be careful."

*   *   *   *

"In *here*!" Clarence Mingle shouted, almost as soon as the echo of the last shot had faded away.

"Quiet, Clarence," Vince Gilkey whispered. "What if the other guy won?"

"I heard Todd and Andy shoutin', you shit-stained moron," Clarence snarled. "They're back, and we may be able to help 'em, if they can cut us loose."

"Okay," said Vince. "On three. One, two, three."

"*IN HERE*!" they shouted in unison.

*   *   *   *

"I hear somebody shoutin' down near the tents," said Andy, working his way along the ventilated side of Todd's Ford. "The cruiser's gone, and it looks like he's tampered with the other rigs."

"Watch your step," said Todd, pointing down at the snow near the front of the truck.

"You musta got him," said Andy, kneeling to get a better view of the blood spots. "He's not hit too bad, though. Just a drop here and there."

"You want to take the sled out to the highway, to see if we can get a direction of travel?"

"I think we need to check for casualties, first," said Andy. "With all that shootin', I just want to make sure we're still workin' only *one* homicide."

With Andy in the lead—keeping his revolver at the ready, Todd followed a couple of steps behind, watching the distant tree line for any sign of their assailant. It only took them a minute of careful walking to reach the main tent.

"Anybody home?" said Andy, pushing back the tent flap with his gun muzzle.

The sight before him would've been comical under less hazardous circumstances, but Andy wasted no time in freeing the two captives. His folding pocket-knife was no match for the flex-cuffs, so he used the wire cutters on the multi-tool he also carried.

Clarence quickly rolled away from Vince as soon as he was freed.

"Did you guys get on each other's nerves while I was gone?" asked Andy, as he folded up the multi-tool.

"Hell, no," Clarence replied, shaking his head. "The boy's shit his britches, that's all. We've been trussed up like this for an hour or better."

"It was them Polish sausages," Vince said sorrowfully.

"I told you not to eat 'em," said Andy, helping Vince to his feet. "I've got a jumpsuit in the Bronco. I'll go get it while you find a way to get cleaned up."

"Is that little woman around?" Vince asked, a worried look in his eyes.

"Oh, shit," said Andy, turning toward the tent door.

*   *   *   *

Todd found Natalie right where he'd left her, and a wave of relief swept over her at the sight of him. The image made him pause for a few seconds. It had been quite a while since someone appeared to be actually glad to see him. The fact that the someone was a very pretty little woman didn't bother him, either.

"Is everything okay?" she asked, shivering a bit in her wet socks.

"Actually, I think I need a bandage on my arm, and our base camp's trashed all to hell," Todd replied with a smile, "but it sure is good to see *you* again."

"What's that smell?" she asked, wrinkling her button of a nose.

"Ah, he did…something to the other vehicles. He didn't want to be followed, that's for certain."

Without another word, Todd walked over to her and took her in his arms. She smiled broadly as he lifted her.

"A girl could get used to this," she said, wrapping her arms around his neck.

"Careful what you say. You're talking to a guy whose take home pay might not equal a couple of *months* of your salary."

"Listen here, cowboy," said Natalie, pulling her lips close to his. "My whopper salary came to an end when you zipped up that body bag. You're holding a thirty-three-year-old woman with no foreseeable future and with almost nothing in her work background that she'd want to see listed on a resume.

"I've got no place to go and nobody to answer to, and I'm scared to death."

"Welcome to the club," Todd said with a smile, before silencing her with a kiss.

"Thank God," Andy shouted, looking almost as relieved as Natalie had been a moment earlier. "I forgot all about little Miss Weinberg—but I'm glad to see *you* didn't."

"What? Did you think I was just gonna leave her to freeze out here in the trees," said Todd. "I saw a pot of coffee on the kitchen stove when I cut those guys loose. Think we can round up a cup for a shivering woman?"

"I believe we can do that," Andy replied with a twinkle in his eyes.

✳   ✳   ✳   ✳

"What the hell did he do, Clarence?" Vince Gilkey asked, as he struggled with the long pant legs of Andy's jumpsuit. Andy had to be six inches taller than the stubby deputy.

"Thermite grenades," Clarence replied with a sigh. "We used 'em on a Cuban motor pool in Grenada. They melt right through an engine block."

"He had a machine gun and this…other stuff you said," Vince whined, turning to see the smoke rising from beneath the upraised hoods of the other parked vehicles. "Who the hell *has* stuff like that?"

"He meant business, I can tell you that, and I think he was lookin' for some-thin' in particular, too," replied Clarence, giving his left front tire a kick. "And now he's got *me* lookin' for another 392 International V-8."

*   *   *   *

"News from Carlton," the broad-shouldered man said, as soon as Yancey Fitzgerald ended a hushed telephone conversation.

"Success, I hope," said Fitzgerald, annoyed at the untimely interruption. The old man had just learned that his favorite hooker was free for the evening.

"Partially, sir," the big man replied, enjoying the idea of prolonging the exchange.

"Just tell me what we've got," Fitzgerald snapped.

"He's on his way to meet a covert flight at a small airstrip just south of Inter-state 90. The people there will dispose of the vehicle, and he's going to leave a package for them to ship. I'm having the next Bozeman flight held over for its arrival."

"He found the *laptop*," Fitzgerald said excitedly.

"Yes, sir."

"The man has done very well, indeed. I assume he'll be suitably rewarded."

"He was slightly wounded in the left leg. There was some shooting. I instructed him to make use of the account he had access to."

"How much is in there?" the old man asked.

"Seven figures—"

"Tell him it's his," Fitzgerald said quickly. "I'm feeling especially magnani-mous this afternoon. And have the package sent here under the corporate top pri-ority label."

"I'll relay your instructions, sir. The laptop should be here by tomorrow morning."

"Where will he go from Montana?" asked Fitzgerald, his thoughts ready to return to the evening's diversions.

"Out of the country, sir, but I didn't inquire further. It's best we don't know."

"I'd have to agree with you on that point."

*   *   *   *

"Well," Andy Freund said to Clarence Mingle and the others gathered in the large wall tent. "We've lost two county vehicles and three personal rigs—four, counting Todd's shot-up truck. Except for the sleds, we're pretty much afoot. He trashed our portable radios, too, so I've put in a call to the highway patrol by telephone. The closest officer is in Big Timber, though, and he's tied up on a tipped over semi. I guess what I'm sayin' is we're lucky nobody got hurt too bad. He even left Vince's gun in the cruiser, so it doesn't look like he took much of anything."

"Wrong, Andy," said Todd, as he threw open the tent flap. "I was wondering what he was doing around my truck. The bastard took my computer."

*   *   *   *

"What do you mean, he's not in the office?" Rudy Rosser asked, concealing his delight from the Missoula CIB secretary. "Did he list where he's out at on the board?"

"Yes, he did," the woman replied, turning in her chair. "It says he went to Park County—on Sunday morning. He's got a homicide listed."

"Does he have a cell phone?" Rosser asked, not wanting to look up the number himself.

"I'll get the number for you," said the woman, putting him on hold. "Asshole."

*   *   *   *

"There *is* a car available, sheriff," Natalie said, after swallowing a mouthful of doughnut. It tasted pretty good, and she could understand why so many cops seemed to crave them.

"I forgot about your little road-scorcher," said Andy, taking a peek over at the melting pile of snow. The sloped black roof was plainly visible.

"Where do you need to go?" she asked.

"How about takin' me back to my place for the Travelall?" Clarence asked. "My house is the closest, anyway. The Travelall will haul all you guys, and we can take the body outa here with it, too."

"Sounds like a plan," said Andy. "Let's get her shoveled out."

Natalie followed the other men, as they grabbed up shovels, and she watched patiently while they cleared the snow away. They were careful not to hit the Porsche with the blades of the shovels, although she really didn't seem too concerned that they would.

"Can you drive in those heels?" Todd asked, as he threw his shovel aside.

"Nah, I like to drive barefooted—is that legal in Montana?" she asked.

"I don't think the judge'll mind if it isn't," Todd said with a laugh.

Clarence had a little difficulty lowering himself into the front passenger seat, and he couldn't resist the urge to fondle the padded roll cage. Natalie dropped lightly into the driver's seat—a seat that had been specially modified to fit her little frame, and she gave the ignition key a twist. The engine roared to life, with a deep howl.

"What the hell is this thing?" Clarence asked, as the men outside stood back to give her some turning room.

"Have you ever heard of a 993, your honor?" asked Natalie, as she shoved the transmission into first.

"Hell no. What's she got under the hood?"

"Hopefully, there's still a Haliburton suitcase under the hood," Natalie replied, flashing him a mischievous smile, "but behind us is a twin turbocharged 3.6 liter flat six, turning out a little over four hundred ponies."

"Now hold on a minute, missy. It's kinda slippery around here for a sports car, and I don't want us windin' up on our heads," said Clarence, buckling his seat belt with shaking hands.

"Not to worry, your honor," said Natalie, giving the Porsche some gas. "This thing's got all-wheel-drive, too."

Clarence couldn't keep his mouth from hanging open, as they roared out toward the highway.

*   *   *   *

Rudy Rosser let his fingers drum on his desk, as his call through to Todd's cellular telephone began to ring. Rosser had already scurried down the hall to gripe to the division administrator, and he was now anxiously waiting to exert his limited and temporary authority. His only worry was that he'd not taken the time to prepare some notes for a proper verbal admonishment.

"You got me," said Todd, as he flipped his cell phone open.

"Who gave you authorization to go to Livingston?" Rudy asked rudely.

"Who the heck *is* this?" Todd asked back. The connection wasn't the best.

"This is Rudy in Helena."

"What are you callin' *me* for?"

"Meacham left me in charge while he's in Salt Lake."

"How was I supposed to know that?"

"It went out as a bureau-wide E-mail memo at 8 a.m. this morning," Rudy replied. "I'm acting chief for the whole week."

"Good for you," said Todd, "but did you ever think that I've been down here since *yesterday*? How am I supposed to get E-mails on the road?"

"That don't matter," Rudy said angrily. "Freund should've called to me to request an agent."

"If *I* didn't know you were in charge, Rudy, how's he supposed to know?"

"Well...I'm tellin' you both officially right now. Livingston's way too far for a Missoula agent to go, anyway."

"Andy said he tried to call the Helena office, but nobody answered, and Dave's on vacation, so the Bozeman office is all shut down. He called me as a last resort, I guess."

"Billings is closer," said Rudy. "He shoulda called them."

"He doesn't know any of the agents in Billings, and he had my home number. Now let's quit arguing. While I've got you on the phone, I need a case number on a homicide, and it looks like we've had at least four cases of unlawful restraint and two cases of attempted deliberate homicide—"

"Whoa, whoa, whoa," said Rudy. "Who says this is your case? I might want to send somebody else."

"Maybe you should," Todd agreed. "I could use a little help, 'cause I've got two cases of criminal damage to government property and four cases of criminal damage to private vehicles—one of which is my own."

"You mean *you're* a victim?" Rudy asked in disbelief.

"Double victim, Rudy," Todd replied. "The same suspect shot me in the forearm. I'm an attempted deliberate homicide victim, too."

"How bad is it?" asked Rudy, his voice a little lower.

"The whole scene or my arm?" Todd replied with a laugh. "Actually, I got lucky. The bullet just cut the skin on top of my right arm, just above the wrist. I've got a sterile dressing on it, and the bleeding's stopped.

"As for the rest of this place, we've got a ten million dollar house burned to the ground—along with a garage and high-dollar Mercedes, so I guess we've got a healthy case of arson, too. My truck's shot up from one end to the other. Two of the Park County sheriff's vehicles are toast, and the same guy cooked the engines in three other rigs.

"Oh, and we've got a dead guy who looks like he's been force-fed some antifreeze—but we've had him since Sunday. He might have some fresher bullet holes in him, though. He was in the back of my truck when the shooting started."

"Where's your state car?"

"In the shop for brakes. Just my luck, huh?"

"Listen, Todd, I gotta think about this," said Rudy, drawing circles around the GSG 800 number on his desk blotter.

"Well think fast, because we've got a material witness in protective custody down here—sort of, but we're real short on the resources and personnel we need to protect her. I think she might be able to help us with the original homicide, and I think she can steer us in the right direction on the other stuff, too."

"What do you mean, 'sort of' in custody?" asked Rudy.

"Right now, she's the only one with a car that's still running, so she's hauling the judge up to his house to pick up another rig."

"You let her out of your sight?" Rudy asked, hoping his joy didn't extend over the airwaves.

"I think being with Judge Mingle could still be considered 'in custody,' Rudy," said Todd, "and I don't think anyone else could fit behind the wheel of her car."

"Fit? What are you talkin' about?"

"It'll take me a week just to write what's happened to this point, Rudy," said Todd, beginning to lose his patience with the snooty acting chief. "Is there any way you might be able to ferry me a car down here?"

"The only spare we got is funded through the Medicaid Fraud Unit, and you can't have it," Rudy said firmly. "And I still haven't decided to assign this case to *you*."

"You're right, Rudy," Todd said with a sigh. "I'm here. I can't go anywhere without my truck or a fresh car. I've already processed the homicide scene. I've just finished taking taped statements from the folks here at the base camp. I photographed the fire yesterday, and I took pictures of the damaged vehicles half an hour ago. Hell, I even took a picture of my own damn arm. Why should *I* have to work this case?"

Todd flipped his phone closed without waiting for an answer. Rudy, however, stayed on the line for a few minutes more, trying to come up with a reply.

"Damn," Todd said, as Andy began to laugh. "I forgot to tell him I lost my computer, too."

∗   ∗   ∗   ∗

"Daddy's got a new car! Daddy's got a new car!" Clarence Mingle's youngest daughter went shouting through the house, after seeing the black Porsche pull into the driveway. Before the judge could fight his way out of the seatbelt, his entire family had surrounded the shiny sports car.

"Get back, children," Clarence scolded, as he literally crawled out of the low-slung door. "I need you older boys to go get your huntin' rifles. We've got problems in the county, and I don't want to be without a gun until things settle down."

Natalie had much less trouble exiting the car, but she drew as many stares as the German racer. Clarence looked from Natalie to Christine, his nine-year-old daughter. They were about the same height and size, and the similarity gave him an idea.

"Chrissy," he called, drawing the girl to his side. "Take this little lady in the house, and see if you can find your old snow pacs. She's been runnin' around in wet socks for too damn long."

The little girl took Natalie by the hand, and the two of them headed for the front door.

"Get her a coat that fits, too," Clarence shouted, as the miniscule pair climbed the front steps.

The abundance of activity seemed to satisfy Clarence for the moment, and he headed back toward his shop, where his '64 International Travelall was parked. The big rig had been sitting idle since the hunting season, but he knew it wouldn't let him down.

*   *   *   *

"He just hung up on me," Rudy Rosser whined from his chair in front of the division administrator's desk.

Arthur Yost gave the brooding agent a forlorn stare. Without the real bureau chief present, Rosser could refer potential problems directly to him—thereby distracting him from his proper duties, as head of the division. For example, Yost was working on a proposal to rename the division, since the Law Enforcement Services Division had too much of an ancillary ring to it. Yost also had hopes that a new name might shed some of the tarnish his division had accumulated over the years. The last thing he needed to do was serve as referee for a pair of at-odds agents.

"Rudy," Yost said evenly, "I think Chuck Meacham put you in charge to handle little problems just like this one. As acting chief, everyone knows your authority is only temporary, but it's up to you to exert that authority while it *is* yours."

"My job here is to run a whole division. If I didn't trust Chuck's judgment, I'd take over CIB myself under these circumstances, so why don't you prove to him—and to me—that he made the right choice."

"But this sounds like a pretty big case, Art," said Rosser, leaning forward in his chair. "I don't like the idea of Freund disregarding CIB policy, either."

"Sheriffs can often be that way, though," said Yost. "You've got to keep in mind just how limited our authority really is. Without a request, our original jurisdiction authority extends only to welfare fraud and a few other areas. We can't work major cases unless the sheriffs and police chiefs ask us to."

"Do you want me to…give Milton the spare rig from Medicaid Fraud? I don't know how that'll look if we get audited."

"From the sound of things, he might need the assistance of another agent—"

"When I started here," Rosser shot back, perhaps trying to demonstrate his authority a bit too effectively, "it only took one agent per crime—no matter what it was. If I send Park County another agent, it'll be to *replace* Milton, not help him."

"Whatever, Rudy," Yost said, swiveling in his chair and showing Rosser his back. "Just handle the problem and keep me informed."

"What about media interest?"

"If there are any inquiries at the CIB offices, have them referred back to the Park County Sheriff's Department. I don't like the idea of our office making public comments on another agency's case."

"What about me?" asked Rudy. "Can't I give 'em a statement if they call?"

"Since we haven't seen a report from Todd, I'd discourage any press releases from here. It's one thing to get a verbal assessment, and quite another to see it in writing. In the past, I haven't been especially enamored with any of Chuck's press releases, and I certainly don't want to see an *acting* chief give one."

"I'll take that as a 'no,' then," Rosser said meekly.

"Very good, Rudy," said Yost, not bothering to turn back around.

*   *   *   *

"Why don't you stick it out here?" Clarence said to Natalie, as he loaded a scoped hunting rifle into the front seat of the Travelall. He also had a cocked-and-locked .45 automatic stuffed haphazardly into his waistband. "The boys all know how to shoot, and I pity the fool that'd try to force his way into my house. We've got enough ammo to start a revolution."

"Thanks for the offer, judge," Natalie replied, "but I think I'd better meet back up with Todd and the sheriff. I might be able to help them if they've got questions about GSG, and I think the sheriff had some ideas about where I should stay for the time being."

"Follow me, then," said Clarence, climbing behind the wheel of the big International, "and don't even think about passin' me, 'cause I know I can't keep up."

Natalie gave him a thumbs-up, and she made a dash for the Porsche. In Chrissy's coat and boots, she could've been mistaken for the judge's daughter.

As the Travelall lurched forward, Natalie fired up the twin turbos, and the two vehicles made a strange looking procession heading out of the Mingles' short driveway. With its oversized mud-grips, the International was tall enough to run over the Porsche, and Clarence had to do a little weaving just to catch a view of the black speedster in his side mirror. Natalie, on the other hand, was afforded an excellent view of the Travelall's dusty undercarriage. More than once, she had to remind herself to look up for the taillights.

The highway was almost dry from the warming afternoon sun, but the usual Yellowstone-bound traffic had yet to materialize. It took Clarence about twice as long to make the return trip, though.

Andy and Todd were waiting in the parking area—both of them talking on separate cellular telephones.

"Got back quick as I could," said Clarence, stepping from his high-rolling rig.

"You did great, judge," said Andy, returning his phone to his coat pocket. "Our nearest highway patrolman is now out on a cattle truck in the median, just east a the Livingston exit. The truck's still upright, but the view is too much for some a the tourists. He's already got four cars spun out up there."

"Everybody's busy in Billings," Todd said with a shrug, flipping his own phone shut. "There's an outside chance I could get some help from Kalispell or Great Falls, but I don't think Rudy would stand for it."

"Why in hell does Meacham keep puttin' *him* in charge?" Andy asked, throwing his hands in the air.

"Consolation for coming in last in the bureau chief race, I think," said Todd, looking beyond the judge's rig.

"She's parked behind me," Clarence said with a laugh. "I think she's doin' a woman thing, like puttin' on some makeup or fussin' with her hair."

Todd found Natalie doing just that, leaning forward to use the rearview mirror. Fresh lipstick. He could almost understand the need.

"You holding up okay?" he asked, kneeling beside her door.

"Hey," she replied, motioning to her new attire. "I'm even kinda stylish."

"Where'd you get that stuff?"

"The judge's daughter, Chrissy. As it turns out, we're both the same size."

"But she's just…ten—"

"*Nine*, cowboy. She won't be ten until December. We managed to get in a little girl talk, while I was going through her closet."

When she stepped from the Porsche without her heels on, Natalie was even shorter than he'd remembered, her, but he had to admit the boots she wore were much more practical. He didn't even check to see if anyone was watching before he lifted her in his arms. Natalie liked that—and she didn't seem to mind messing up her newly applied lipstick, either.

"Hey. Are those two…uh…" the judge started to ask.

"Yeah," Andy said quickly. "Makes you kinda wonder how this is all gonna turn out, don't it?"

"She's a city girl," Clarence said with a frown. "She'll start missin' it, and the next thing you know she'll be gone."

"I hope you're wrong, judge," said Andy, trying not to time their kisses. "Todd needs a good gal to get him settled down. He brought this one girl from the U of M down here two-three years ago, and she was a head case from the get-go. She saw this bear makin' a stalk on a moose calf, so she wrecks her car tryin' to *hit* the damn bear. She managed to scare the critter off, and she felt like a hero for savin' the moose. When I cussed her for interferin' with nature, she got all huffy and didn't ever speak to me again—not that I minded, but I was pretty worried that Todd might marry the dizzy broad. She's history, though, and it's high time he caught himself a keeper."

"Hell, Andy," Clarence scoffed. "I bet her car cost more than his *house*."

"You know, Clarence," said Andy, giving the judge a serious stare. "For a guy with so many kids, you sure got a lot to learn about love."

*   *   *   *

"The package is on the way from Bozeman, sir," said the broad-shouldered man, passing a computerized shipping record across Yancey Fitzgerald's desk.

"Tomorrow, you think?" Fitzgerald asked, leaning back for a better view in the mirror on his credenza. He was trimming the hair in his nostrils.

"It'll go through the collection center in St. Louis, then on to our Douglasville routing center," the big man replied. "I could wait on it there, if you'd like, but it'll probably be delivered to my office with the first shipments tomorrow morning."

"I think its importance warrants…special handling," said Fitzgerald, checking his shirtfront for clippings. "Why don't you take a drive out I-20 tonight, just to be certain?"

"Would you like me to bring it directly to you, sir, or should I destroy it immediately? There's a large incinerator in the routing center."

"I think I'd like to see it before it's destroyed—just to see what that fool kept in the way of information. If it's password protected, we'll know our Miss Weinberg had a hand in Draper's other affairs, and we can take appropriate action.

"Did…Carlton have anything to say about *seeing* our little missing employee?"

"No, sir. But if her car was there, there's still a chance she met the same fate as Mr. Draper—although we still don't know *where* Mr. Draper was killed. Carlton didn't learn much from the local sheriff."

"Just to be on the safe side," said Fitzgerald, "let's keep her company account active. Have the audit division keep you informed of any new activity. Without Draper, she might not know where to turn, but it troubles me she hasn't made an attempt to contact the home office. Her corporate card might be the best way to track her down."

"Shall I bring the laptop here as soon as it reaches the routing center?"

"Yes," said Fitzgerald, canting his head toward his personal suite. "I'll be working late this evening."

*　　　*　　　*　　　*

"I've got Vince on the way to the crime lab with your dead guy," Andy Freund said over his shoulder, as he drove Todd and Natalie away from the Mingle residence. "Miss Weinberg's car'll be safe and outa sight in the judge's back garage bay. Clarence put a tarp over it, too—probably just to keep his damn kids out of it."

"I'm sorry Vince had to use his own truck for the crime lab run," said Todd, leaning over the back seat of Andy's unmarked Crown Victoria.

"Hell, don't you worry about it. The boy was happy to make some travel mileage," said Andy. "Now, Jeanie's got a pot roast almost done, so I thought we'd get us a bite before I got you folks settled in for the evenin'. I think she got the big guest cabin all spruced up for you, too."

"What does your wife think about all this excitement?" Natalie asked. She was sitting so low in the passenger seat beside Andy, he'd almost forgotten she was there.

"Actually," Andy replied, gritting his teeth in thought. "After I gave her a quick rundown on all the stuff I could remember, the only thing Jeanie seemed to be interested in was gettin' a closer look at *you*."

"*Me?*" asked Natalie, unable to suppress a giggle.

"Well, I guess I should've just said you were kinda little, but I told her you weren't much bigger than Red," Andy replied.

"Who's Red?" she asked.

"Our cat," said the sheriff.

"You've still got that cat?" Todd asked with a laugh.

"Yeah," Andy said with a sigh, turning quickly toward Natalie. "He's a *big* damn cat, though."

The sheriff's house was north of Livingston, with a nice view of Crazy Peak to the northeast. It was a two-story log home—but nothing like The Manor. As Andy parked in the gravel strip in front of the house, Natalie was surprised to see there was no evidence of the snowstorm. The area around the Freund house was dusty and dry.

Todd and Natalie followed Andy into the house. The table was already set and waiting, as Andy awkwardly introduced Natalie to Jeanie. The sheriff's wife seemed genuinely pleased to meet a new woman in town, and she gladly accepted Natalie's offer to help in the kitchen.

"What's next?" Andy asked, as he and Todd took seats at the table.

"I don't know, Andy," said Todd, running his fingers through his close-cropped hair. "I really need a computer, so I can get started on my reports. This'll be a tough one to explain on my expense voucher, too. I've never heard of an agent losing his personal rig on an investigation, and Rudy'll jump for joy when he hears I lost that laptop."

"I think you know why *I* can't stand the little prick," said Andy, listening for the women in the kitchen. "But why's he so mad at you?"

"I beat him out in the bureau chief interviews, too," said Todd. "That, and he's just stuck in the past when it comes to procedure."

"I'll never forget how he screwed up the motel murder in '93," said Andy. "I never called him, but he heard Dave's radio traffic on the highway patrol channel, and he waded right into the crime scene like he owned the place. Talk about a violation of CIB policy. When the Billings television people got there, he went right out and started spouting off with these wild theories. Six months later, the killer's defense attorney was calling him as *their* goddamn witness."

"Don't gripe too loudly, my friend," Todd said with a sigh. "Rudy's liable to show up here at any moment. That is, unless he's too busy trying to get me in trouble with Yost."

"I don't want to hear any shop talk during dinner," said Jeanie, as she and Natalie entered the dining room with serving bowls.

"Aw, shucks," said Natalie. "I kinda like listening to it."

"Then it's okay if Natalie likes it," Jeanie said quickly, anxious to please the new girl, "but no cussing—and I'm not talkin' about Todd, neither."

"Yes, ma'am," Andy said, hanging his head.

"So, where do we go from here, cowboy?" Natalie asked Todd, raising her eyebrows hopefully.

"Andy and I were just discussing that. I still need a written statement from you," Todd replied reflectively, "and we never did get a taped interview, either. Just the particulars of the homicide case. You know, like where you were the day before and so on—right up until the time you got here. If you've got your plane tickets, that'd help, too, so I can positively eliminate you as a suspect.

"*I* know you didn't do it, but it's my job to *show* that you didn't do it, too."

"Let her eat, Todd," Jeanie scolded. "She needs to get some warm food inside her. She can help with the investigation after dessert—carrot cake with my *special* frosting."

"Oh, it's fu—I mean, it's good," said Andy, scooping up a forkful of potatoes.

"But you won't even get a crumb if I hear one foul word," Jeanie said sternly.

Natalie and Todd exchanged smiles, as they, too, got busy with their silverware.

✳   ✳   ✳   ✳

"Working late," the stranger said to himself, as he sat in his rented car. The high-rise parking garage was only thirty stories tall, but it offered him a view of Yancey Fitzgerald's office windows, some twenty-five floors above.

Behind the blinds, Fitzgerald was enjoying the company of a tall black woman, who was actually lighter skinned than her client, thanks to the way-too-many hours the old man spent in a tanning bed. Sitting astride him, she watched Fitzgerald's watery eyes follow the sway of her perfect—though perhaps too big for her slender frame—artificial breasts.

"You can touch 'em, if you want to, honey," the hooker cooed seductively.

"I wouldn't want to leave a mark," Fitzgerald replied between gasps.

The buzzer at Fitzgerald's outer office door sounded, causing the woman to tighten the wrong muscles. The old man let out a howl, and she leapt to her feet and stood beside his leather sofa. Fitzgerald managed to sit up, but he was a little too dizzy to stand.

"That ain't your wife, I hope," said the hooker.

"My wife's on vacation in Australia," said Fitzgerald, pulling at his trousers. "She's there until the end of the month. I'm expecting a business associate, however, if you'll excuse me for a moment."

"You know our price only covers you," she felt compelled to remind him. "I can do him, too, but the price—"

"That's not why he's here," said Fitzgerald, finally able to rise.

"Want me to let him in?" the hooker asked with a devilish smile.

"Yes, do that," the old man replied, trying unsuccessfully to emulate her expression.

Making her way to Fitzgerald's outer office, the woman stepped into her platform heels, but she ignored her panties and skimpy gown. The old man followed her, just to see the expression on the face of his late night visitor.

As tall as the hooker was, she was still dwarfed by the broad-shouldered man. His impressive appearance left her speechless, and he walked right past her after only looking her in the eyes. All she could do was stand in awe with her hands on her hips, wondering what it might be like to share the sheets with him.

"So nice of you to come," Fitzgerald said. "Shall I introduce you?"

"No need, sir," the big man replied, placing the flat shipping box on his boss's desk.

"You didn't open it," said Fitzgerald, annoyed by the thorough packaging.

The big man produced a knife from beneath his coat, and he sliced open one end of the box. The folded compact computer slid out easily, and Fitzgerald anxiously lifted the screen. The liquid crystal display came to life, and an immediate problem arose.

"I knew it," Fitzgerald said, turning the screen toward the big man. "That little Jew bitch of his has programmed some kind of a password. There's no way that idiot Draper could've done this."

"It's worse than that, sir," said the big man, as the nude hooker strode up to stand beneath his shoulder. "There's a property tag on the top of the computer. This machine belongs to the Montana Department of Justice—"

"God *damn it!*" the old man shouted, lifting the machine up over his head. Only the big man's firm grasp kept Fitzgerald from throwing the laptop across the room.

"Before you act too hastily, sir," the big man said calmly, "there may be information we could use on this machine. Investigative notes, witness statements, anything that might help identify the actual crime scene and...perhaps, the person responsible for Mr. Draper."

"Who's working in the data center tonight?" said Fitzgerald, rising from his chair with the laptop still clutched in his bony fingers.

"I think the night supervisor presently on duty could do this for us...discretely," the big man replied.

Without another word, the old man was through his office door, leaving the big man and the hooker standing at his desk. The slender woman couldn't resist giving the broad-shouldered man's biceps a feel. His arm was bigger around than her waist.

"I got my money up front, honey child," she whispered, ignoring his blank expression. "Wanna use up the rest a his hour?"

✳   ✳   ✳   ✳

There were three guest cabins in a little hollow, below the Freund's house. They were leftovers from the days when Andy was a deputy. He used to supplement his income as a hunting guide, and the cabins served as a base camp for nearby excursions.

Jeanie showed Natalie to the largest of the three, a rustic two-story structure with a downstairs bedroom and bath and an upstairs loft bedroom. There were coat closets and a living room area with a woodstove and an entertainment center, but there were no kitchen provisions. Antlered game heads decorated the walls, and the hardwood floors were also covered with hides and skins.

"I thought you'd like the downstairs bedroom, since it's got a door that locks," said Jeanie, ushering her little visitor into the lower bedroom. "The bathroom's right next to your room, so you won't have to walk far."

"I can get another cabin ready for Todd, if you want more privacy."

"Having made it through my first gun battle unscathed, thanks to Todd," Natalie said, taking a seat on the side of the double bed, "I think I'll take the extra protection over the privacy, if you don't mind."

"Suit yourself, sweetie," Jeanie said with a smile, turning to leave. Before she could reach the bedroom door, however, Natalie was tapping her on the shoulder.

"What can you tell me about...Agent Milton?" the tiny woman asked softly.

"Todd? He's a good man," Jeanie said thoughtfully. "One of the best friends Andy has. Pleasant and respectful—and he's always welcome under our roof."

"Has he got a girlfriend?"

"He had one—a real loony, if you ask me. He hasn't been with her in…oh…two years or better. She was a Missoula girl, working on her PHD or maybe her master's, I think, but those university girls can be strange. She was pretty, mind you, but not near as pretty as you.

"Andy used to tell me he'd stand up and object if Todd was fool enough to ask that girl to marry him. I think…Linda was her name. Lisa. Something like that. It didn't work out, though, and he's a lot better off—even if he doesn't know it."

Natalie took a step back from the doorway, and Jeanie waited for a moment to see if her answers had satisfied the diminutive girl.

"What kind of work is there to do around here?" Natalie asked. "I mean, if a person had to make a living here."

"Like for you? Can you type?"

"Maybe…eighty words a minute, give or take."

"I'll talk to Andy, but I think he needs a dispatcher. He's got a part-timer, but she looks like she's ten months pregnant with quadruplets, so she might not be workin' too much longer."

"Thanks," said Natalie, returning to the edge of the bed.

"You do like Todd, don't you?" Jeanie had to ask.

"Did Andy tell you?"

"Didn't have to," Jeanie said with a wink. "I could see the way you were lookin' at each other at the supper table. I never really thought of Todd as tall, since Andy's got a good two or three inches on him, but you and Todd do make a right cute couple—and he's not the cute one!"

"I appreciate that," said Natalie, resisting the urge to yawn. The big meal and the long hours were catching up with her.

Jeanie gave Natalie a smiling nod, and she left the bedroom door open when she walked out. When Jeanie reached the front door of the cabin, she met Todd, carrying his travel bag and a large polished-aluminum suitcase.

"I think this thing weighs more than she does," said Todd, stepping aside to let Jeanie out.

"The TV's hooked up to our satellite," said Jeanie, continuing on toward the main house. "I'll give you folks a wakeup call around seven."

"Thanks, Jeanie. That'd be great."

"You take good care a that little gal, now," she said, without turning to look back.

Todd dropped his bag on the living room couch, and he lugged Natalie's suitcase over to her bedroom door. He found her sprawled on the bed, having kicked off the loaner boots.

"Where's your rifle?" she asked, propping her head up on a pillow.

"It's still in the back seat of Andy's car. I guess I oughta go get it, huh?"

"You're pretty good with it, and I'd feel a lot better if we had it in here with us."

"Anything else I can get you?" Todd asked. "There's a little refrigerator on the other side of your bed. Andy said there's bottled water in it."

"Once you get back with your rifle," Natalie replied, "I'll feel safe and sound."

"Start the stopwatch," said Todd, as he disappeared from view.

*   *   *   *

"Pretty simple files," said the GSG data center supervisor. "The only recent ones are for an application for a search warrant, what appears to be the actual search warrant document itself, some kind of receipt form, a form titled 'photograph log,' and something called a search warrant return.

"Would you like them opened, Mr. Fitzgerald?"

"Yes," the old man replied breathlessly, "and remember this is a strictly confidential matter, the importance of which will be reflected in your next paycheck."

"Absolutely, sir," the man said, manipulating the keys almost too fast for Fitzgerald to follow. "The search warrant is for a property in unincorporated Park County, Montana, known as The Manor, on U. S. Highway 89, 7.2 miles north of Corwin Springs, Montana. The warrant covers all dwellings, structures, and improved and unimproved areas of the property. Pretty much the typical vague boilerplate wording, but the crime being investigated is the apparent deliberate homicide of an unknown white male adult. This document was last modified on Sunday morning."

"What does the receipt form list?" Fitzgerald asked anxiously.

"Let's see," said the data center supervisor. "It's more a recent document. Last modified on Monday morning. I see clothing, shoes, a wallet containing…twenty-two credit cards in the name of…Matheson Draper. Would that be *our* Mr. Draper, sir?"

"As I told you before, this is strictly confidential. Please continue."

"Uh, two bottles of antifreeze, pieces of duct tape, a wooden chair, a vial of urine recovered in snow and now melted, two plaster casts of footprints, a video tape labeled 'blonde,' another tape labeled 'redhead,' a third labeled 'Arabs,' and a fourth labeled 'February 1997.'"

"Draper and his videos. Jesus, Joseph, and Mary," Fitzgerald said with a sigh. "Please go on."

"The remains of a white male adult tentatively identified as…Hugh Matheson Draper, dressed in white boxer-style underwear, bearing numerous attached strips of duct tape and with an…aluminum funnel duct taped in his mouth."

"Anything about a laptop?" asked Fitzgerald, ignoring the supervisor's growing discomfort.

"Not on this list, sir."

"Try the one called…photograph log."

"It's another Sunday document, last modified in the afternoon. The entries are numbered. Exterior structure south wall, same for the east wall, same for the north wall, and same for the west wall. Outbuilding, south and east sides. Outbuilding, north and west sides. Outbuilding interior, four-wheeler. Structure main floor living area from front doorway. Structure main floor living area from base of stairway. Structure main floor living area from south wall facing north—"

"Does he say *what* structure he's talking about?"

"Uh…no, sir."

"What does this…search warrant return form say?"

"It's only a template, sir. It was never completed."

"How about the application?"

"Pretty much the same language as the search warrant itself. It says there's reason to believe the offense of deliberate homicide was committed, and pretty much what the county attorney's responsibilities are. The agent who was supposed to sign it is a Todd Milton, of Montana CIB, Missoula Office.

"Nothing about a laptop, though. Is that something important, sir?"

"It's something you will never mention again," Fitzgerald replied sternly.

"I could search these other stored documents, sir, although none has been modified during the month of June."

"I really don't see any point," said Fitzgerald. "Go ahead and shut it down."

*   *   *   *

Todd propped the rifle beside the twin bed in the loft, and he pulled a pair of nylon jogging shorts out of his travel bag. The flimsy shorts made great summertime sleep attire, and he could get away with walking around in them without drawing too many stares. He took a peek over the loft railing, but there was no sign of Natalie. He heard the bathroom shower sputter to life, and he knew the time was right for him to change.

Pulling on a long sleeve CIB T-shirt, Todd took the tight circular stairway down from the loft, and he switched on the television. The Braves were playing on the West Coast, and the game was only in the seventh inning. He took a seat on the couch and propped his feet on the head of a bearskin rug.

"*You* are a Braves fan?" Natalie asked from somewhere back in the darkness of her bedroom.

"They're on just about every night," Todd replied without turning around. "Even though there are other teams closer to Montana, I wouldn't make special a trip just to see them. Missoula's working on a minor league team, though, so we'll have real baseball to watch one of these days."

She stepped up behind him and put her hands on his shoulders. What her fingers lacked in length they made up for in strength, and she began to work the tightness from his neck muscles. He relaxed with the massage, and she followed the game while her hands remained busy.

"Think you could teach me how to shoot?" she asked, wincing at a high pitch that almost nailed Chipper Jones.

"As a matter of fact," said Todd, leaning back to get a look at her. Her face was a lot closer than he expected. "I'm also certified as a firearms instructor for CIB."

"I'm not talking about your rifle. That thing makes the ground shake when you pull the trigger."

"It was just the muzzle blast you felt. The Marlin's chambered for the .357 Magnum handgun round, so it's pretty easy on the shoulder, but it still has plenty of power. A regular .357 revolver like the one Andy carries might be a handful for you, but we can start you out with something like a .22, so you can learn sight picture and get the feel of trigger control."

"What kind of handgun do *you* carry?" she asked, changing the focus of her massage to his tight shoulder muscles.

"Don't tell anybody, but I carry a .357 Smith & Wesson revolver, too—just to go with the carbine. It makes sense to have a rifle and a handgun that use the same round. The state issued me a 9mm, but I leave it locked in my office in Missoula most of the time, and that's where it is right now."

"What are you, some kind of a rebel?" Natalie asked with a laugh.

"I don't know," he replied with a sigh. "Sometimes I think I'm more at odds with Helena than I am with the crooks."

"Who's Helena?" she asked, taking her hands away.

Todd had to smile at her reaction, and he reached back for her hands. She didn't resist when he held her.

"Helena isn't a *who*; it's a *what*," he said with a laugh. "Helena is the state capital. That's where all my bosses hang their hats."

"Aren't they happy with your work?" she asked, resuming the massage.

"It's hard to tell. I've gotten letters of commendation from sheriffs like Andy and the county attorneys who prosecute my cases—for all the work I've done for them, but Helena is pretty stingy with pats on the back. The only way you know you're doing a good job for CIB is when someone else thanks you."

"How long have you been a state agent?"

"Eight years, but prior to that I was a deputy in Missoula County for six years."

"Why didn't you stay a deputy?"

"I like to travel—and I really like to work major cases like this one. State agents are few and far between, though, and we have to cover an awful lot of ground. When the opportunity came up to go to work for CIB, I jumped at the chance, and I've got no real regrets."

"So, where do you go from here—as far as your investigation goes?"

"I don't know what to tell you on that one, darlin'," he replied, leaning away from her welcomed touch. He motioned for her to join him on the couch, and she walked around to stand before him. She was wearing the same baggy Dallas Cowboys jersey. "I'm kinda in limbo until I can get transportation, and I couldn't even get the *acting* chief in Helena to give me a case number. Be prepared, because somewhere down the road another CIB agent might be asking you all the same questions."

"Will I...see you again?" she asked softly, lifting the jersey just enough to allow her to sit astride his lap. In the flickering light of the television, it was hard to tell if he was blushing, but his swallow was loud enough to be heard outside.

"You mean...like...in Atlanta?" he asked cautiously.

"I don't know if I'll be going back to Atlanta," she said, leaning forward and resting her elbows on his chest. "My...*work*...with GSG is over. Like I told you: I'm a woman without a foreseeable future."

"Do you...like me—I mean...*really?*"

"Yes, I do," she said quickly.

"Don't get me wrong, but...I'll understand if you were caught up in the moment. When all the shooting started, well, it was my *job* to protect you. I want you to know that. You really don't owe me any more than what you'd owe your typical public servant."

"Do you always try to talk women *out* of liking you?" Natalie asked, running a finger across his lips.

"Is…is that what I'm doing?" he asked uneasily.

"Let's get something straight, cowboy," said Natalie. "Do *you* like *me*?"

"Very much."

"Do you believe me when I say I like you?"

"You don't…seem like a liar to me."

"Do you find me…attractive?"

"You're darn right I do."

"Then quit talking in circles and kiss me you fool," she demanded, trying to make her voice sound deep.

"Yes, ma'am," he said, before pulling her lips to his.

It was their longest kiss to date, and she let his hands move over and under the thin fabric covering her body. Her hands were busy, too, in his hair, brushing his eyebrows, tracing the outlines of his ears.

Her hands also found the bottom of his T-shirt, and she lifted it up to his chin. He pulled his arms from the sleeves to help, but she was already busy with the hair on his chest.

Natalie leaned away briefly, to slip out of her jersey, and Todd pulled her close and let his tongue taste her freshness. She wore nothing else, and he was quick to show his appreciation. Strong but gentle, he let her feel things even a billionaire couldn't provide.

Todd turned to lie on his side, and Natalie slid down beside him. Rolling onto his back, he lifted her up onto his chest. Their lips were close again, but their kisses were more brief and repetitive.

"I…guess it would be fair to say you've…slept with a woman before," Natalie whispered, unaware that the Braves had blown a five run lead.

"Yeah," Todd replied, letting his fingers run down her slender back. "You don't find too many thirty-five-year-old men who haven't—straight ones, any-way."

"But you do remember what I said…about me?" she asked, even more softly than before. "I…I've never…"

"What's the rush," he said, wrapping his arms tightly about her. "I'm not gonna hurt you, if that's what you're worried about. I'd never do that.

"If it's all right with you, I think we can make each other happy with-out…well, you know, and I'm getting kinda old to be thinking about starting a family. A guy over fifty shouldn't have to be bothered with beating up his six-teen-year-old daughter's pesky boyfriends."

"But I've…never even made a man *happy* before—at least not directly. I've never *touched* a man before. All through school, I was afraid—even in college. I think I'm…still afraid."

"Like I told you before," Todd said, giving her tight little bottom a squeeze, "welcome to the club."

*   *   *   *

"Where's Yolanda?" Fitzgerald asked, as he burst through his own office door.

The broad-shouldered man was seated in one of Fitzgerald's overstuffed office chairs, but the hooker was nowhere to be seen.

"She said her hour was up…sir," the big man replied. "Were you able to learn anything from the agent's machine?"

"Nothing of value," said the old man, flopping into his own chair. "The agent had a photographic log of some kind, but his description of the location was inadequate. It's obviously a smaller building than The Manor, but he didn't say where it was."

"It must be in Park County, though," said the big man. "He wouldn't be doing an investigation at The Manor unless the crime scene was within the same jurisdiction. As large as it is, I don't believe the GSG property extended into another county. Were there any other structures on the property besides the garage?"

"At The Manor? Why should there be? The place would easily accommodate forty guests. There was no need. But you're absolutely right about the scope of his investigation. His search warrant seemed to concentrate solely on the GSG property."

"If there was no mention of any other address…"

"Then it must be close by," Fitzgerald said, mostly to himself.

"Perhaps someone should make another visit, sir."

"It doesn't matter," Fitzgerald said dismissively. "There was no mention of Draper's computer in the agent's evidence log. It's obvious the man was at the crime scene, however. His list included the bottles of antifreeze and Draper's remains."

"Then, forgive me for asking, sir, but what are we concerned with now? If the laptop wasn't destroyed in the fire, what information could it contain that might damage the company? It's obvious Mr. Draper's murder will be investigated. We were expecting that all along, although, personally, I doubt it will ever be solved.

Would Mr. Draper keep such damaging information, knowing what might happen if it was discovered?"

"Do you believe in evolution, my friend?" Fitzgerald asked, sniffing a familiar scent on his fingertips. The big man remained silent, knowing better than to interrupt what would be a typical Yancey Fitzgerald lecture. "Matheson Draper was an evolutionary anomaly, make no mistake about it.

"I'm not talking about the man's sexual aberrations and physical deformities. I'm speaking of the next…level of Homo sapiens. If the early examples of mankind can be given unique names like *Peking* man, then I propose we give Matheson Draper the title of *Business* man.

"He had no real book smarts. He suffered from dyslexia and an attention span disorder, but he had an *instinct* for making money. A certain foresight for the opportune monetary moment.

"He would've been a billionaire *without* working. His family left him more money than he could ever conceptualize, but he could see the future. Railroads, trucking, airfreight, oil tankers, real estate, mining, onshore and offshore drilling, precious stones and metals. Nothing of value escaped him. No force—natural or governmental—could resist him. He knew the proper time to strike. And that's what concerns me now, my fine friend.

"He had no conscience. The concepts of remorse, contrition, guilt, shame— they were all foreign to him. Like any predatory animal, he stalked his prey. His needs were much more basic than we can ever imagine. He viewed any competition as a potential—make that probable—victim. And he spared no expense when it came to…problem solving.

"You'd said recently that Draper's…*contractor*…was unknown to you. Draper was way too stupid to memorize what he'd spent and when he'd spent it and whom he'd spent it on. The information contained on his office hard drive was useless gibberish—a silly string of letters and numbers with no rhyme or reason, so his laptop represents an unknown quantity, if you will, and that might be the *last* thing we'll ever have to worry about."

*   *   *   *

From twenty-five floors below, the stranger lowered his binoculars.

"I don't know if you guys are going to be any help at all," he muttered.

*   *   *   *

A violent shiver went through Natalie's body, and she tensed in the unfamiliar surroundings. It was dark, and in her sluggish half-sleep she felt the familiar restrictions of close confinement. But her wrists were free, and so were her ankles. The realization brought her to complete consciousness.

Todd felt her stir, and he tucked his arm more tightly about her waist. They were sleeping on their sides, and her back was pressed against his chest. He felt a sudden tautness come over her body, but then she relaxed and curled more deeply into his grasp.

"For a moment there, I forgot where I was," she whispered.

"I knew where you were all the time," he said in a hoarse, unused voice.

"Does it always get this cool during the summer nights?" she asked, taking in a deep breath. "It sure does make a warm bed feel good."

"That's just Montana. You can sleep under a blanket during the summer, but when winter arrives there never seems to be *enough* covers."

"Shared body heat helps," she said, turning onto her back. "Although I'm not sure I'm providing an equal share."

"When you decided to quit impersonating Emmitt, you made me warm enough to sleep outside in January."

"I think I have to…visit the little girls' room," she said, sliding her hands along his outstretched arm, "but I'm afraid to go down there by myself."

"Where did you leave your jersey?" Todd asked, rolling onto his back.

"I think we left it on the couch with your shirt, but I don't really need it."

"Lead the way, then," he said, lifting the covers.

There were still glowing coals in the woodstove, and they gave off just enough light through the glass-front stove door for Natalie and Todd to find their way down the spiral stairs. Todd waited outside the bathroom door, as Natalie slipped noiselessly inside.

There was a wind building outside, and the strong gusts whistled through a nearby stand of juniper. In the distance, a coyote sang with joy at the discovery of a fallen fawn.

The flushing toilet brought Todd back to reality, and he listened to the sound of water running in the sink. After a moment of silence, Natalie reappeared in the dull orange light of the embers.

"I…uh…cleaned myself up," she said, making no effort to cover her nakedness. "In case you want to…"

"Yes," he said, lifting her chin with a gentle touch. "I want to."

Todd could see the flash of her smile in the fading glow, and he let her lead him back to the warmth of their loft bed.

*   *   *   *

"What do you think a her?" Andy asked in the darkness. The lighted alarm clock numerals told him it was way past time to be asleep.

"How'd you know I was thinkin' about her?" asked Jeanie, reaching a hand across to her husband's sprawled form.

"This is little Natalie we're talkin' about, ain't it?"

"Well, what other *her* would I mean?"

"Do you think she's good for Todd?"

"Do you?"

"I…"

"It doesn't matter what *we* think, hon," Jeanie said soothingly. "What matters is what he thinks, and he sure seems to like her."

"I just wish I knew more about her, that's all," Andy said with a tired sigh. "I don't want him rushin' into things."

"I meant to tell you, but I got busy with the dishes—"

"What?" Andy asked, sitting up in the bed.

"Oh, lay yourself down," Jeanie scolded. "They aren't gonna elope. I wanted to tell you she asked me about finding work."

"Work? You mean around here?"

"Yeah, around here. I told her I'd talk to you about the dispatcher job. Dawn's gotta be leavin' to have her baby soon, and Natalie said she can type eighty words a minute."

"That damn car a hers cost more than the courthouse, baby doll," Andy said, mostly to himself.

"What car?"

"Ah, I had her hide it down in Clarence's garage. It's a jim-dandy, though. It's sorta like the one that movie star fella drives."

"The kung fu guy?"

"No, the whiny, liberal, tree-huggin' cocksucker. You know who I mean."

"Yes, I do, and I told you not to cuss," Jeanie hissed.

"It's just us, honey," Andy said softly, reaching out to take his wife's hand.

"You tired?" she asked, her tone subdued.

"Not really."
"Wanna fool around?"

CHAPTER 5

▼

If there was one thing Rudy Rosser was good at, it was hunting. Big game. Varmints. Waterfowl. Upland birds. Rudy lived for the hunt, and he put more effort into that pastime than anything else. He went hunting so often that an early morning departure was almost his daily routine.

The nighttime stars were still in Rudy's rearview mirror, as he drove through Bozeman on Interstate 90. Up ahead, the dawning of a new day was prefaced by a clear gray sky. Rudy checked his watch: 5:35 a.m.

Officially, this Tuesday morning was still one day shy of the *hump* day of Rudy's temporary duty as acting CIB bureau chief, and it was especially uncharacteristic for him to stray too far from the halls of power in Helena. Rudy was still smarting from his meeting with Arthur Yost, however, and he reasoned that a decisive act might bring him some much-needed favor, although he hadn't thought far enough ahead to identify just what act might be necessary or what particular favor might be gained.

Patting his right pant leg to see if his spilled coffee had dried, Rudy raised his chin during the final downhill stretch into Livingston. A quick stop at the courthouse would get him on the right track, and then he'd have his showdown with Todd Milton.

*   *   *   *

The stranger assembled the false identification he'd used to rent the car, before dropping it into a waste receptacle on the curb at the south terminal of the

Atlanta-Hartsfield International Airport. In the swarming crowd of summer travelers, he was hardly noticed in his rather drab company uniform.

Making his way through the security stations, he flashed his company credentials at each checkpoint until he arrived at the commercial shipping terminal. There, he paused for a moment at a company computer cubicle to access a pair of shipping code tracking numbers. No activity.

Another check revealed a soon-to-depart flight, and he entered his own employee number on the shipping manifest. He then walked through the GSG warehouse and boarded a plane to Boston.

*   *   *   *

A fist pounding on the cabin door brought Todd out of a deep sleep. Natalie had her head resting on his chest, and she felt him shift beneath her.

"Wha-what is it?" she asked, wiping at some saliva at the corner of her mouth.

"I don't know, but you'd better stay up here," he said, slipping from beneath the covers.

"I wanna go with you," she said lazily, pulling back the blanket.

"Then put this on," he said, offering her a Montana Law Enforcement Academy T-shirt from his travel bag.

After putting the shirt on backwards, Natalie finally managed to get the logo on the front, but Todd's offering only fit her slightly better than her discarded football jersey, and the broad crew neck exposed her bare right shoulder. The length was fine, though, covering her knees with fabric to spare.

Still dressed in his nylon shorts, Todd armed himself with the carbine, and he led his bedmate downstairs to the living room. The stove had cooled during the night, and the effect was noticeably pronounced through the flimsy cotton of Natalie's T-shirt. When Todd reached the door, Natalie hid behind him.

If someone had told Todd that Rudy Rosser was waiting outside the cabin door, Todd could've predicted the acting chief's pose from memory. Rudy's natural posture was defensive, although he actually thought crossing his arms over his chest accented what he regarded as an heroic stance.

"Where is she?" Rudy demanded, as Todd lowered the muzzle of the Marlin.

"Good morning, Rudy," said Todd, without moving out of the doorway.

"The jailer in Livingston said you had that material witness gal up here," Rudy went on. "Where'd you put her?"

"She's in here with me, Rudy," Todd replied, feeling Natalie's hands on his back.

"Well, I'm takin' over the case," Rudy said, leaning back in an effort to look down his nose at the taller man. He was still hesitant about barging into the cabin, however. "I assigned myself the case number, so I'll be the lead agent."

"What did Andy have to say about that?" Todd asked, taking a step forward.

"I'll deal with Freund later," Rudy replied, backing up a step to keep a distance between them. "He's movin' to the top of my shit list, anyhow, for not followin' proper CIB request procedure."

"I don't think he'll be too pleased to hear that—"

"I don't give a fuck if he is or not. Now where's that girl?"

"I'm right here," Natalie said, peeking from behind Todd.

The sight made Rudy do a double take, for it wasn't often that he got to look down at someone.

"What the fuck is *this*?!" Rudy shouted, stepping to the side to allow himself a better view of the tiny woman.

"Easy, Rudy," said Todd. "You don't need to talk like that in front of a lady."

"Lady, huh?" Rudy said, giving the MLEA T-shirt a closer look. "What's she doin' in *your* shirt? Or is that how *you* guard a material witness?"

"I'm not denying anything, Rudy," said Todd, propping the carbine in the corner behind the door. "Natalie and I have been…getting to know each other, but she's *not* a suspect, and she really *does* need protection."

"I hope to hell you were *usin'* protection," said Rudy, motioning for Todd to back up.

"There's no call for that kinda talk, either," said Todd, his eyes narrowing.

"Are you gonna let me in or what?" Rudy went on, still unwilling to openly challenge the younger agent.

After a few seconds of cold staring, Todd stepped aside and allowed Rudy to enter the cabin. Todd kept his arm around Natalie, and he was careful to stand between her and the man with the suspicious brown stain on his khaki pants. For the moment, however, Rudy seemed preoccupied with the rest of the cabin.

"Did she make her bed already?" asked Rudy, canting his head for a better view of the downstairs bedroom. "Or did she sleep on the couch under your CIB shirt?"

"Knock it off, Rudy," Todd said firmly, ushering Natalie to the bedroom door. She ducked inside, and Todd closed the door behind her. "We're adults, and you came here uninvited. She's here because she *wants* to be. And I want her here, too."

"You've fucked up good this time, buddy," Rudy said, strolling over to an end table next to the living room sofa. Todd's CIB badge case was resting on the tabletop, along with his keys and wallet. Rudy picked up the badge case. "Art's gonna be hearing about this, as soon as I get your little girlfriend booked into the Lewis & Clark County Jail."

"You really need to rethink this, Rudy," said Todd, walking up to the grinning weasel. "This is still Andy Freund's call, and he's not going to let you take Natalie out of Park County."

"Fuck Freund," said Rudy, stuffing Todd's badge case into his coat pocket. "I'd say 'fuck her, too,' but I guess you already did—"

A smug smile is not the best expression to have when a fist meets your face, as Rudy learned all too quickly. The blow filled his eyes with tears, and blood spurted from his nose and mouth, but it was the cabin wall against the back of Rudy's head that hurt the worst.

Todd stood over the blinking worm, as Rudy's world slowly returned to focus.

"She's staying right here," said Todd.

"For now, maybe," Rudy whined, trying to get some traction with his sprawled legs, "but you're gonna get canned like a tuna. I'm takin' your badge and ID back to Helena, and I'm gonna tell Yost about this. You can't go around hittin' a fellow agent."

"You and I have never been 'fellow agents,' Rudy," said Todd, offering the squirming toad a hand. Rudy took it reluctantly, and Todd helped him to his feet.

Brushing himself off—but ignoring the blood still dripping from his nose and upper lip, Rudy strutted to the cabin door.

"I'll be back," he said defiantly, "and I'll put that little bitch of yours in jail until *my* investigation is over."

Turning to make a hasty departure, Rudy almost bumped into Andy Freund—fully dressed in his duty uniform—on the small front porch of the cabin. Andy didn't move, so Rudy sidestepped around him, and the still-bleeding skunk scurried toward his parked car without looking back.

"Got somethin' else for you to take back to Helena," Andy said from a step behind the fleeing acting chief. The sheriff of Park County then planted one of his size 13EE boots between Rudy's butt cheeks.

*   *   *   *

The stranger's drive from Boston was a pleasantly uneventful one. He'd been tired after his early morning arrival, and he'd opted to sleep a few hours in a motel room near Logan. The sleep had done him good, with the added benefit that he was able to check out long after the morning rush hour. The downtown traffic was still heavy for the first hour, though, as he kept just below the speed limit while still within the Interstate 95 loop. Once he'd left the Boston suburbs, he turned west on roads less traveled. His destination was still hours away.

*   *   *   *

Natalie sat on the edge of the couch, with her knees pressed tightly together, as Andy tried to act distracted by goings-on outside. At her suggestion, she and Todd had flipped a coin for the first shower, and he'd won the toss, but the sound of running water made Natalie wish she hadn't raided the water bottles in the downstairs refrigerator. At least Andy had been kind enough to stoke up the stove.

"Do you really think he'll lose his job over this?" she asked, as Andy tried to follow the flight of a camp robber.

"I don't know," Andy replied, shaking his head. "After givin' Rudy a good kick in the ass, though, I was sorta worried about losin' my foot. For such a squatty turd, that Rudy's got a damn big butt."

"Please don't make me laugh," Natalie said, crossing her legs in agony. "I've gotta pee something awful."

"Hang on, then," Andy said quickly, rushing to the bathroom door. "Hey, Todd! Get a move on. The little lady needs take a squirt."

Andy turned back with a wounded expression, having realized how uncouth he must've sounded, but Natalie was gripping her sides with laughter.

"Tell her to come on in," Todd called back. "I can't see her from behind the shower curtain, anyway."

Before Andy could pass the word, Natalie was by him and through the door. A moment later, Andy heard her scream, but he knew better than to interfere.

"Are you okay?" Todd asked above the patter of the shower.

"You left the seat up, and that porcelain is *cold*," Natalie said with a gasping laugh. "I should've known better than to sit down without checking."

"Sorry," said Todd, smiling at the thought of her discomfort. "Bachelor's habits are hard to break."

"I'm gonna work on that," she said softly, pulling back the shower curtain. The MLEA T-shirt was hanging over the towel rail, and Todd wasted no time in offering his soapy washcloth.

She stood with her back to him, as he ran the cloth from her neck to her heels. Todd's touch was a world away from the ordeals she'd suffered for the sake of a paycheck. After lathering the cloth again, he raised her arms one at a time and cleaned them from shoulder to fingertips. Only when she turned to face him did he hesitate.

"Sorry," he said, looking down into her eyes through the passing clouds of steam. "I didn't want you to think I was…like…in those films."

"You're not a bit like him," she said, taking the washcloth from his hand. Instead of washing herself, though, she began to run the cloth over his dripping form.

"I was almost through," Todd said shyly.

"I know," she whispered, "but I've never done this before—until last night I'd never *touched* a man before, and I really want to…with you."

"Just pretend like I'm not here!" Andy shouted from the living room.

"We could, if you weren't so *noisy!*" Todd hollered back.

＊   ＊   ＊   ＊

"And then he hit me right in the mouth for no reason at all," Rudy wailed on his cellular telephone, unable to wait for a face-to-face meeting with the division administrator. He knew Art Yost would be in early, and Rudy had called just as Yost was sitting down to a freshly heated Danish.

"No reason," Yost echoed, watching as the warm frosting on his pastry began to harden. "From what you've already told me, Rudy, Todd might've had a reason. Why did you have to go down there in the first place?"

"I assigned myself the case, that's why," Rudy replied defensively. "It's in the ledger book, now, so it can't be changed. I'm the official lead agent of record."

"Who says it can't be changed?" Yost asked, as he reached for his policy manual.

"That's been bureau procedure for…twenty years, at least. I came up with it myself, in…1979. When it's written down in the ledger book, it's as good as carved in stone. That's what I've always said."

"1979 was only eighteen years ago, Rudy," said Yost, flipping through the pages of the manual, "but there's no mention of the case ledger book in CIB policy. I think that's just Meacham's way of keeping a personal record, but it's certainly not in the manual."

"Didn't need to be. The ledger book's been around since the sixties. Way before we had a manual."

"You know something, Rudy," Yost said with a sigh. "There's a saying in management, and it goes something like this: practice can make policy, but whiteout can make changes. Now I'm going down to Meacham's office with my little bottle of Liquid Paper, and as soon as it dries Todd Milton will be the lead agent on the Park County homicide case. Do I make myself clear?"

"But I fired Milton," said Rudy. "I left a voice mail message for the county attorney down there, too. I told her I wanted to prosecute him for assault on a law enforcement officer. I'm gonna get a warrant issued for his arrest."

"Have you recently run out of some kind of medication, Rudy?" asked Yost. "I know you can't read my lips at the moment, but listen carefully. Even the bureau chief of CIB doesn't have the authority to fire an agent, so no *acting* chief is ever going to get away with such a stupid stunt. As for Agent Milton's relationship with his witness, there's nothing in CIB policy about that either. Agents aren't allowed to fraternize with jail inmates or known criminals—unless the interaction is of an undercover nature, but there's no restriction on personal relationships with witnesses or victims. From the sound of things, this woman just might be both."

"Well, there's the section about accepting gratuities," Rudy said quickly.

"I'm...not sure I'm following you."

"Like, uh, if she gave him a piece of ass, that's a gratuity, ain't it?"

Yost held the phone away from his ear, but he resisted the urge to throw the receiver across the room. It took him a moment to calm himself.

"How long have you been married, Rudy?" Yost asked stiffly.

"Me an' Emma have been together...twenty-six years next July," Rudy replied.

Again, Yost gritted his teeth in anger, but he was still able to control his growing frustration.

"Do you mean twenty-six years next *month*?" Yost managed to ask. "Or are you referring to July of 1998?"

"Oh, uh, '98," Rudy replied.

"Then wouldn't that mean you'll have been married twenty-*five* years next month?" said Yost, trying to keep from shouting. "Oh, never mind all that! What I'm getting at is this: while a man celebrating his twenty-fifth wedding anniversary might perceive *any* type of sex act as a gratuity, a younger, single, more physically active man like Todd Milton might just view it as a mutually rewarding experience."

"I beg your pardon?" Rudy asked, drifting onto the shoulder of the road.

"You won't get it," said Yost, slamming down the telephone.

*   *   *   *

"You're sure ready in a hurry," said Andy, as Todd came down the stairs from the loft bedroom.

"My hair's easy to dry, and I don't have to put on makeup," Todd said with a smile.

"It's in my *suitcase!*" Natalie shouted from behind the bedroom door.

Andy and Todd got caught in the doorway, as they burst into the room in response to her cry. The sight of Natalie in bra and panties was enough to freeze Andy in his tracks, and he remained in the doorway.

"Are you all right?" Todd asked, stepping up to give Natalie a little needed cover.

"Look," she said, pointing to her opened case.

Some of her clothes were pulled aside, and Todd could see the corner of a flat black object.

"What is it?" Andy asked, still wary about moving closer.

"It's Math Draper's laptop computer," she replied.

*   *   *   *

"Montana Department of Justice," the administrative assistant answered in her most pleasant tone. "How may I direct your call?"

"Yes, ma'am," Yancey Fitzgerald replied. "I would like to speak to the acting chief of CIB. I believe he said his name was Rosser."

"I'm sorry, sir, but Agent Rosser is signed out on the board, can I take a message for you and have him call you back when he returns?"

"Did he leave anyone else in charge? This is Yancey Fitzgerald, with GSG in Atlanta, Georgia. I don't mean to sound impatient, but there seems to be an investigation going on in Park County, Montana, and I understand your agency has an agent on the scene there. It's very important that I talk to someone about this."

"According to the board, Agent Rosser is *in* Park County today, sir. He's listed the courthouse in Livingston as a contact point. I think Mr. Yost, our division administrator, spoke with Agent Rosser earlier this morning. Mr. Yost is in his office now. Would you like to talk to him?"

"That would be wonderful," said Fitzgerald.

"I'll transfer you, sir," she said, before placing him on hold.

"Arthur Yost," the division administrator answered on the first ring.

"Good morning to you, sir. This is Yancey Fitzgerald, with GSG in Atlanta, Georgia. I was calling about the CIB investigation in Park County. The investigation is being conducted on GSG-owned property there."

"Yes, Mr. Fitzgerald," Yost said, scribbling notes as he went. "We've had an agent there since Sunday morning, actually, although I didn't learn of the investigation until yesterday. I've yet to see anything in writing, however, so I wouldn't be able to brief you on our progress at this point."

"I'd spoken with an Agent Rosser, yesterday," said Fitzgerald, "and he told me he would check on the case. The lady who answered your telephone told me Agent Rosser had traveled to Park County this morning. Is there anything our office can do to speed things along? The brief call I had with Sheriff Freud wasn't very informative."

"His name is *Freund*, Mr. Fitzgerald," said Yost. "Andrew Freund. He happens to be the president of the Montana Sheriffs and Peace Officers Association, making him one of the more powerful and politically active public servants in the state, although his department is one of the smaller sheriff's offices. I guess what I'm telling you is that his agency resources might be taxed at the moment, and that's why he's asked for our assistance. Andy Freund is a very direct individual, Mr. Fitzgerald. I'm sure if he didn't want to tell you anything over the telephone he had a good reason."

"Yes, sir," Fitzgerald said uneasily. "Sheriff Freund did tell us an expensive building on our property had been burned in an apparent case of arson, but we're still trying to locate two missing employees—one of them is Mr. Matheson Draper, the CEO of GSG. The other employee is Mr. Draper's...personal assistant, I guess you could say, a Miss Natalie Weinberg. We would certainly like to know if they've been located, as we've had no word from either of them."

"As I said before, Mr. Fitzgerald," Yost replied cautiously. "I've not been in contact with Sheriff Freund or our agent in Park County, and no reports have been forwarded to our office here in Helena. Your best bet would be to telephone Sheriff Freund again. If there *is* any news to report, he would be the one to release it."

"Ah, yes," said Fitzgerald, staring up at the decorative ceiling tiles as though they might hold an answer. "I'll do just that."

The old man's hand was still resting atop the telephone receiver in its cradle when his secretary rang back on the office intercom.

"What is it?" Fitzgerald snapped, as he searched for the telephone number to the Park County Sheriff's Office.

"We have a call on the 800 line, sir," the woman replied sheepishly. "He says he's a state agent in Montana."

"Well, put it through," said Fitzgerald, his finger poised over the call buttons.

"Hello," Rudy Rosser said, as he heard a clicking on his cellular telephone.

"This is Yancey Fitzgerald."

"Yes, sir, Mr. Fitzgerald. Rudolph Rosser, Montana CIB."

"Agent Rosser," Fitzgerald said in the best syrupy tone he could concoct on such short notice—which wasn't much. "So kind of you to call back. I hope you have some good news for us."

"I'm afraid not," said Rudy. "I made a quick trip down to Livingston early this morning. I didn't go down to the site of the fire, but I did see Todd Milton."

"Now…who is he?"

"He *was* the state agent Freund called out over the weekend."

"What do you mean, 'was the state agent'?" Fitzgerald asked warily. The old man wondered if some of the shooting done by the man called Carlton had resulted in yet another casualty.

"Well, I had to suspend him, sort of," Rudy replied. "I've got his badge and ID, but I've still got some…issues to discuss with our division administrator."

"Would that be Mr. Yost?"

"Yeah. Do you know Art?"

"I spoke with him a little earlier. That's when I learned you were out in Park County. You were saying something about some news, I believe."

"Yeah, it's a homicide investigation, all right. The body's on the way to the crime lab, if it ain't over there already."

"Just…one body?" Fitzgerald asked, afraid to take a breath.

"Yeah. That Draper guy you told me about. I guess he was your boss."

"Were they able to locate…Miss Weinberg?"

"Is she a real small gal?"

"Yes, tiny, you might say, uh, dark haired, very pretty. *Extremely* pretty."

"I saw her this morning. She's being treated as a material witness at the moment. I hope to get her transferred to the Lewis & Clark County Jail sometime today."

"You mean she's in *jail?*" Fitzgerald asked in disbelief.

"Not yet," Rudy replied, "but she will be soon."

The thought of Natalie behind bars reminded Fitzgerald of his own porno collection, and he was buoyed by the thought.

"If your Agent Milton is suspended," Fitzgerald said slowly, still preoccupied with a vision of Draper's little sex-servant being pursued by a 300-pound dyke, "who is conducting the state's investigation?"

"I'll be doing that," said Rudy. "I've just got to clear some things up back in Helena, and I'll probably get started by tomorrow morning, at the latest."

"Then...I can count on *you* for progress reports?" Fitzgerald asked hopefully.

"I got your phone number. You bet."

"I look forward to hearing from you, sir," said Fitzgerald, "and I hope you have wonderful day."

After hanging up the phone, Fitzgerald pressed a button on the underside of his desk. Within a few seconds, the broad-shouldered man was walking through his door.

"She's alive," Fitzgerald said, in answer to the man's questioning stare.

"Where, sir?"

"I'm not sure, but she'll soon be in the Lewis & Clark County Jail. Wherever that might be."

"Do they think she...did it?" the big man asked.

"She's being called a...material witness, I think he said. Does that sound like 'suspect' to you?"

"In legal terms, that would cover a witness who might not be cooperative—or one in need of protection."

"Maybe she's regarded as both," said Fitzgerald.

"How did you find this out, sir?"

"The acting chief of CIB called," Fitzgerald replied with a self-satisfied grin. "*His* boss in Helena was pretty tight-lipped, but this Agent Rosser freely confirmed Draper's death and Miss Weinberg's present status."

"What would you propose we do next?"

"There was no mention of Mr. Draper's computer?"

"No, but this Rosser would probably tell me, if I made such an inquiry."

"Showing an interest in a specific item might be a bad idea, sir," said the big man, rubbing his chin in thought. "If this Rosser is so free with information, it might be best to continue to express concern, and he very well may tell us all we need to know without prodding."

"How should we deal with the issue of Miss Weinberg?" asked Fitzgerald, still obsessed with the jailhouse vision.

"If she's in need of a lawyer—or any other services for that matter, she'll need the use of her corporate debit account. Did you deactivate her GSG credit card?"

"No. Only Draper's status was changed," Fitzgerald replied. "After you told me about the fuel stop, I thought we might be able to track her through any purchases she might make."

"And we still can, sir. At least until we know for sure that she's behind bars."

"Have her accounts and her employee identification number flagged for your notification, and let me know if there's any activity. Now that we've found her, I don't want her to slip away again."

The big man nodded slowly, before turning to leave.

✻   ✻   ✻   ✻

The note—actually a small piece of yellow self-adhesive paper attached to the top of the portable computer—was simple and brief:

N—

4 got 2 put it in the Merk, so I paked it in yore sootkase. Bring it with U.

—M

Natalie placed the laptop on the Freund's kitchen table, and she took a seat while Andy and Todd stood behind her. In her haste to dress, Natalie had put Todd's MLEA T-shirt on backwards, but it was tucked neatly into her jeans. She wore her own Nikes.

"What the hell kinda writin' is that?" Andy asked.

"It's Matheson Draper's kind of writing," Natalie explained. "He could never spell my name, so he'd just write my initial. If he ever had to spell out his own name, he'd transpose some of the letters most of the time, so he preferred to use his initial, too.

"The rest is his typical bonehead spelling. Whenever he could, he'd use a number for a word, like the '2' and the '4,' and he'd also use single letters that sounded like words, such as the 'U.'"

"'Merk'?" asked Andy. "Ain't that the medical manual?"

"It's what Math called his Mercedes," Natalie replied. "Even though it's really American slang for a Mercury, and, of course, he couldn't begin to spell either Mercury *or* Mercedes."

"The guy writes like an idiot," Andy said, shaking his head.

"Want to know the real shame of it?" asked Natalie, turning in her chair to face both men. "It probably took Math a couple of minutes to write those two simple lines, and, based on his annual salary, he was paid well over ten thousand dollars for those two minutes."

"Holy sheep," said Andy.

"I guess he must've had his car shipped out before mine," said Natalie. "He knew I'd be coming back from LA on Sunday.

"The important thing is that Math had to pack this himself—he'd never trust anyone else to do it, so nobody in the company knows we've got it—or even where it is. But I'll bet my little ass they'd like to know where it is."

"Can you get into it?" Todd asked, resisting an urge to glance at Natalie's wager.

"Nothing to it," Natalie replied, lifting the screen. The liquid crystal display came on almost immediately. "From the looks of things, he didn't use it for much, though. I only see two short documents stored here. Labeled 1 and 2, since he'd be the only one concerned with them."

"I thought you said you showed him how to use the machine," said Todd.

"I just showed him how to save and name documents," she replied. "I never saw what he wrote, but you can be sure whatever's in here will look just like his note."

"Can you open Number 1?" Todd asked.

With a click of the cursor, the single page document filled the left hand edge of the screen. Unfortunately, it was more confusing than Draper's normal writing. It appeared as:

2–12

D-4,4

JR-5,6

MR-5,10

MY-5,5

O-5,10

N-5,5

F-6,10

JE-6,5

JL-6,5

S-6,10

AL-7,5

JE-7,5

JE-8,10

N-8,5

JR-9,5

D 2,10

AT 3,10

O 3,10

MY 4,10

JE 5,10

N 6,10

D 6,10

JR 7,20

"And that list is supposed to mean something?" Todd asked.

"It meant something to him," Natalie said with a shrug. "But it shouldn't be too tough to figure out. If *he* was able to keep track of something this way, it's got to be pretty darn simple."

"Open Number 2," said Todd. "Maybe he actually tried to write something."

Natalie closed the first document, and she clicked onto the next. The display came up as follows:

2–69

-6,2

-7,2

-8,2

-9,2

0,2

1,2

2,4

3,4

4,4

5,6

6,6

7,10

"Shit on a stick," said Andy, leaning back from Natalie's shoulder. "That's even crazier than the first one."

"It's got to mean something," said Todd. "There's almost a logic to this one if we could figure out what the number sequence means. He left out the goofy letters."

Natalie remained silent, but her eyes were glued to the screen.

"Is there *anything* else on that machine?" asked Andy.

"Just the two numbered documents," said Todd. "He wasted a whole laptop computer to store a few characters of information."

Natalie pushed her chair back, and she rose to her feet. She turned to look at both men, who were momentarily silenced by her worried expression.

"I know what it means," she said softly.

When Rudy Rosser walked through the front door of the Montana DOJ offices, he could've been mistaken for an automobile accident victim. The bloodstains on his shirt and coat had dried to a dark red, and his coffee-stained trousers only added to the effect. When he turned at the front desk, on his way to Art Yost's office, the front office staff was afforded a view of the whites of his faded briefs through a rip in the seat of his pants.

"What an asshole," one of the women typists said under her breath.

"I only saw his underwear," said another, bringing uncontrollable giggles from them both.

Art Yost had his back to his open office door, as Rudy walked in and took a seat in front of the division administrator's desk. Rudy placed Todd's badge case on Yost's desk, knocking over a framed photo in the process. The noise got the boss's attention.

"You're back," said Yost, taking a moment to assess the damage to Rudy's nose and lip. Rosser's upper lip had a broad split, but his nose was outwardly intact.

"I figured you'd change your mind, once you saw what he did to me," said Rudy.

"Change my mind about what?"

"Like I told you," Rudy whined, sitting as tall as possible in his chair. "He hit a law enforcement officer in the performance of his duty, and I'm gonna swear out a warrant for his arrest."

"When one cop hits another, Rudy, I'm not so sure a judge will view the case as strictly one-sided. You might get him for an ordinary assault, though. It looks like he nailed you pretty good."

"And I didn't hit him back, either. You can ask. That girl was witness, too."

"Oh, I believe you," said Yost, standing to look over the top of his desk. The stain in Rosser's lap caught his eye. "Did you lose that much blood?"

"Coffee," Rudy replied.

"Did he hit you while you were holding a cup of coffee?" Yost asked in surprise.

"No. He hit me when I said somethin' about fucking his witness."

"You said *what*?!"

"I can't remember it all, Art," Rudy replied, shrinking lower in his chair. "She was in there—proud as can be with *his* T-shirt on and her nipples standin' straight out like two doorbells, and I figured he'd fucked her, so I said so."

"Did you happen to…dictate a report tape on this already?" asked Yost, dropping back into his chair. "Because I really would hope there's a lot more to this incident than what you've just told me."

"I'll get right on it," said Rudy, starting to rise.

"Hold your horses," said Yost, spying Todd's badge case on his desk. "What's this?"

"Milton's badge and ID," Rudy replied. "I took 'em from him."

"And what's he going to use for identification while he conducts his investigation?"

"It ain't his investigation; it's mine," said Rudy. "I put it in the ledger before I left."

"And I changed the ledger—"

"You really meant that?" Rudy whined. "The ledger's never been changed before."

"Then today is a new day in CIB," said Yost. "Now, tell me. How do I get in touch with Todd?"

"But I've done some work on this case already," Rudy protested.

"Do you call taking the lead agent's badge *work*?"

"Not just that," replied Rudy. "I took some calls—and made some."

"From whom—to *whom*?" Yost asked, leaning forward in his chair.

"Uh, I think his name is Fitzgerald—"

"Yancey Fitzgerald?" Yost asked quickly, checking the notes he'd taken earlier in the morning.

"Yeah. I told him about his boss croakin', and he asked about that woman I'm gonna put in jail."

"I specifically told you *not* to release *any* information," said Yost, standing once again. "This is still a Park County case until we get a request letter, and I don't want anything leaked—even if it's true. For all you know, that man's nothing but a reporter."

"Oh, no. He gave me a 1-800 number, and they answer...as...some company."

"Christ on a *crutch*, Rudy. Anybody can get an 800 number, and who's this woman you want to put in jail?"

"She's the one who Milton fucked—"

"Stop saying that, Rudy," Yost growled, hoping none of the office staff was eavesdropping just outside his open office door. "You make it sound like you've done a rape kit on this woman, and what's she done to warrant a trip to jail?"

"She's a material witness in my case. I want easier access to her, so I'm gonna have her brought to the county jail up here."

Yost walked to his office window, and he took a series of deep breaths to calm his elevated heart rate. Some three floors below, there was a group of children lining up on the sidewalk for a tour of the nearby Capitol building. One of the kids was taking a leak on the tire of their school bus.

"I need you to excuse me for a moment," Yost said, without turning away from the window. "I want to telephone Todd on his cell phone, and I'd like some privacy."

"Can't," said Rudy, making no effort to rise.

"What did you say?" asked Yost, his face glowing red as he turned his back on the laughing children.

"Can't call his cell phone," said Rudy, digging into his briefcase. "I took it. Suspended agents don't have cell phone privileges. And if that ain't in CIB policy, it sure oughta to be."

"Do you have *your* badge case with you, Rudy?" Yost asked, returning to his desk.

"Always keep it in my coat pocket. You never know whe—"

"Put it on the desk next to Todd's," Yost said firmly.

"You...you mean," Rudy said weakly.

"Leave it and get out," said Yost, lowering himself into his chair.

Rudy removed his badge and identification with a shaking hand, and he did as Yost had directed. He stood at the edge of Yost's desk for a moment, hoping his show of submission might give Yost cause to grant him a reprieve, but the division administrator's only response was an unwavering glare. With a shoulder-slumping shrug, Rudy finally turned to leave.

"Hey, Rudy," Yost called out, as Rosser was walking out the door. "Who kicked you in the ass?"

*   *   *   *

"He raised my annual salary—*three* times," Natalie said, as she stared down at document Number 2.

"What are you talkin' about?" asked Andy, still unable to fathom the short list of numbers on the screen.

"Like I said before," Natalie replied, pointing to the top of the page. "Math used numbers for words. '2–69' means: to GSG employee number 69."

"With all those employees," said Todd, "how'd you wind up with number 69?"

"Simple," said Natalie, her wounded expression offering more of an explanation. "The first one hundred employee numbers have always been reserved for top level corporate personnel. There aren't really a hundred of them, so all of the numbers aren't in use, but Math made a special point of assigning me number 69, for reasons we don't need to go into.

"Since the company has over four million employees worldwide, though, each employee number is preceded by enough zeros to extend it to seven figures. My real employee number, according to the company payroll records, is 0000069.

Math couldn't keep track of a long number like that—even though it's mostly zeros, therefore he listed it as just 69. His own employee number was 0000001."

"So, what's this about your salary?" asked Todd.

"Math wasn't good with dates, either," Natalie explained. "He took over GSG from his father in '82. Up until then, he had some ass-wipe corporate job, learning at his daddy's knee. Before I showed him how to use the computers, he kept records by hand in a personal diary. After he got the computer, though, he burned the diary.

"He's only had the laptop since '92, but he had trouble with *decades*, too. Whenever he'd write something about his early years as CEO, he'd list the previous decade as a minus sign, indicating the eighties.

"On this list, the '–6' is 1986, and so forth. This list covers my income for the entire time I've served as GSG employee number 0000069."

"I thought you said you made two hundred thousand dollars a year," said Todd, running down the right hand list of numbers.

"That was what my original contract called for," she said absently.

"You mean you didn't *know* how much money you made?" Andy asked in disbelief.

"No," Natalie replied weakly.

"What about when you paid your taxes?" asked Todd.

"The GSG audit department did them for me," she replied. "I always signed blank forms every year, and GSG took care of the rest of it."

"Didn't you see the money in your personal bank accounts?" Todd went on.

"I only have one account, but I've never seen how much is in it," said Natalie. "I know this sounds crazy, but I've never had a need for money. I had an unlimited expense account through GSG. I never had to spend my *own* money."

"So…you wouldn't even know if you were overdrawn. What about when you bought your car?" asked Todd.

"I used the corporate expense account to buy my car as part of a fleet purchase, and GSG automatically debited my personal account during the following month. They sent me a debit notice through inter-office mail," she replied. "If there hadn't been enough cash available, I'm sure I would've heard about it, but I've never had to directly access my personal account since I've been working for GSG."

"These numbers here…do you mean all this money is in the *bank*?" Todd asked, blinking at the figures on the opened page.

"I don't see what money you're talkin' about," said Andy, leaning closer to the screen.

"The numbers following the commas," said Natalie. "They represent hundred thousand dollar increments. It was Math's way of identifying amounts. He used to always say life would be a lot easier for him if they'd bring back the hundred thousand dollar bill. It was the smallest denomination he could deal with."

"Then according to his list here," said Todd, adding in his head, "you've made $4,600,000.00 since 1986."

"Exactly—less the cost of the car, of course, but I really didn't know he'd raised my salary so often," Natalie said, closing document Number 2 and reopening Number 1.

"This one looks a lot more complicated," said Andy.

"No, it isn't," said Natalie. "Not since I've seen the other one. These are payments to GSG employee number 0000012."

"Well, what do the letters mean?" Andy asked.

"Math couldn't spell anything with much more than three letters—even though he could make reasonable sense in normal conversation," Natalie replied. "In school, his family hired tutors, who grilled him orally until he could memorize what he needed to know. He still couldn't write, but they bought him an educational record, mainly for looks.

"The letters listed before the date numbers are just months. 'D' is for December. It's the only month with a D, so there was no need to designate it any other way, and that made it simpler for Math to memorize. 'JR,' however, is for January. His tutors probably chose 'JR' because June and July don't have an R in them. 'MR' differentiates March from 'MY,' which is May. The same reasoning throughout. 'O' is October. 'N' is November. 'F' is February. June is 'JE' and July is 'JL.' It's not the way an educated person would tell them apart, but it obviously worked for Math. 'S' is September, since there's no other S-month. 'AL' is April, and, farther down, 'AT' is August. Those last two appear to be a little more sophisticated and logical, since the first and last letters are used to designate the A-months, but I'm sure it's just a coincidence. Math would never be able to come up with this kind of logic on his own, but his tutors trained him as well as they could. In fact, the only thing I find especially shocking is his use of commas, but he probably didn't know the punctuation he'd chosen even *was* a comma."

"Well, he's paid old number 12 a shit-load a money," said Andy, without bothering to try to add it up.

"Nineteen million dollars since December of '84," said Natalie.

"Number 12 has got to be a muckety-muck with GSG to have such a low number," said Todd. "Would all those low-numbered folks make salaries like that?"

"Those figures are much too irregular to be a salary," said Natalie, "and none of the GSG execs bring home money in chunks like this. *My* salary is unusual in that it's all cash. The regular company pooh-bahs get things like stock options or other kinds of benefits as supplements to their regular salaries—but nothing like nineteen million dollars, and there are a couple of years here—'90 and '91—showing *no* payments to employee number 12.

"But look at the last three entries, here. Number 12 made four million dollars in three months, and those dates stink the worst."

"Worldwide," Todd said, just above a whisper.

"What's Worldwide?" Andy asked, looking from Todd to Natalie.

"The plane disappearance in January—" Natalie started to say.

"You mean the one over in China?" asked Andy, blinking with dismay.

"They *think* it went down in the South China Sea," Natalie corrected him.

"You're talkin' better than…what…*fifty* dead people? Are you sayin' they were *murdered*? Would somebody do that for four million dollars?" Andy asked.

"We're missing the point here," said Todd. "This is the kind of information that'd get Draper killed. Maybe number 12 didn't think he got paid enough, or maybe Draper stiffed him. Even though he shows a four million dollar payout, who's to say number 12 didn't want a lot more? Maybe Draper didn't pay him at all. Somebody who's capable of the Worldwide crash sure wouldn't have any trouble finding Draper and killing him."

"What about the other dates?" Andy asked. "Are all those payments to some…corporate hit man?"

"We've got to move fast on this," said Todd. "This guy moves around internationally. He's not just gonna go home and be content for the rest of his life. For all we know, he's already flown the coop."

"How do we identify him?" asked Andy, turning back to Natalie.

"The employee number might help—if he's really listed in the corporate database," Natalie replied. "If my employee status hasn't been cancelled, I might be able to pull up the information on a networked terminal."

"You mean, like the place you had your car shipped to in Bozeman?" Todd asked hopefully.

"We don't even need to go that far," said Natalie, looking from Todd to Andy. "Have you got a place in town that accepts GSG shipments?"

"Their logo is on a little shipper outlet on the south edge a town," Andy replied. "It's just north a the interstate."

"If they ship for GSG, there's got to be a terminal there," she said. "Who's drivin'?"

"I will," said Andy, "but first, you gotta put another shirt on."

*   *   *   *

The stranger's driveway threw up spirals of dust, as he made the last few yards of his journey. His mail would be waiting at the post office, and the box was large enough to hold a several-day accumulation. He could let it wait another day, he told himself.

He parked his Jeep in a vacant garage bay and left it unlocked. He felt no need for tight security at home.

Silence greeted him, as he entered the house. The usual ticking of his hand-carved German cuckoo clock had stopped when the counterweights reached the floor. The hands on the clock were frozen at 10:33.

The inaccurate time gave the stranger cause to ponder. On the previous Friday, Matheson Draper had died at almost exactly the same evening hour.

The stranger walked to his mantel, where a dusty photograph stood alone in its dull brass frame.

"One down," he said, before wiping away a tear.

*   *   *   *

"Hey, Shirley," Andy said, as he walked into the small shipping outlet. "Don't you ship for GSG?"

"The *black gang*," the elderly woman said with a laugh. "They're here every morning. She's come and gone already."

"I've got some GSG people with me now," said the sheriff, motioning toward Todd and Natalie, "and they need to check on a shipment."

"They'll have to do it themselves," said Shirley. "I can only find out by calling their 800 number. The GSG computer terminal is in the back corner of the cubicle. It's the black one, of course."

Natalie smiled and nodded politely, as she drew a confused stare from the wrinkled woman. With Todd in tow, she entered the tight cubicle and pulled a chair up to the keyboard. She paused with her fingers poised above the keys.

"This might be a very brief attempt," she whispered, as she entered her corporate identification code.

The monitor screen came to life in an instant, and Natalie tensed with excitement. Before Todd could put his hand on her shoulder, she was pounding the keys at over eighty per. Just to support the ruse, Andy had remained at the front counter, and his voice drowned out Todd's and Natalie's hushed words, as he chatted pleasantly with Shirley.

"I can't believe it," said Natalie, scrolling down to another page.

"What?" Todd whispered.

"This is worthless...crap."

"Not even a name?"

"According to this, GSG employee number 0000012 is just listed as an ordinary vendor account number, but hold on. There's still a couple of pages left."

Todd wanted to pace, but the cubicle was only big enough for him to stand right over Natalie's shoulder. He felt helpless, as line after blank line traveled up the monitor screen.

"It's something," Natalie said, pulling a pen from her purse. She jotted down a quick note, before scanning the balance of the data.

Natalie exited the personnel record program, and she logged off the computer. When she turned to rise, she faced Todd with a finger pressed to her pursed lips.

"Don't keep me in suspense," he whispered.

"It might not be enough," said Natalie, "but let's talk about it outside."

"Done?" asked Andy, glad to be moving along. Shirley had shown him way too many pictures of her grandkids.

"Thanks," said Todd, as he followed Natalie from behind the counter.

Taking Andy by the arm, Todd tried not to seem rushed as the three of them made an abrupt departure. Todd only let out a sigh when they were safely back in Andy's car.

"Tell me something good, darlin'," said Todd, as Natalie pulled out a slip of notepaper.

"Time for you to be a detective, cowboy," she said lightly. "According to the vendor account routing, all the wire transfer payments go to the Wilbraham Road branch of the Sixth National Bank of Hampden County."

"Where the hell is that?" asked Andy.

"I don't know," said Natalie, "but I do have an account number."

"We should be able to find the bank on a regular Internet search," said Todd.

"I'll bet I can do you one better, cowboy," said Natalie, getting the undivided attention of both men. "Ready to take me for a ride?"

*   *   *   *

"She's in Livingston, Montana," said the broad-shouldered man, handing a tracking printout across Yancey Fitzgerald's desk.

"Her code was used...twenty minutes ago," Fitzgerald said with a frown.

"It's one of our shipping outlets, sir," said the big man. "We have no staff there. It's just a rural pickup point."

"What was she doing there?"

"She accessed personnel records, but the tracking program we utilized can't identify where she was searching."

"Maybe she was just checking her own status," Fitzgerald mused. "The program was only accessed for...fifty-one seconds, it looks like. Enough time for her to see if her personal account is still active. If she's not in jail, she might be trying to leave the area."

"What does your source in Helena have to say about that?"

"I don't know," Fitzgerald replied with a sigh. "I only get Rosser's voice mail, and the secretary there says he's signed out for the balance of the week. Someone's told them to keep their mouths shut, I'm sure."

"If she does travel, we can easily track her movement, either through the account or by her personnel payroll number."

"Keep me informed," said Fitzgerald, slipping the printout into his shredder. "And see what you can do about identifying the information she might be accessing."

The big man nodded, and he walked briskly to the door.

*   *   *   *

"*You* have done enough, young lady," Todd said sternly, as Andy and Clarence Mingle stood outside Clarence's backyard garage bay. Natalie tried to pout, but Todd's bright grin prevented her from maintaining the expression. "There's no way I'm going to put you in that kind of danger."

"What about you?" she asked, taking his hands in hers. "You might be up against a lot more than one man, you know."

"There was only one set of tracks up on the mountain," said Todd, "and, besides, I'll have the help from the cops in the local jurisdiction."

"With what kind of authority? That miserable prick took your badge. You don't even know if you're still a cop."

"Andy took care of that," said Todd. "He's got a new deputy who's still in the academy. He loaned me the guy's badge until this thing is over. I've even got official Park County deputy credentials."

"But what am I gonna do while you're off chasing some...mass murderer?"

"What do you mean? You've got over four million dol—"

"Oh, right," she said with a laugh, her eyes filling with tears. "GSG probably drained my account as soon as they realized Math was dead. Right now, I'd bet the only record of it is on Math's laptop, and who with GSG would be willing to confirm it?"

"If you need somewhere to stay, Jeanie can drive you back to my place in Missoula," he said, offering his handkerchief. "I live in the South Hills. There's a pretty view of the valley and the mountains."

"I don't want to be alone," she said softly.

"Then stay put right here," Todd said firmly. "I just don't want anything to happen to you, and Andy is the best protection a girl could ever want."

"Next to you," she said, drying her eyes. "Aren't you scared?"

"Only of losing you," he whispered, wrapping her in his arms.

"Oh, kiss her and be done with it!" Clarence shouted. "I gotta get to work on her car. Unless I take out that spacer rail, you're never gonna be able to fit behind the wheel."

Rather than answer, Todd followed the judge's orders. Then he escorted Natalie back into the Mingles' house, while Clarence went to work on the Porsche. Andy joined Todd and Natalie, who were seated in the living room on a well-worn loveseat. The sheriff took a chair across from them.

"If there's one thing GSG does well," said Natalie, holding up a plastic card with a magnetic strip, "it's to instill the fear of management in all of its employees. Just displaying this card will get you carte blanche at any GSG property. There's no photo ID involved. The average GSG employee never even sees one of these cards in a lifetime, but they've all been trained to recognize the corporate management card, and they know what it means.

"Rather than risk early detection, though, I think you'd better fly out of Billings. It's a little farther to drive, but I've never been there, and no one there would recognize the car. The GSG shipping terminal always has its own gate, and the magnetic strip on the card will open it.

"Once you get inside, flash the card to the terminal supervisor, and have him show you to the computer. Use my access code to enter the product shipping number assigned to the Porsche, and ship it—and yourself—to the vendor account code we got off the records of employee number 12. I have no idea where you'll be going, but GSG *does* go everywhere.

"Once you reach the destination, just flash the corporate card again, and people will know to stay out of your way. It shouldn't be too hard to figure out where you are once you've landed, but be prepared to be moved from plane to plane. It would be rare for a shipment from Billings to go anywhere directly, other than to a Midwestern routing depot like St. Louis or Oklahoma City, and you might be in transit for hours at a time. Any cargo plane they put the Porsche on will have a bathroom, though, so just ask."

"Won't they wonder about me flying along with the car?" asked Todd.

"I'm sure they will, but only to themselves. They wouldn't be stupid enough to question you," she replied. "Hell, there was this one time when Math had his favorite corner hotdog stand shipped from Chicago to Atlanta for a Falcons game. The poor guy who pushed the cart had to fly with it, and it was pretty cold in the cargo hold of that plane."

"I was wondering about that, too," said Todd.

"Just dress warm, and be sure to carry enough clothes to tide you over," Natalie told him. "If you need money, my personal code will also get you cash from any ATM, but I wouldn't use it to charge anything like a motel room. Keep 'em guessing."

"Can I travel with a gun?" asked Todd, patting the .357 on his side.

"They'll never ask, so they'll never know," Natalie replied. "Why don't you put your rifle in the front trunk of the Porsche, too? You're pretty handy with it."

Todd nodded, and he looked across to Andy. The sheriff was brooding, but the pause gave him time to voice his thoughts.

"Are you sure you want to do this?" Andy asked. "I can go with you, if you'd feel better about it."

"I'd feel better knowing you were right here, my friend," said Todd, nodding with appreciation. "This is a crazy case—and it's probably going to be my *last* case, but I'm not so sure everything is over in your neck of the woods. For one thing, you've got to be on the lookout for Rudy's return, and you'd sure better keep him from dragging Natalie off to jail."

"I'd eat him for supper first," Andy said with a sneer. "You leave it me. Jeanie and I'll keep tabs on your sweetie until you get back, and, if Yost does decide to fire you, I'll figure out a way to juggle my budget. I'll find you somethin' around here, even if it's just catchin' stray dogs."

"Now there's a reassuring thought," said Todd, wrapping an arm around Natalie's narrow shoulders. He gave her one last hug, as they heard the Porsche roar to life.

"If he got it started," said Natalie, "I guess that means Clarence can fit behind the wheel. You'd better get rolling."

"If I can get cellular service on this phone of yours, I'll call as soon as I touch down," said Todd. "I'll charge it up in the car."

"Just make sure you're in the right place first, before you call in," said Natalie. "Don't jump to conclusions. I'll see what I can find on an Internet search, and I'll try to relay the info to you before you arrive. Remember what I said about changing planes, too."

"I will," he said, rising from the loveseat. She followed him out, as the judge revved the twin turbos in the driveway.

✳   ✳   ✳   ✳

"Is there any way you might be able to raise him on the radio?" Arthur Yost asked the Park County dispatcher. "It's very important for me to reach Sheriff Freund or, better still, Agent Milton."

"They were together earlier today, sir, and I think the sheriff picked up a spare portable," said the young girl. "I'll see what I can do."

Yost watched the second hand on his wall clock, while the dispatcher called Andy's unit number.

"Park County One?" she called for the third time.

"Yeah, Dawn, what is it?" Andy finally answered.

"Got a call from DOJ in the dispatch center. Are you near a landline?"

"Give 'em Clarence's number," said Andy, "but if it's that Rudy Rosser, you hang up on him."

"Will do," said the dispatcher, reconnecting with Yost. "Is this Rudy Rosser?"

"No, ma'am. It's Art Yost," he replied clearly, cringing at the thought of Rosser.

"Yes, sir," said the girl. "Let me connect you."

There was a click on the line, as Yost's call was forwarded, and then the telephone began to ring.

"Sheriff Freund," said Andy, picking up on the second jingle.

"Andy, this is Art Yost. I've been trying to reach you since noon."

"We've been pretty goddamn busy down here, Art," said Andy, "and things haven't cooled down yet. What can I do for you?"

"It's about Todd. I've only gotten bits and pieces, but I take it you do want him working your case down there."

"I wouldn't have called him, if I didn't want him. You, more than anyone, should remember the cases he's worked for me. I've sent you a thank-you letter each time."

"Well, what I really need from you at the moment is a request letter, Andy, as soon as you've got a spare minute. I've got Todd listed as the lead agent, but I was wondering if you'd like some help from another office? I might be able to scare you up an agent from our Billings crew."

"From what I heard, your Billings guys are all tied up on the two floaters in the Musselshell."

"Oh, yes. I'd forgotten about that," said Yost.

"It doesn't matter," said Andy. "We're pretty much on top of things down here."

"Is Todd nearby? I'd like to speak to him."

"I've sent him on a mission. Can I have him call you once he checks back in?"

"That would be good, Andy, and tell him this thing between him and Rudy…we'll get it straightened out later."

"Just keep that little shit-head outa my jurisdiction, Art," Andy said firmly. "If I lay eyes on him, he's gonna have more than a sore butt next time."

"So that was you," Yost said with a chuckle, "but that reminds me, what's the status of this tiny woman I've been hearing about? Is she really being held as a material witness?"

"We mighta given it some thought at first," Andy replied, "but she's been a big help to our investigation. I'm keepin' tabs on her, but it's more informal than it sounds."

"Is she really shacked up with Todd?" Yost asked, lowering his voice lest there be sharp ears in the corridor beyond his office door.

"Uh, not at the moment," Andy replied awkwardly.

"Well, you know how Rudy can exaggerate things," Yost said with a sigh of relief, "but I should warn you that Rudy leaked some information to GSG—a man named Yancey Fitzgerald. He told this Fitzgerald about the murder victim, and he also told him about the girl you've got with you."

"I guess it's gettin' too warm to freeze that little bastard in a block a ice," Andy growled.

"I've done the next best thing," said Yost. "I've pulled his badge, but I've got Todd's badge here, too. Is there some way I can get it back to him?"

"Just hang on to it," replied Andy. "I gave him a temporary deputy ID, for the time being. He can get his work done with that."

"Well, thanks for the information, Andy, and I'll wait to hear from you or Todd."

"Good enough," said Andy, hanging up the phone.

Natalie watched him standing over the now silent telephone, and she stooped even lower to catch his down-turned eyes.

"You are one convincing liar, Sheriff Freund," she said with a laugh.

"Say that again, sweet cakes," said Andy, returning her smile, "and I won't hire you as a dispatcher."

"Yeah," Natalie fired back. "Like there's another unemployed person around here who can type eighty words a minute."

"Give me a break, shorty," Andy said, extending a hand to help her up from the loveseat. "I feel like havin' a beer. Wanna join me?"

"Beer? Yuck! I might be willing to nurse a Coke, though."

"You don't drink beer, huh?" Andy asked lightly. "You and Todd got somethin' in common—I mean aside from mixin' spit."

"A silver-tongued devil you are *not*," said Natalie, as she accepted Andy's hand.

✳   ✳   ✳   ✳

"She's on the move," said the broad-shouldered man, as Yancey Fitzgerald was gathering his briefcase to leave.

"Where?" asked Fitzgerald, motioning for his subordinate to come closer.

"She accessed the shipping database through the terminal computer in Billings," said the big man, pointing to a line on the tracking printout. "The program shows the shipping code number assigned to her car. It's being sent to a secondary routing center in Hartford."

"She wouldn't send the car there without going with it, would she?"

"I doubt it. Corporate card holders do it all the time, sir," the big man replied. "I ship myself with my car more often than not, and I use the vehicle number to allow for the load calculation. Our employees can—and often do—ship only *themselves*, just by using their employee numbers. As long as there's no critical weight restriction on the aircraft, the company allows it."

"*Her* car would get top priority, anyway," said Fitzgerald, walking over to his office wall map. "Is Hartford the final destination?"

"No, sir. According to the manifest, it's bound for Springfield, Massachusetts, but Bradley International is almost exactly between Springfield and Hartford. The last leg would have to be made on the ground, if need be."

"When will she get there?" asked Fitzgerald, his finger on Springfield.

"There'll be a plane change in St. Louis," the big man replied, scanning the routing schedules. "She might make it there by 2 a.m. Wednesday."

"Does the Billings flight have enough fuel to go straight through to Bradley?" Fitzgerald asked, tracing a line from Missouri to Massachusetts.

"I don't know, sir, but it's still on the ground in Billings—"

"Then send them word now," Fitzgerald said quickly. "Have them travel straight through to Bradley International. Top priority. They should be able to carry enough fuel."

"It'll take some...governmental intervention. What reason should I give the crew in Billings?"

"Tell them it's by my direct authority," Fitzgerald said smugly. "*I* don't need a reason. As for the FAA, well...you know what to do."

"Yes, sir," said the big man.

*   *   *   *

"Mr. Smith?" a man on the telephone asked.

"Yes," said the stranger. "This is Mr. Smith."

"This is Harry, with GSG St. Louis. I'm calling about the lost item number you reported, sir."

"I reported two."

"Well, sir. I think we've found one of them. Number 6900000PV is on the way to Springfield right now."

"Do you have a projected arrival time...at the terminal, I mean?" the stranger asked cautiously.

"It should be at our Bradley International shipping terminal by early this morning, so you can expect a delivery before 7 a.m."

"Very good," said the stranger. "Thank you."

"You're very welcome, sir, and thank you for using GSG."

The stranger hung up the phone, and he glanced at his reset cuckoo clock. There was no real hurry, but he busied himself with his uniform jumpsuit.

*   *   *   *

"Where do you think he is right now?" Andy asked, checking his watch.

Andy, Clarence, Natalie, and Jeanie were all seated in a back booth of the Branding Iron Saloon, on the outskirts of Livingston.

"Still in the air," said Natalie, "unless they're movin' him to another plane."

"Where's that bank?" asked Clarence.

"It's in Springfield, Massachusetts," said Natalie. "They've got quite a website. They've also got the best mortgage interest rates I've seen in a while."

"Do you know where they'll have him switch planes?" asked Andy.

"St. Louis, for sure, since that's the direct routing center for the Northeast," she replied, "but I'm not so sure after that. He may have to go on to New York City, and then catch a third plane going north."

"Lots a hours in the sky," Jeanie said dreamily. Her four beers were taking their toll on her. "I hate to fly. Did you fly much, honey?"

"Yeah," said Natalie, using her straw to making a slurping sound in the bottom of her empty Coke glass. "Do you know what that sound means in Saudi Arabia?"

The others exchanged confused looks, but the best answer she could get was a shrug from Clarence.

"It means it's empty," she said with a sly smile.

After a moment, she was rewarded with a chorus of snorts and groans.

"You guys need to get out more," said Natalie, holding up her empty glass for the bartender.

The old man came out from behind the bar, and he waddled up to their booth.

"Did I card you before?" he asked, trying to make out Natalie's features in the dim lighting.

"She's drinkin' nothin' but Coke, Phil," Clarence snarled.

"Sorry, Clarence," the man said, hanging his head. He took Natalie's empty glass and crept back behind the bar.

"Thanks to you, judge," said Natalie, "he'll probably piss in it."

"I'll take the first sip, if you're worried," Clarence offered.

*   *   *   *

"Everything's been arranged, sir," said the broad-shouldered man, speaking with Yancey Fitzgerald on the telephone. "There was our usual problem with FAA routing clearance, but it was handled through the fund we've set aside for that purpose."

"Who says you can't buy happiness—or anything else?" Fitzgerald said over the traffic noise. In the back seat of his limousine, the old man was relaxing while Yolanda was busy between his knees.

"Her new projected arrival time will be…11:15 p.m. our time."

"Do you have some of your people up there?" Fitzgerald asked, frowning at a tuft of unsightly lint trapped in Yolanda's Afro.

"I've got one of my more experienced men on the way from New York," the big man replied, "and an internal security man on the way from Newark. I don't know if they'll both be able to arrive in time…"

"She weighs less than one of your *arms*, my good man," said Fitzgerald, finally feeling the stirrings of orgasmic activity somewhere below the beltline. "I'm sure one man can handle her."

"Yes, sir," the big man agreed, resisting the urge to remind his boss that Natalie Weinberg was probably used to being handled by only one man.

"Dear *LORD!*" Fitzgerald exclaimed, unable to ignore Yolanda's oral and tactile skills any longer.

"Are you all right, sir?" the big man asked, confused by the background noise.

"Call me…when you've…you've got her," Fitzgerald gasped, before terminating the connection.

*　　　*　　　*　　　*

There was a problem. The stranger smiled at his good fortune, however. The tracking record showed an updated arrival time, but he'd gotten himself dressed early, and there was still enough time for him to reach the Bradley terminal. He logged himself off and trotted to his Camaro.

*　　　*　　　*　　　*

"Hello…Natalie?" Todd asked, as he heard a familiar voice on the Freunds' home phone.

"Todd," said Natalie. "I've got some information for you."

"Great. We've just touched down."

"Your final destination is Springfield, Massachusetts," she said quickly, unsure of how long the cellular connection might last. "That's where the bank is. You'll probably change planes at least once, but there's no direct flight into Springfield. The closest routing point is at Bradley International Airport in Hartford, Connecticut, about thirty miles south of Springfield. Once you get there, you'll need to find your way to I-91 and go north."

"What's the name of that airport again?" asked Todd, reading signs as the cargo plane taxied off the runway.

"Bradley…in Hartford…"

"Well…that's where I am right *now*," said Todd, reading the sign on the main terminal building. "I never had to change planes."

"*Damn them*! GSG must be on to you," Natalie said, the fear rising in her voice. "It takes something just short of an Act of Congress to reroute a scheduled cargo flight, so if they're willing to go to that much trouble they've got to be tracking you.

"The good news is that they'll be looking for me, though, so you might be able to slip out unnoticed. Let 'em keep the damn car. I just want you to get outa there."

"I might be able to get both me *and* the car out," said Todd, walking to the rear of the loading bay. "They backed the car in, so it's pointed out, and it was the last thing they loaded. We're slowing down, too, baby, so I'm gonna get the car started. I'll call you back."

"Todd?" Natalie said, but the connection was gone.

The roar of the jet motors met Todd's ears, as the rear loading ramp began to drop. There were men in GSG uniforms milling around near the tail of the plane, but the noise of the Porsche engine was drowned out by much larger turbines. When the ramp was still six inches from the concrete, Todd floored it.

All four tires of the Porsche threw up smoke, as Todd fought the tight steering wheel. The cargo handlers scrambled for cover, but a man in a black overcoat tried to block the sports car's path. Todd liked the idea of playing chicken, though, and the man dove out of the way at the last instant.

He expected shots to follow, but Todd could only hear the high-pitched howl of the turbochargers. He raced along the row of cargo bays until he saw a lighted gate. There was a guardhouse there, but the guard seemed to be busy with an incoming van. Todd blew by him at eighty miles an hour—and he was only in third gear!

There were plenty of signs just outside the gate, and Todd had no trouble finding his way to Interstate 91. At first, he revved the Porsche up to a hundred and twenty, but then he realized how much attention the speeding car would attract, so he dropped back to half that velocity. Merging into the other traffic, he felt safe among the group of darkened vehicles.

Todd never noticed the red Camaro, keeping pace with him from some two hundred yards back.

*   *   *   *

Yancey Fitzgerald was ill at ease with the surroundings. The motel room was large and relatively clean, but he was more accustomed to high-priced hotel suites and room service. This place reminded him of the rooms his sniveling employees must endure during their hard-earned vacations.

Still, it was better than risking a trip home. Yolanda had a way of leaving evidence behind, as his office janitorial staff had learned just this morning. Fitzgerald wondered how a woman could forget one of the only two things she'd been wearing.

The running shower made the old man's bladder ache, and he tried the door on the only bathroom. Locked! He couldn't believe it. After another minute of agony, he aimed a stream at the bedside wastebasket, thankful that he'd only had to urinate.

His cellular telephone was on the bed, just out of reach—even if both hands had been free. It began to ring annoyingly, and Fitzgerald tried to hurry. He should've let it ring. The end result was wet pants.

"Yes," he said, as breathless as his last conversation.

"They lost her, sir," said the broad-shouldered man.

"You've got to be *kidding*!" Fitzgerald shouted. "A woman no bigger than a child, and she got away from *two* men."

"Only one of my men made it to the terminal in time. The flight was fifteen minutes early. She drove her car straight out of the aircraft hold as soon as the ramp was lowered. I don't doubt she suspected something, though, since the flight had been rerouted."

"Where was she trying to ship herself?"

"Some…bank in Massachusetts, sir. That particular branch is on our local pickup-delivery route—along with hundreds of other businesses. I'm not sure of its significance, however. Our contract shows irregular pickups there, and we only deliver their office supplies to them on a regular every-other-Monday schedule, but my men will be staking out the location, nonetheless. If there's any sign of her, she'll be picked up immediately. They have her description, should she choose another form of transportation."

"Do I need to tell you what else to do?" Fitzgerald asked, letting the question hang there for a moment.

"My men will…inquire about the laptop, sir," the big man said hesitantly.

"And?" Fitzgerald went on, imagining his subordinate's discomfort.

The big man chose to remain silent, however.

"I've given some thought to the Kuwaiti offer," said Fitzgerald, smiling at the sudden appearance of Yolanda. "If the logistics can be worked out discreetly, see that she's…shipped to them. I find a certain degree of…comfort in that solution, don't you? Comfort in her *discomfort*, you might say."

The big man did not reply, as Fitzgerald had expected.

*   *   *   *

"I'm in a motel room in East Longmeadow," said Todd, using the extension in his room rather than the cellular telephone. "They've got a parking lot behind the building and away from the street, so I don't think anybody will be able to spot the car."

"What was it like?" Natalie asked, her knees still shaking with worry.

"You were absolutely right, darlin'. GSG sent somebody out there to stop me—or maybe you, since they couldn't see through those tinted windows. I gave 'em the slip, though, and, come sunup, I'll be checking in with the Springfield Police. I don't think the GSG goons would be fool enough to get in the middle of a bunch of cops."

"For all you know, they may own some of those cops," said Natalie, unconvinced.

"Still, it's a chance I've got to take, and, listen, I'm really sorry I had to cut you off back there," Todd said softly, "but it was your warning that got me through, Natalie. I know you've been worried, but I just couldn't call you any sooner. I had to make sure I'd gotten away clean."

"I know you're being careful," Natalie whispered. Andy and Jeanie had given up waiting, and Natalie was the only one still awake. "This is just something new to me, that's all. How do cops' wives and girlfriends stand it?"

"Sometimes they don't," said Todd, leaning back on a pillow. "Police work can be monotonous for months on end and suddenly life-threatening for just a few seconds. Until I met you, nobody had ever shot at me before."

"You make it sound like you're grateful," Natalie said, finally able to smile.

"I could've done without the shooting," Todd said lightly, "but I am thankful…that I met you."

*   *   *   *

Despite efforts to conceal it next to a row of thick shrubbery, the black Porsche looked painfully out of place in the back parking lot of the $28-a-night motel.

Not so, the red Camaro.

*   *   *   *

Wearing only her platform heels, Yolanda looked especially inviting, as she stood seductively in the bathroom doorway. Her toothy smile made Yancey Fitzgerald dismiss all the earlier problems of the moment, and he patted the empty space beside him on the bed.

The hooker's strides across the room were reminiscent of a fashion model's on a runway, but then she stopped abruptly and wrinkled her Michael Jackson-like designer nose.

"It smells like *piss* in here!" she shouted.

CHAPTER 6

▼

A man. Just one man, too. The stranger watched as the driver of the Porsche prepared to leave the motel. The man was carrying a gym bag, and his windbreaker hung open when he put the bag in the front trunk. A badge and holstered handgun were clearly visible under the light jacket.

But where was the girl? The stranger knew the car belonged to Draper's hired mistress, but there was no sign of her.

As the black sports car moved gracefully out of the parking lot, the stranger let the mystery man get a bit of a lead before following.

*   *   *   *

The headquarters building of the Springfield Police Department was larger than any law enforcement office in Montana, but public access was limited to a spacious lobby overseen by the cubicle of the traditional desk sergeant. Todd walked up to the glass windows of the elevated platform, where an elderly man in a spotless uniform stood stiffly above him.

"Todd Milton," Todd said in way of introduction, as he held up his freshly issued identification card, "Park County Sheriff's Office, out of Livingston, Montana. I'm doing a follow-up on a homicide investigation. Is there a detective I can meet with?"

"Just have a seat, bucko," said the old sergeant. "I'll call back to the dicks' office to see who's in. It's been a wee bit busy this morning, but I think I can find someone for you."

"Thanks," said Todd, turning back to the expansive lobby. There were rows of chairs against the windows near the front of the building, and he headed for them.

There were only a few other people waiting in the lobby, and Todd found a chair at the end of a row. He took a moment to review his few pages of handwritten notes, and he shook his head in frustration over the loss of his laptop. The information he'd stored on the computer would've made the job a lot easier, he silently told himself.

"Tony!" said a man standing a few feet in front of him. The man was dressed in casual clothes, wearing well-worn work boots, but his bearing appeared familiar. He had a two-day growth of beard, on what was an otherwise clean-shaven face. He looked to be in his late forties. "Tony Danzig. Don't you recognize me? Hank Cotterman. Iron Worker's Local 434."

The man extended his hand, but Todd could only stare back in confusion.

"Look, mister," said Todd, not wanting to hurt the man's feelings. "My name's Milton—Todd Milton, and I...don't think I've ever seen you before."

"No way!" said the persistent stranger. "We worked side by side on the Mass Mutual job for...what was it? Nine months? I know it's been a few years, Tony, but damn."

"Really, Mr. Cotterman. You do look kind of familiar to me, but I'm not from around here, and I've never worked construction. Have you ever been to Montana?"

"Montana?" the man said with a laugh. "I haven't been farther west than...Pittsfield. Are you sure you're not trying to put one over on me, Tony? I remember what a kidder you used to be."

"Sorry, Mr. Cotterman. You'll have to look for Tony somewhere else. I'm a cop from Montana, not an iron worker."

"You look just like him," the man said, the disappointment showing in his eyes. "Sorry to bother you, Mr...."

"Milton," Todd said with a shrug. "Don't worry about it, sir. The world isn't as small as we think it is, sometimes."

The man nodded and turned back toward the exit. His shoulders were surprisingly squared as he walked away. Todd tried to watch him all the way out the door, but someone else walked up to block his view. He looked up to see a young black man, dressed in a sport coat and tie.

"You from Montana?" the man asked amicably.

"Yeah," said Todd, fishing for his identification.

"I'm Gaddis Johnson. I work burglary, but I'm the only detective in the office at the moment. You wanna come on back?"

Todd nodded and extended his hand. The young detective took it firmly.

"I've got one heck of a case going on back home," said Todd, following Johnson's lead, "and I think I may have a suspect in your jurisdiction."

They entered the detective offices through a controlled-access door. Johnson used a swipe-card to release the lock. There were several rows of empty desks, but only a couple of busily typing women were present in the large room. The shoulder-high cubicles offered a little privacy, and Johnson showed Todd to an extra chair next to a desk bearing the Springfield detective's name.

"The desk sergeant said you were workin' a homicide," said Johnson, pulling out a pad to take notes.

"Yeah," Todd replied. "It happened a few days ago—I'm not really certain since I haven't gotten an autopsy report, but I got the call on Sunday.

"An anonymous tip led the sheriff in Park County to the crime scene. From the looks of things, the victim, a guy named Matheson Draper from Atlanta, Georgia, was poisoned with antifreeze."

"Did somebody slip it to him in a drink or somethin'?" asked Johnson, his pen busy.

"That's the weird part. He was actually tied up with a funnel in his mouth, and it looked like somebody forced it down his throat."

"That's a mean way to go, man," said Johnson, frowning at the thought, "but the whole day watch homicide squad is out on a drive-by. I know the shift lieutenant will want to hear all this, but he's out with 'em, too."

"Is there any way you might be able to help me with an investigative subpoena?" asked Todd, pulling out the information Natalie had found on the bank account. "It looks like our suspect had wire transfers made to the Sixth National Bank of Hampden County, at the Wilbraham Road branch. All I've got is an account number. If you can help me with a subpoena for the records, I might be able to positively identify the suspect, or at least see whose name is on the account. Right now, all I know is that he wears size eleven boots.

"Is this something I need to work out through an audience with one of your prosecutors, or do I need to go straight to a judge?"

"I…think I can speed this up a little," said Johnson, rising just high enough from his chair to see over the top of his cubicle. They were still alone. "My partner's run off with the car, though. Can you give me a lift?"

With an enthusiastic nod, Todd rose with his newfound coworker, and the two of them walked briskly back through the building and out into the public parking lot. There was a small group of admirers standing near the Porsche, as Todd produced a key.

"If this is a rental," said Johnson, running his hand along the sleek roofline, "I gotta get me a job with you guys."

"Actually, it's a loaner," said Todd, unlocking the doors.

Johnson's face lit up with a broad smile, as the throaty Porsche engine came to life, and he leaned his head back in anticipation of the thrust, but Todd disappointed him with a legally slow exit.

"Turn right," said Johnson, as they left the parking lot. "It's a few blocks down to Roosevelt. The bank's on the left."

"I don't mean to tell you your business, detective," said Todd, "but Wilbraham Road is back the other way. I saw it on the wall map in the lobby."

"We don't need to go there, my man," said Johnson. "I got my car loan from Sixth National, and I've got me a special lady friend in charge of new accounts at the Roosevelt Avenue branch."

"Good idea," said Todd.

"Is it good enough to let me drive this thing back to the office when we're done?" the young detective asked hopefully.

"Show me some results," Todd said with a smile, "and we'll see."

*   *   *   *

"A cop from Montana," said the stranger, as he followed the Porsche from four car lengths back. "Todd Milton."

*   *   *   *

"Any sign of her at the bank?" Yancey Fitzgerald asked anxiously, as the broad-shouldered man entered his office.

"No, sir, but I've got an extra man up there, now, so they can cover the building in shifts—at least during business hours."

"She may just need to use an ATM," Fitzgerald said nervously. "She could do that after the bank closed."

"But why *that* particular branch, sir?" the big man asked. "The Sixth National Bank of Hampden County has fourteen other branches—two of them in shopping malls.

"Were you able to get any news from your CIB contact?"

"No," Fitzgerald hissed. "It looks like I'll have to call that tight-lipped sheriff in Livingston. Did you have our route driver quiz the manager of the shipping outlet there?"

"Yes, sir. It was Miss Weinberg, all right, although the sheriff and another man were with her. The woman didn't recognize the other man, but she said the sheriff seemed to know them both."

"What did *that* critical piece of news cost us?" Fitzgerald asked, rolling his eyes.

"A...box of glazed doughnuts, sir."

Fitzgerald inhaled loudly through his yellow teeth, but he was sure of what he'd heard. He closed one eye but fixed the other firmly on the big man.

"It never ceases to amaze me," the old man said softly. "The price of information can vary so much, but it's nice to know there are still those out there somewhere who can be bought for a few hundred calories. The route driver did well. Make a note of his name."

"The driver is a woman, sir," the big man informed him.

"Well...see that there's a little bonus in *her* pay envelope, then."

*   *   *   *

The Montanan and his black associate were only in the bank for a few minutes, but they seemed to be satisfied with their visit. They were both talking animatedly as they returned to the Porsche.

The stranger waited until they'd passed him, before pulling out behind them in his Camaro.

*   *   *   *

"Do you know this guy?" said Todd, looking over the printout Johnson's friend had provided. At one time, the man had had funds totaling forty-six million dollars in hundreds of separate Sixth National accounts, but his present assets were down to about half that amount.

"Never heard of him," said Johnson, unable to resist the urge to make the tires bark. "What's the name again?"

"Curtis Tremain."

"Don't ring any bells with me."

"Well, he's one rich fella," said Todd, checking the address. "Is Lyon Street a pretty upscale part of town?"

"Yeah, I think so," Johnson replied, giving some thought to passing by the headquarters building, just to extend his driving time. "I don't get up there much, you know, but the lots are real big. I know that. Those folks have alarms, too. They don't get burglarized."

"Would you be interested in taking a drive over there?" asked Todd, hoping to tempt his newfound associate. "Just to pass by and see what the house is like."

"Better not, man," said Johnson, shaking his head. "From the way this sounds, you're gonna need to brief the shift lieutenant. I think I've done about as much as I can do for you."

"I figure if we showed up unannounced," said Todd, hoping Johnson might have a change of heart, "we might take him by surprise. If we did it like that, we might find evidence there to tie him to Draper's murder."

"Shit, man, I'm just a measly little burglary detective," said Johnson, shaking his head. "I only got one gun. We need make some kinda plan. Talk tactics. Stuff like that."

"I've got a gun—two if you count the carbine in the trunk," said Todd.

"A *gun*! You!" the young detective shouted, quickly lowering his voice since they were almost in front of the police headquarters building. "This is Massa-*fucking*-chussetts, man. The Kennedys don't want no guns 'round here. It's against the law."

"But I'm a cop," Todd protested.

"I don't matter to them, my man. The chief don't even like us carryin' our duty weapons home with us."

"Sorry," said Todd. "I didn't want to cause any problems."

"Then you just keep your mouth shut about a gun, okay?"

"You got it," said Todd, as Johnson whipped the wheel toward the parking lot.

*   *   *   *

Albert Boyle, the Attorney General for the State of Montana, was a lonely Democrat in an otherwise Republican administration. Someone once said: in a perfect world, all the cops would be Republicans and all the lawyers would be Democrats. Whoever said it had sheep-dip for brains, of course, but Albert Boyle liked to believe it.

As the Attorney General, Boyle was also directly in charge of the Montana Department of Justice, an agency he occasionally meddled with, as he was hoping to do on this Wednesday morning.

Art Yost's intercom line buzzed, and he picked up the receiver to hear a quick "boil-on-the-ass, boil-on-the-ass" warning from one of the outer office staff. He just had time to hang up before the Attorney General appeared at his door.

"Art," Boyle said amicably. "Always good to see you."

"Good to see you, too, sir," said Yost, offering Boyle a chair.

"I got a call from Rudy Rosser this morning," said Boyle, jumping in almost before his rump met the cushion. There was no indication of a boil on *his* ass.

"I'll be sure to tell him to leave you alone, sir," Yost offered, knowing full well that was not the purpose of the AG's comment. "I know what a pest he can be."

"Oh, no. Nothing like that, Art. Rudy calls me from time to time, just to chat. We go way back, you know. He was assigned as my driver for a while."

"I'm sorry to hear that," Yost said, just above a whisper.

"I beg your pardon—"

"Never mind, sir. Is there something *I* can do for you?"

"This business…in Park County," Boyle replied, squirming as though a boil might've suddenly surfaced after all. "I think Rudy can handle the case, don't you?"

"If I thought so, sir," Yost replied with a sigh, "I have him down there, but I spoke with Andy Freund yesterday afternoon, and he told me to keep Rudy out of his county. I think that's a pretty strong admonition, coming from Andy."

"But Rudy's been with DOJ for so long," said Boyle, in an apparent effort to sway Yost. "I think it's silly to send him home with a nasty note to his mommy, so to speak."

"If I thought his mother could read, I would've included one."

"Oh, Art. I know running the division isn't the easiest thing to do, but with Chuck gone you can delegate some of the chores to Rudy. Chuck thinks enough of him to put his trust in Rudy, so why can't you?"

"Chuck put Rudy in charge because all the agents in Billings are busy, Dave is on vacation in Bozeman, we've loaned out our agent in Kalispell to help with courtroom security in Libby—"

"Please, Art, spare me the details," Boyle interrupted. "I just came by to pick up Rudy's badge case, and I don't want any more arguments."

Yost nodded weakly, and he removed the case from his desk drawer. He handed it over the desk to Boyle.

"I've made arrangements for the highway patrol to pick up this woman who's a witness on the Park County homicide," said Boyle, pocketing the badge case. "I drew up the material witness warrant myself, so I don't expect any trouble from Andy Freund."

"Nobody ever does," Yost mumbled.

"What was that?" asked Boyle, leaning closer.

"Nothing, sir," Yost replied with a pained smile.

*   *   *   *

"I thought that chair would raise up pretty high," said Dawn, the pregnant Park County dispatcher, "but you're gonna have to hop up to get in it."

"Wait a minute," said Natalie, walking across the cramped radio room.

Natalie found a wooden box on the floor, and she placed it in front of her freshly adjusted chair. When she stood on the box, her bottom was elevated to seat level.

"Mission accomplished," said Natalie, looking over the control panel.

"Transmit button," Dawn said, pointing as she went. "Microphone. Switchboard, but there's only two incoming lines. We type in all incoming calls, but the computer will give you a call screen to fill in the blanks. I like the keyboard on my left, but I'm left handed. It'll move wherever you want it. There's enough cable."

"How about letting me take the next call?" Natalie asked, rolling up the sleeves of her sweatshirt and bringing her watch and bracelet into view.

"Oooooh," said Dawn, admiring the diamond bracelet. "Who gave you that?"

"Do you like it?" Natalie asked, the bracelet suddenly feeling heavy on her wrist.

"Yeah, but…well, with three kids already," said Dawn, looking away. "I'll never have anything like that."

"Do me a favor," said Natalie, removing both the watch and the bracelet. "Take care of these for me, will you?"

"Are you serious?" Dawn asked, her big brown eyes almost falling out on the counter. She was only twenty-three, but she was already showing signs of the hard life of a Montana ranch hand's wife.

"I'm not givin' 'em to you to wear, Dawn," Natalie said, placing the jewelry in Dawn's trembling hands. "Just seeing them reminds me of what I had to do to get 'em, and I wouldn't want their bad luck to rub off on you. I want you to sell 'em and use the money for your kids. Will you promise to do that?"

"Oh, Jesus. Yes, ma'am," the young girl replied, tears welling in her eyes. "These things sure will pay for a lot of diapers and baby food."

"Manage the money right," Natalie said, reaching for the call ringing into the switchboard, "and you might have enough left over to put your kids through college.

"Park County 9-1-1."

*   *   *   *

Todd checked his watch, as people filed in and out of the police building. He'd been left to wait in the lobby, and several times he caught the desk sergeant giving him the eye. He knew something was going on behind the locked detective office door, but the longer he waited the more discouraged he became. The buzzing sound of the door distracted him from his notes, and he saw a familiar face approaching.

"I don't know what to tell you," Gaddis Johnson said, hanging his head. "I gave the shift lieutenant a rundown on your case, but this Tremain guy is connected."

"You mean…like the *Mafia*?" asked Todd, drawing stares from an elderly couple seated nearby.

"I…I hope not, but he *does* know the chief and the mayor," Johnson replied.

"Well, what kinda guy is he? A businessman? Maybe he just hired somebody to kill Draper," Todd said with a shrug.

"You didn't hear it from me," Johnson whispered, "but I could overhear 'em in the shift lieutenant's office. My LT, he just don't know how to keep his voice down. Anyway, I think this Tremain dude is some kinda diplomat—or he used to be. He gives money to political campaign funds and the patrolman's union and…shit like that."

"Listen, Gaddis," said Todd, lowering his own voice. "Along with Draper, this Tremain fella looks like he might be responsible for international killings, too. If he *is* some kinda diplomat, he's sure not the kind who's working for world peace."

"I really do want to help you, man," said Johnson, "but I'd be up to my narrow ass in it if my lieutenant found out. I've only been a detective for a year, and I don't want to lose the gold shield, if you know what I mean."

"Hey," said Todd, extending his hand. "I know the feeling. Sometimes it's tougher fighting the office politics than it is chasing the crooks."

Johnson shook hands and nodded, then he started to head back to his office.

"One more thing," said Johnson, pausing a step away. "I didn't tell 'em about your guns, and I got you a map to Tremain's house."

"Thanks," said Todd, rising from his chair. He took the map and slipped it into his case file folder.

"Thanks for lettin' me take a spin in your *loaner*," Johnson said with a smile.

The young detective watched Todd leave the building, and his eyes followed the Montanan all the way to the parking lot. Johnson felt a chill when he heard the Porsche motor roar to life, but his rookie detective skills didn't notice the red Camaro following Todd out of the parking lot.

*   *   *   *

"What time does that bank branch close?" Yancey Fitzgerald asked the broad-shouldered man, seated before his desk.

"5:30 p.m.... during the summer, sir," he replied.

"Two hours," said Fitzgerald, his eyes on the traffic headed to the stadium. "We've been waiting all day. What's keeping her?"

"Call for you, sir," his secretary said over the office intercom. "It's from Montana."

"Yancey Fitzgerald," the old man said before the telephone had reached his ear.

"Hey, Mr. Fitzgerald," said Rudy Rosser. "Got some things straightened out down in Park County."

"I'm very glad to hear that, Agent Rosser," said Fitzgerald, easing himself into his chair. He motioned to his subordinate, who picked up another extension to listen in. "I hope you have enough evidence to find the party or parties responsible."

"Yeah, all the evidence has been sent to the crime lab with the stiff," Rudy said haughtily. "I'm on my way down to Livingston, right now. I'll get all the pieces picked up, and then I'll have a better idea about where we need to go."

"It's a shame about Miss Weinberg," said Fitzgerald, drawing a wide-eyed stare from the big man. "I'm sure you wanted to interview her."

"I'll do that in Helena. I've got a couple a highway patrolmen on their way down to Park County, to pick up the little lady for me. The Attorney General issued a material witness warrant for her arrest, and I've got it in hand."

"But...she's not in Livingston."

"Sure she is. One of the dispatchers with the patrol just got off the phone with her. Freund's got her workin' their radio, for Christ's sakes."

"You mean to say she has a...*job*...with the Park County Sheriff's Office?"

"Not for long, though. I'll have her behind bars in Helena by tonight."

"Well…that is most interesting, Agent Rosser," Fitzgerald said, looking to his subordinate for guidance. The big man only glared back in silence. "Is there anything else you can tell us?"

"Are you a bettin' man, Mr. Fitzgerald?" Rosser asked.

"On occasion," Fitzgerald replied hesitantly.

"Then mark my words," said Rudy. "With me on the job, the people behind these crimes will be in jail before the weekend."

"That's…very reassuring," said Fitzgerald, flinching at the sound of a slamming office door.

✻   ✻   ✻   ✻

Gaddis Johnson's map was right on the money, and the houses in the area were just as he'd described—so far off the street they were utterly invisible. The entrance to the Tremain estate was bordered by a pair of massive brick columns, but there was no gate to keep him out, so Todd drove the Porsche slowly up the sloping driveway.

At the crest of the noticeable incline, the polished brick drive wound around through heavy woods. It was only a quarter of a mile long, though, emerging from the trees in front of a large Williamsburg-style house. Of course, Todd didn't know a Williamsburg from an iceberg, but that's what it was.

In the shade of the surrounding forest, the house looked especially dark. Todd climbed the front steps to the entryway, taking note of the absence of much-needed interior lighting. He was about to reach for the bell, but he took a moment to pause and listen.

And then the world dropped from beneath him.

✻   ✻   ✻   ✻

"I hope you're making preparations to go out there and *finish* this," Yancey Fitzgerald shouted, as he entered the private office of the broad-shouldered man.

"Things have…gotten out of hand," the big man said, closing his briefcase.

"And that is what you're paid to resolve."

"Who did we ship to Springfield?" the big man asked, walking up to Fitzgerald and casting a shadow across the old man.

"I…I don't know," Fitzgerald replied, taking a step back.

"What information did Mr. Draper keep from you and the rest of the company?"

"Nothing," Fitzgerald said defensively. "I knew...I *know* everything."

"That's a *lie*. You've lost all control, and you know it," said the big man, brushing the frail old man aside.

"Where will you go?" Fitzgerald called out, as the big man walked out the door. "Where can you hide?"

"Sir," Fitzgerald's private secretary said, stepping into the office. "There's a woman on the telephone who says she knows you. She sounds hysterical, sir, but she keeps saying she's...positive about something."

"Put the call into this office," said Fitzgerald, shuffling over to the taller desk of his subordinate. He lifted the telephone on the first ring. "You're positive about what?"

"Huh?" Yolanda said, unable to control her sniffles. "That ain't what I said. I tol' that bitch I'm...*HIV positive*."

*   *   *   *

The stranger parked his red Camaro in a turnout used for the snowplows during the winter. He was over two hundred yards from the driveway where the Porsche had pulled in, but he was sure the property across from him was still part of the same parcel.

He crossed the road quickly, and he ducked into the shadows of the woods.

*   *   *   *

Ammonia. Todd leaned back quickly, but his head hit something solid. All was dark, too, and his arms and legs were immobile. He tried to turn his torso, but he felt straps across his chest and waist. There were even straps across his bent knees.

"How?" said a voice in the darkness.

Todd licked his lips, tasting blood at the corner of his mouth.

"How?" the word came again, but this time closer.

Todd turned his head to the side, feeling a stiffness in his neck, but at least his head was free to move.

"How?" the voice went on, becoming monotonous, but then the word was followed by a vicious slap across his face. Todd shook his head, as blood dripped from his nose.

"How—"

"Hey," Todd shouted. "Just 'cause I'm from Montana doesn't make me a Native American. What's with the 'how' business?"

Nothing. Except for a breath exhaled loudly through nostrils.

"What do you think you're doing here?" the voice from the darkness finally asked.

"Investigating a homicide—"

"I can see that," the voice snapped back. "The pitiful little list of notes you brought. Useless scribbled nonsense. What do you think you've found?"

"The man who killed Matheson Dra—"

"*Fool,*" said the voice, punctuating the word with another slap. "You can't *prove* any of this…conjecture."

"He…kept his own record."

"I should hit you again," said the voice, "but I knew him better than that—and his father before him. Matheson Draper *couldn't* keep a record. He was a hopeless idiot. He couldn't *spell* his own name."

"Maybe so, but he managed to lead me to his killer—"

"Nonsense. I'd be the last person he'd suspect. And who was he to point a finger?"

"Then…how do you explain my being here?"

Footsteps. Fading away. A metallic clicking, somewhere behind Todd. Something pinching his left shirtsleeve—and then his right pants leg. Another noise, almost a voice. A body straining, and then the splash of water, soaking Todd from his head down.

"How?" the voice asked. "It's a question, not a greeting from some goddamned shit-faced redskin!"

"I'm not following you," Todd said. Shaking the water from his close-cropped hair.

"I've attached electrodes to your arm and leg," said the voice. "In a moment, you'll tell me more than everything."

"But I don't understand," Todd shouted, testing the strength of the straps. They were wide and tight. "'*How*' what? '*How*' did I get here? '*How*' did I find you?"

The electrical surge was strong, sending Todd's body upward against the restraints. He could feel the contacts burning his arm and leg, and then it stopped.

"A laptop!" Todd cried out. "He kept it in his own…code…on a laptop."

"Don't even begin to think you can convince me that Math Draper was computer literate, young man."

The second charge was shorter, but to Todd it seemed twice as long. He could smell his clothes and flesh burning, and he thought he could see flashes of light. His head fell forward as the current was turned off, and he had to fight to keep his wits about him.

"It was his own…stupid…code. He didn't need…computer skills. It was…simple…easy to figure…out," Todd gasped.

"What the *fuck* are you rambling on about?" said the voice, now in his left ear. "I want to know *HOW?*"

The next surge threw his head back against the restraint chair, and Todd lost consciousness. It was almost welcomed, but it didn't last. Another dousing brought him back to a painful reality.

"I…want to talk," said Todd, the warmth of blood flowing down the back of his neck. "I want to…tell you. But you've…gotta…tell me what…you want."

"*WHAT I WANT! WHAT I WANT!*" the voice shouted. "You God damn well *KNOW* what I want—"

"Wait…wait," Todd cried, the tears soaking the tape across his eyes. "Just tell me…what do you…mean by 'how'?"

"*HOW*," the voice shouted, now in Todd's right ear, "did Draper *DIE?*"

There was silence for a moment, and then Todd turned toward the voice.

"What do you mean…how did he die?" Todd asked, his mind just a bit sharper than a total blur. "You know damn well…how he died. *You*…killed him."

"If I *did* know, Deputy Todd Milton, of the Park County Sheriff's Office," said the voice, now moving in front of Todd, "why would I need to ask?"

Current again, but this time in spurts, bringing spasms to Todd's arms and legs. The water soaking him was joined by the contents of Todd's bladder. There was no way he could stop it.

"It was…it was," Todd said quickly, taking short breaths. "*Poison!*"

"Not *good enough!*" the voice shouted, as the current returned.

"Eth…eth…" Todd tried to say between the charges. "Ethylene…ethylene glycol."

The current was turned off, and Todd hung loosely in the restraints. He'd bitten the sides of his tongue, and blood flowed down his damp shirtfront.

"What?" the voice asked softly.

"Eth—" Todd tried to say, but his swollen tongue wouldn't allow the word to form. He swallowed back a mouthful of blood and took a ragged breath. "Anti-freeze…"

Except for some dripping water and urine, there was almost complete silence, but the pounding in Todd's ears made it difficult for him to hear.

"Oh, shit," said the voice. And then he was gone.

One minute. Two minutes. There was movement on the floor above. Frantic movement. Then the unmistakable aroma of gasoline.

*   *   *   *

The broad-shouldered man took a deep breath of downtown Atlanta smog, and he scanned the eyes of the people on the sidewalk around him. Wherever he went he drew stares. Fitzgerald was right; there was nowhere for him to hide.

Tucking his briefcase under his arm, he began climbing the stairs toward the offices of the United States Attorney.

*   *   *   *

Rudy Rosser's spirits were buoyed by the sight of the two highway patrol cruisers on the curb in front of the Park County Courthouse. With the proper reinforcements, Rudy felt confident he'd be slapping the handcuffs on a woman much shorter than himself.

Rudy parked his state car in an empty space marked as reserved for Judge Mingle, and he strode into the sheriff's office entrance with warrant in hand. The dispatcher's control panel was just inside the door, and Rudy was surprised to see Natalie answering the telephone.

"It's all over, teeny-weeny," said Rudy, holding up his handcuffs in one hand and the arrest warrant in the other.

"It sure is, you little prick," said Andy Freund, taking Rudy from behind by the scruff of the neck. "I'm gonna let you cool your shit-kickin' heels for a while."

Rudy made the mistake of reaching up for Andy's powerful arm, and the sheriff used his free hand to relieve the agent of his sidearm. With his feet touching the floor only occasionally, Rudy was hustled off to the cellblock. Andy put him in a cell next to the two young highway patrolmen.

"I got what I wanted," said Andy, as he released the two uniformed officers. "You guys go back to Helena, and you tell Boyle-on-my-ass he'd better keep his baby storm troopers outa my Republican county.

"We've got us our own highway patrolman stationed down here, and he knows who the *law* is in Park County."

"But I got a warrant," Rudy cried from behind the bars.

"Good," said Andy. "You can use it to wipe your butt, 'cause there ain't no toilet paper in that cell."

Andy turned back to the two young patrolmen, and he looked them up and down. The oldest of them had to be younger than Andy's favorite cowboy hat.

"I locked your guns in the trunks a your cars," he said, motioning toward the exit. "Don't get 'em out until you clear the county line."

The two patrolmen nodded, and they made their way back to the courthouse parking lot. As they climbed into their cruisers, Clarence Mingle was busy with his wrecker, hooking up to Rudy Rosser's state car.

∗   ∗   ∗   ∗

There was the familiar crackling sound of a fire now coupled with the almost overwhelming aroma of high-test. Todd could even detect a faint whiff of smoke, too, and he could feel the heat from the floor above him through the dampness in his hair.

"*Hey!*" he shouted, ignoring the pain from his swollen tongue. "Get me *outa here!*"

Todd's breaths became more frantic, as the heat continued to rise. He could smell the smoke growing thicker through his one nostril not clogged with dried blood, and his eyes began to water beneath the tape.

Twisting at the straps only made him breathe more deeply, and he could feel himself fading as the oxygen was depleted by the fire. His head felt heavy, but his arms and legs felt light, as he slipped into the depths of a smoke-induced unconsciousness.

The heat became intense at times, bringing blisters to his exposed skin, but then he'd feel surprisingly cool. He was back on the mountaintop, placing stones on a familiar grave.

Something covered his mouth, and he felt his cheeks stretch. His lungs filled with stale air, and he began to cough uncontrollably.

"I think he's gonna be okay," a vaguely familiar voice said.

Todd reached up to touch his eyes, and he found the tape gone. He squinted into the fading sunlight, and his eyes slowly focused on the grinning face of Gaddis Johnson.

"Man oh man," Johnson said, wiping at Todd's bleeding face with a gauze pad. "When I heard the fire call go out, I knew it had to be you, Montana-boy."

"I couldn't see him," said Todd, recoiling from a paramedic's touch on his left arm. The skin there bore the black crispness of a third degree electrical burn. "He got the drop on me, I guess. I never saw it comin'."

"Don't talk, man," said Johnson. "The brass is on the way. You need to keep your mouth shut, like I told you before. I don't know where your gun got off to, but I got the file cabinet drawer for you. You don't need to worry about that."

"Drawer?" Todd asked, the dizziness returning.

"I'll take care of your loaner car, too," Johnson went on. "But you knew I was gonna do that, anyway, didn't you?"

The light faded, and the choking returned. Todd felt himself being lifted, and then an oxygen mask was placed over his mouth. He thought he heard sirens, but he couldn't be sure. The movement made Todd think he might be floating on water.

The departing ambulance made a sweeping turn onto Lyon Street, and it sped away from the scene of the fire. While Todd was being hustled away, even more fire trucks were responding, and the local traffic had to pull to the curb to allow the emergency vehicles to pass. A school bus driver was thankful for the snow-plow turnout, and he quickly pulled off the road, effectively obliterating the tire tracks left by the absent Camaro.

*   *   *   *

"Do we still have a court reporter in the office?" the United States Attorney for the State of Georgia asked his staff assistant.

"I think they're about to leave for the evening, sir," she replied.

"Not *this* evening," he said firmly, "and I need you to put a call in to Justice, too."

*   *   *   *

Rudy Rosser sat up on his bunk, as Natalie Weinberg carried a Styrofoam plate of food into the small cellblock. She brought the plate to the food trap in the door of Rudy's cell, and she placed it on the shelf.

"Would you like anything to drink?" she asked, as Rudy continued to stare bullets at her. "We've got some canned soft drinks in the break room refrigerator."

"I want you to know, I'm gonna lock you up as soon as I get outa here," Rudy said. "I got the warrant right here."

"What's with you, mister?" Natalie asked. "What did I ever do to you?"

"This is *my* case, honey. Milton didn't have a right to go off on his own. He's gonna be in a world a shit the next time I lay eyes on him."

"Okay, let's say it *is* your case—hypothetically. What would you do to solve it?"

"Well, uh, collect evidence—"

"Todd already did that."

"Then I'll collect *more* evidence," Rudy said defensively.

"Todd's already on the killer's trail, mister," said Natalie, turning to listen out for the switchboard telephones. "He left here yesterday."

"Where did he go?" Rudy asked, walking up to the cell door. The food looked inviting, and he used his fingertip to taste the gravy.

"Massachusetts," Natalie replied, waving in the direction she thought was east.

"What county's that in?" asked Rudy, taking his plate from the shelf.

"It's not a county; it's a *state*," Natalie said with a laugh. "You know. The Bay State. Plymouth Rock. The Pilgrims."

"But…but that's all the way over on the other side of the damn country."

"I know," Natalie said with a nod. "So, you see, he's way ahead of you."

Rudy carried his plate back to his bunk, and he took a seat on the edge of the mattress. He seemed to be momentarily preoccupied, but Natalie waited patiently to see if he needed a drink to go with his meal.

"Have you got any Pepsi?" he asked, his eyes still fixed on his plate.

"A Pepsi drinker. I knew there was somethin' I didn't like about you," she said, turning back toward the communications console.

✳   ✳   ✳   ✳

"All this stuff can't be real," said Bettie Page—not *the* Bettie Page, but a young assistant prosecuting attorney for Hampden County who just happened to get saddled with the pinup girl's name. Her narrow fingertips grew damp, as she flipped through the folders in the file drawer Gaddis Johnson had carried into her office.

"It's gotta be real," said Johnson, pulling one of the folders from the drawer. "That Montana cop almost got himself killed just to find it."

"This looks like lots of money," Bettie said absently. "There are wire transfer and deposit records going back…to the early seventies."

"Did you see this one?" asked Johnson, holding up a two-inch thick folder. "It's stuffed full of newspaper clippings from Texas."

For some reason, Johnson's offering didn't attract Bettie's attention, and he started thumbing through the pages in the folder.

"Hey! This one's all about a kidnapping!" Johnson said excitedly.

But Bettie still didn't look up. For her, all the sounds in the room seemed to have faded away. Her mouth hung open, and she was frozen in place by the contents of an even larger folder titled "Worldwide."

Johnson put the folder he was holding back down on Bettie's desk, and he walked around and put his hand lightly on her shoulder. His touch seemed to bring her back around.

"I gotta call the boss," she said breathlessly, a look of terror in her eyes. "And we've gotta make sure nothing happens to any of this stuff. I want to make copies...*now!*"

*   *   *   *

"Worried?" Andy asked, as he took a seat at the radio console.

Natalie nodded, and she swiveled in her chair to face him. Her feet dangled freely, and Andy bit his lip to keep from making the wrong comment.

"Dawn said you did a real good job, while she was here," he went on. "I think you're gonna work out just fine."

"It's not all that hard," said Natalie. "I think I can get the hang of it in a day or two."

"You better already have the hang of it," Andy said with a smile. "Dawn's water broke an hour ago. She won't be back for a couple a months."

"No pressure, in other words," said Natalie, unable to suppress a grin.

"I think the work'll keep your mind off what's goin' on back East—at least for the time bein'," said Andy, reaching for her empty coffee cup. "Just remember. Todd's a big boy and a good cop. He can take care of himself."

"Thanks," said Natalie, reaching for a switchboard call. "Park County 9-1-1."

"Is this the sheriff's office?" a man asked.

"Yes, sir. What's the nature of your call?" asked Natalie, her fingers poised above the keyboard.

"Uh, this is Detective Gaddis Johnson, Springfield Police Department in Springfield, Massachusetts," the man said, opening Natalie's eyes more effectively than a gallon of coffee. "I'm callin' about a deputy of yours, a guy named Todd Milton."

"Just tell me...he's okay," she said softly.

"Oh, you know Todd, do you? Well, I guess you would if you work there," Johnson went on. "I'm just callin' to tell you we've got him in the Wesson Hospital here. He's pretty doped up, but I thought he'd want me to give you folks back there a call."

"In the hospital," Natalie echoed, as Andy reached for the other extension.

"This is Sheriff Freund," said Andy.

"Hi, sheriff," said Johnson. "Gaddis Johnson here. Detective with Springfield P.D. I was callin' about your man Todd."

"Did I hear somethin' about a hospital?" asked Andy.

"Oh, yeah. He's in the Wesson Hospital, all right. I knew he couldn't call on his own, 'cause they got him under sedation, you know."

"What happened to him?" asked Andy, gripping one of Natalie's hands.

"Hell, sheriff," Johnson replied with a chuckle. "It'd almost be easier for me to tell you what's *not* wrong with him. I wouldn't put him in any beauty contests for a while. I'll say that. He's got burns on his face, arms, and legs. He's got a…somethin' called a…basal fracture—I almost said baseball, 'cause the way the doctor wrote it looked like baseball. Oh, and I think his nose might be broke, too. If it ain't, it's pretty damn swollen. All that, and he's got eyes blacker than mine—that's a joke, sir."

"He…was workin' on a case for us," Andy tried to say.

"Oh, I know all about it, sir," said Johnson. "I got the boss man prosecutor himself goin' through the whole pile of stuff Todd found out. He says it'll take a task force to get it all straight, but he just took a call from the U. S. Attorney in Atlanta, so somethin' else has gotta be in the works.

"I know one thing. The chief here is sweatin' like a soul brother at a Klan meetin', and we got us a rich white man's mansion burned right down to the cellar."

"That's just like our case out here, detective," said Andy. "Was anybody else hurt?"

"As far as I know, nobody but Todd, and he was almost cooked with the rest of the place. My lieutenant called in the ATF arson investigators, but the place is still too hot to go through. We'll probably know more about the fire tomorrow mornin', but the prosecutor said he wasn't gonna leave until he'd gone through the whole damn file drawer, and that may take all night. The thing's gotta be two feet long."

"What's all that about a file drawer?" asked Andy.

"Todd got it outa the house somehow. I found it next to him when I got there," Johnson replied, lowering his voice to a whisper. "Don't tell Todd, but I had to give him mouth-to-mouth. Some white folks don't wanna know things like that."

"Listen, detective," said Andy, wrapping a long arm around the now shaking Natalie. "I want to personally thank you for what you've done for Todd—and for my department. If there's anything I can do for you, I hope you won't hesitate to ask."

"Well," said Johnson, raising his voice just a bit, "there is this one…minor thing. This here loaner car Todd's been drivin'. Now, that is one wicked ride, sir. Todd was even nice enough to let me get behind the wheel for a few blocks, after I helped him get some information from the bank. Do you think anybody would mind if I…took care of it—just until he's back on his feet? I think the doctors said he'd be out for a few days, at least."

Natalie tried to speak, but she couldn't make the words come. She wiped at her eyes with her sleeve, and she gave Andy a vigorous nod.

"Gaddis, is it?" asked Andy, giving Natalie a pat on the back.

"Yes, sir. Gaddis Johnson," the detective replied happily.

"I think I can speak for the car's owner," said Andy. "Go have yourself a ball."

"Why…thank you, sir," Johnson said politely.

"No, Gaddis," said Natalie, finally able to speak. "We thank *you*."

*   *   *   *

Daylight. It must be daytime, Todd thought. His eyes were closed, but he could sense a brightness through his eyelids. He squinted into the white light, only to find himself in a lighted room. He tried to move, and a wave of nausea washed over him. The pain felt like pinpricks of fire.

There was a stirring at his bedside, and he cast his eyes toward a blurry shape.

"It's okay, buddy," said a friendly voice. "We're with the State's Attorney's Office. Protective detail. Go ahead and get some sleep."

Todd tried to mouth the word thanks, but his lips felt numb. He closed his eyes and returned to the mountain. There were still more stones to pile.

*   *   *   *

"He has done it *now!*" Albert Boyle shouted, catching Art Yost in the middle of a "boil-on-the-ass" warning call. Yost hung up the telephone as the Attorney General rushed up to his desk. "That son-of-a-bitch Freund has put Rudy Rosser in jail."

"Really?" was all Yost could think to ask, covering his grin with a hand.

"He had a couple of the highway patrolmen locked up, too, but he released them when Rudy arrived with the material witness warrant. The one *I* had only just issued. It seems the less-than-humble sheriff of Park County thinks he can stand up to the power of the State of Montana."

"I don't think it's as serious as all that, boss," Yost said condescendingly. "Why don't you let me give Andy a call? I believe I can get this thing resolved without…calling out the National Guard."

Yost thought about laughing, just to ease the tension, but he held his tongue. Boyle had a determined look in his eye.

"How did you know I asked the governor to call up the Guard?" Boyle asked warily.

"Lucky guess," Yost said with a defeated shrug.

"This is…*war*, Art," Boyle went on, waving his arms.

"A call for you, Art," one of the office staff said from Yost's open doorway.

"See if you can take a message, please," said Yost, as Boyle gave the woman a frigid stare. "You can see we're a little busy."

"It's Sheriff Freund," said the woman. "He said it's urgent—"

"Put him through," Boyle said quickly. "I want him on the speaker phone."

Yost nodded, and the woman disappeared into the hallway.

"Andy," said Yost, pressing the speaker button on his telephone. "I've got the Attorney General in my office with me. I'm glad you called. Now what's all this about Rudy Rosser in your jail?"

"*Piss* on that!" Boyle shouted, stepping closer to Yost's extension. "You listen to me, Freund. I'm going to send as many people as necessary down to Livingston. You won't get the last word this time."

"You need to read your fuckin' protocols, Al," said Andy. "I haven't sent Art a request letter, yet, and you got no right to be here. The DOJ comes to work in Park County when *I* ask em' to, not whenever they fuckin' well feel like it. This is still *my* investigation, in *my* jurisdiction, and I've got this little turd of yours locked up for obstruction."

"*You can't do that!*" Boyle shrieked in a voice more high-pitched than any woman's.

"You got a fax machine up there, Al?" Andy asked. "I'll send you a picture just to show you what I can do. Rudy looks good behind bars."

"He was sent down there on *my* authority," Boyle went on. "He represents the Attorney General of the State of Montana. *I* told Rudy to take over the investigation. After what Rudy told me about Agent Milton, I've already started the process to terminate his employment. Striking a law enforcement officer. Having sexual intercourse with a person in custody. When this case is over, your constituents will be calling for *your* resignation."

"This case *is* over, Al," said Andy, his voice softening only slightly. "I just got off the phone with the U. S. Attorney in Atlanta, and before that I was talkin' to some prosecutor in Springfield, Massachusetts. Todd Milton is in the hospital back in Springfield. He's cut, he's burned, he's got a skull fracture, and he's also recovered enough evidence to shut down one a the biggest companies in the world."

"Is Todd going to be all right?" asked Yost, shouldering his way past Boyle to get closer to the phone.

"The detective I talked to said he was in pretty bad shape, Art," Andy replied, "and they've got him doped up on account of all the burns. Seems he got himself caught in the same kinda fire we had right down the road here."

"Were they able to give you any kind of prognosis?" Yost asked, as Boyle lowered himself into a chair. "Is there anything we can do for him from here?"

"I think he's gonna pull through okay, Art," the sheriff replied. "The detective said some kinda specialist was bein' flown up there from Dallas on a private jet."

"Who's paying for all this?" Boyle asked in the background.

"I don't know, Al," said Andy, "but if they send me the bill, I guess I'll pay it. He was carryin' one a *my* deputy badges, while he was workin' back there."

"How can we be sure you're telling us the truth?" Boyle demanded, leaning forward in his chair.

"Are you callin' me a *liar*, you ball-lickin' liberal bastard?!" Andy shouted.

"Gentlemen, please," said Yost, standing between Boyle and the telephone. "We've got other things to concern ourselves with. Would you like us to send somebody back East to be with Todd?"

"Nah, I don't think so, Art. He made himself a detective buddy while he was there," said Andy, "and I think the kid's gonna keep tabs on him for us.

"As for Boyle-on-the-ass's stupid fuckin' question, though, the story should hit all the big papers by the morning. I've got messages here to call the *New York Times* and the *Atlanta Journal*, too, but Fox News is supposed to run somethin' on the television tonight.

"And one more thing, Al. I turned Rudy loose as soon as I got the word about Todd, but he parked his rig in Judge Mingle's parkin' space, and I'm not sure if he's been able to get his car outa the impound lot, yet. The judge don't take checks."

"What about the material witness warrant?" asked Boyle, leaning to the side to be heard clearly.

"It's not valid," said Andy. "This gal's name's not Wein*stein*. Rudy needs to get the bullshit outa his ears."

"I…I'm…still going to speak to the governor about this," said Boyle. "Unlawful detention of two highway patrolmen and a state agent. We can't just overlook that sort of thing. It borders on anarchy."

"Yeah, right," said Andy, "and I'm not forgettin' you sendin' your three dip-shits down here to try to invade Park County, either. I don't come up to Helena to tell you which hairy butts to kiss, and I'll be damned if you'll tell me which ones I can't kick."

There was a click on the line and then a dial tone. Boyle gave Yost a concerned stare.

"Do you suppose DOJ will get any credit for this?" the Attorney General asked timidly.

*   *   *   *

"We have some fast breaking news this evening," Fox News anchor Shepard Smith announced to his late night television audience. "Law enforcement officers in at least two states have uncovered information implicating the corporate officers of the massive Global Support Group conglomerate, better known as GSG, in criminal activity ranging from extortion to mass murder.

"Confidential sources in Atlanta, Georgia, report that an upper management level GSG employee is negotiating with the United States Attorney's Office there to obtain immunity from prosecution in return for details about what had once been believed to be the terrorist sabotage of the Worldwide corporate jet in January of this year. As reported at that time, some fifty-eight persons were lost aboard the flight, including most of the members of the Augustus Klaus family, owners of Worldwide, a broad-based international shipping company that had challenged GSG in many markets.

"As if that wasn't enough, similar sources close to the prosecuting attorney's office in Hampden County, Massachusetts have disclosed the recovery of a monetary record tying GSG CEO Matheson Draper to the man believed responsible for the Worldwide disaster. The individual in question has been tentatively identified as Curtis Tremain, a man described as a 'contract intelligence operative' and former United States government employee. Government sources deny any association with a man by that name, however.

"This information, as well as allegations of GSG involvement with criminal acts against other market competitors, is being investigated as we speak, and you can expect the most current updates from your correspondents here with Fox News.

"And now an update on an earlier story reported by our Atlanta bureau. The suspicious death of Mr. Yancey Fitzgerald, executive vice president for GSG, had originally been reported as a suicide, but Fox News has now learned that Mr. Fitzgerald was shot to death during an altercation with a prostitute and her procurer."

CHAPTER 7

▼

"Mr. Milton," an elderly man said, his hands on the edge of Todd's hospital bed.

Todd managed to open a crusty eye, and he could see the old man, with Gaddis Johnson standing behind him. There were two other men dressed in suits standing near the door to Todd's room.

"Mr. Milton," the old man said again. "My name's Lonnie Axtell, sir."

Todd licked his lips, tasting the thick salve applied to his burns. He tried to turn onto his side, but he found he was too weak. The effort made him gasp for breath, and he looked up at the ceiling.

"I don't know if he can hear me," Axtell said, turning back to Johnson.

"Todd," said Johnson. "This here's Lonnie Axtell. He's the guy with the trucking company in Texas who had his grandkid snatched."

"Huh?" Todd asked in confusion.

"It was in that pile of stuff you got outa the house before it burned up," Johnson went on. "That Tremain dude was the one behind the kidnapping. We got a hold of Mr. Axtell here, and he had a burn specialist flown up here all the way from Dallas, Texas, just for you."

"I don't think he understands," said Axtell, leaning closer to look into Todd's cloudy eyes. "I think it's the medication."

"It's still early, sir," said Johnson. "He ain't even been here twenty-four hours yet. The doc you sent said he might be able to talk tomorrow or the next day."

"Fine," said Axtell, patting the side of the bed. "I'll come back then. I just wanted to see if he was aware of the reward."

"You can tell him all about it tomorrow, sir," Johnson said with a smile. "I know it'll make more sense to him then."

"Great," Axtell said, rising beside the bed. "I can't tell you how thankful we are, Mr. Milton. You're a godsend to my family, and I'll see that the doctor takes very good care of you. You just rest now, son."

Todd moved his lips, but only air could escape. He watched the old man walk stiff-legged to the door.

"Hey, man," said Johnson, leaning close to Todd's right ear. "Don't you know who that was? The stuff in that drawer was crammed full a crap on the Texas kidnapping. Turns out Tremain passed the kid off to a rich family in some place called Los Mochis. It's a town way down in everybody's-got-the-shits Mexico, if you can believe it. Their cops down there have already picked the kid up, and he's on his way back home to his momma. I guess they'll have to teach him to speak English all over again. He was just a baby when he got took, you know.

"Anyway, this Axtell guy said he's gonna *double* the reward he posted. Looks like you're gonna be able to buy your own loaner car, my man."

Todd squinted in confusion, and he tried to shake his head. The pain in his neck was too great, though, and he only managed to look away from his detective friend.

"I know it's hard to believe, man," said Johnson. "You just get your rest, and I'll be back around soon."

The IV drip momentarily ended Todd's confusion, with a fresh dose of painkillers.

*   *   *   *

"Here's another one," said one of the ATF arson investigators, drawing the attention of his companion. "That's four of these damn things. They're outwardly identical."

"Let's see what his name is in this one," said the other agent.

The polished stainless steel briefcase wasn't locked, and they opened the latches and raised the top. The contents were similar to the other three now tagged as evidence: two million dollars in new hundred dollar bills and supporting identification bearing the same photograph as the ones found in the other three cases. Only the names, birth dates, and social security numbers were different, although all of them were apparently valid. But none of those names was Curtis Tremain.

"Excuse me, sir," one of the firemen called out from the charred debris that had fallen into the basement from the first floor. "We've got a body here."

The ATF men exchanged knowing looks.

"I knew this wasn't going to be easy," said the first.

*   *   *   *

"Do you wanna fly back East?" Jeanie Freund asked Natalie, as she carried two cups of coffee to the kitchen table. They'd been watching the early morning news, where even more recent revelations were being run across the bottom of the screen. After the initial shock of the horrific Worldwide aircraft sabotage, there seemed to be a steady stream of lesser outrages perpetrated by the executives of GSG. Still, there was no mention of Matheson Draper's death.

"I don't know what to do, Jeanie," Natalie finally replied, cringing as a still photograph of Yancey Fitzgerald flashed onto the television screen. It seemed a crowd of Australian youths—angry over the disclosure of the Worldwide crash—had assaulted the old man's wife outside her Sidney hotel. "I'm still not sure if it's safe back there, and I do feel safe right here with you and Andy."

"Well, you know you can stay as long as you like, honey," said Jeanie, fascinated by a shot of the GSG skyscraper in Atlanta. "Did you used to work in that shiny big building?"

"No," Natalie said quickly.

*   *   *   *

After catching the Fox News the previous evening and reading the morning edition of the *New York Times*, Art Yost had a bit of a spring in his step as he entered the DOJ offices. He smiled broadly at his administrative staff, displaying a box of pastries he'd brought to share, and he made his way back to the office coffeepot. He was surprised to see Rudy Rosser there, filling a cup, but the sight of Rudy in no way diminished Yost's pleasant mood. He waited as Rudy added sugar to his cup.

"Good morning," said Yost, wondering if Rudy had even noticed him.

"Yeah, I guess," said Rudy, stirring his coffee.

"I was sorry to hear about your…disagreement with Andy Freund," Yost said, trying to make conversation.

"We…sorta squared things last night, after he talked the judge into givin' me my car back for free."

"I guess you've heard the news or seen the paper," said Yost.

"Yeah. Milton's a big hero around here, I know," Rudy said with a sigh.

"I haven't been able to speak to Todd," said Yost, placing the box of pastries beside the coffee maker. "He's still under sedation. They said he was burned pretty badly."

"You know Al's still got his badge," Rudy said, giving the sweets a careful inspection. "Al's still pretty mad about what Freund did—even if Freund did set things straight with the highway patrol commander, and Al might still go ahead and fire Milton."

"For the moment, I think it's all pretty academic. We can't be absolutely sure that Todd will even pull through, and, besides, he was actually working as a Park County deputy when all this fell into place."

"You act like you're glad the case got solved without us," Rudy said defensively, picking a bear claw from the pastry box.

"I just want to see justice served, Rudy," said Yost, finally able to get to the coffeepot. "Squabbles between agents can sometimes cloud the real mission of CIB. I'd be very disappointed to see the Attorney General fire Todd, but I doubt that the issue is of any concern to Todd at the moment, and I sincerely hope you've managed to acquire a little humility from this experience."

"I still think that girl should go to jail for somethin'," said Rudy, biting off a mouthful of bear claw.

"Well, Rudy," Yost said with a sigh. "I don't always get what I want, either."

$$*\qquad*\qquad*\qquad*$$

"I don't think his real name was Tremain," Gaddis Johnson whispered at Todd's bedside. "The arson guys found a man's body in the basement of the house, but they're havin' trouble gettin' him identified. I think part a the problem is that they've found too many kinds of ID. They also found whole suitcases full of money."

Johnson looked down into Todd's eyes, and he could see a spark of acknowledgement. The Montana cop might not be able to talk, but he was listening.

"At first, I thought this Tremain dude was a soul brother," Johnson went on, "'cause the lieutenant kept callin' him a spook, and the lieutenant talks that way a lot when he's in his office. But then I figured out he was another kinda spook, if you know what I mean.

"The arson guys found a bunch a guns in there, too. None of 'em are registered, but I'll bet a paycheck one of 'em is yours. All of 'em were burned in the fire, so they aren't worth a shit. I'm still stylin' in your loaner car, though, and your rifle is safe in the trunk.

"I got that Axtell guy's hotel room number, and when you're feelin' better he said he wants to talk to you. I'll be glad to make the call, when you think you're up to it. Is there anybody else I can call for you?"

Todd was able to flex the fingers of his right hand, and he lifted it beneath the covers. Johnson saw the movement, and he pulled the sheet down. Todd made a writing motion, and the detective brought out a pen and pad. Johnson placed the pen in Todd's hand, and he held the pad steady so Todd could write. The Montanan was a little shaky, and he only managed to write one name.

"Is that…Natalie?" asked Johnson, as he tried to make out the scribbling.

Todd was able to nod in reply.

"Do you have her phone number stashed somewhere?" Johnson asked hopefully.

"Uh," Todd tried to speak, but his tongue was as swollen as his burned lips.

"Can I get a hold of her through your department, maybe?" the detective asked, taking the pen from Todd's hand.

The question brought another nod, and Johnson smiled broadly.

"You got it, my man," he said. "I'll tell her what's up, and I'll let her know you'll be callin' her as soon as you can."

Todd gave Johnson a tired wink, and the detective took a couple of steps away from the bed. He waited there for a few minutes, until he was sure Todd was asleep, then he made his way out to the nurses' station. There was an empty office there with a telephone, and Johnson dialed the Park County Sheriff's Office number from memory.

"Park County 9-1-1," a woman answered.

"Hey, there, Montana. This Gaddis Johnson again," Johnson said pleasantly. "Didn't I talk to you yesterday?"

"Yes, Gaddis," Natalie replied. "Good morning."

"And a fine good mornin' to you, too, ma'am, but it ain't mornin' here anymore. It's a little after lunchtime, but, anyway, I'm callin' with a purpose. Todd can't quite talk just yet, but he wrote down a name for me, and I was wonderin' if you could get in touch with a girl named Natalie? Is she his girlfriend or somethin'?"

"That's me, Gaddis," she replied, "and, yes, you could say I'm his girlfriend."

"You, huh?" Johnson asked in surprise. "Well, that was easy."

"Is Todd really going to be all right?" asked Natalie, making no effort to hide her concern.

"I know it sounded kinda bad the way I first told it," Johnson replied, "and he really ain't doin' so good right at the moment, but he's gonna be okay down the road. I promise. They got a top-notch burn specialist up here from Texas, and he was sayin' that Todd only has bad burns on a couple a places. I don't know what happened to his tongue, but he was bleedin' from the mouth when I found him. I didn't have time to think about AIDS, with all the other excitement goin' on, but you folks in Montana don't have that shit anyway, do you? Anyway, that's why he can't talk right now, but he wrote down your name for me to call you—for him, that is.

"So…how long have you known my man Todd?"

"Do minutes count?" Natalie asked with a laugh of relief. "I only first met him last Sunday, Gaddis, but we've hit it off pretty well since then."

"Since Sunday, huh?" Johnson said absently. "I gotta take me a trip to this Montana place. Things happen pretty damn quick out there."

"Sometimes they have to."

"Listen," said Johnson, lowering his voice as one of the nurses walked by. "Is there anything you want me to tell Todd for you? I mean, you know, like…you love him and you miss him and mushy stuff like that."

"Yeah, Gaddis. You can tell him I love him and I miss him—and any other mushy stuff you can think of."

"How about anything else, like news or somethin'? I hate to make this so quick, but I'm callin' on one of the hospital phones, and I'm not supposed to use it for long distance."

"Why don't you call me back on my cell phone?" Natalie asked.

"Your cell phone?" asked Johnson, his voice at a higher pitch.

"Yeah. Todd has it. He might've left it in the charger in my car."

"*Your* car?" Johnson asked in surprise.

"Yes, Gaddis. You've been driving my car," Natalie replied.

"Oh, man. What kinda guy is this Todd? You met him on Sunday, and you let him borrow your Porsche Turbo on…Wednesday."

"I think I gave it to him on Tuesday, but only the day before he kept me from getting my head blown off," said Natalie. "That, and he's a nice…gentle…understanding kind of a guy, too."

"Well, you know, people are always tellin' me *I'm* a nice guy, not that I'm tryin' to pull anything fishy while Todd's on the disabled list. But if you've got another one of those Porsches to loan…"

Natalie's laughter brought a broad smile to Johnson's face.

"I'll go get your cell phone right now," he said, "and I'll give you a call when I'm back in Todd's room. He can't talk, but he can listen as good as anybody."

"Thanks, Gaddis," said Natalie. "Talk to you soon."

*   *   *   *

"The cops found this photograph in Yancey Fitzgerald's pocket," said one of the United States marshals. "Who's that in the chair?"

The broad-shouldered man glanced at the picture, and he gave the marshal a quizzical stare. He then looked across to the U. S. Attorney, who also seemed to be waiting expectantly.

"That's Mr. Matheson Draper, the CEO of GSG," said the big man.

"Why's he tied up like that?" the marshal asked.

"Wait a minute," the U. S. Attorney broke in. "Are you telling us Fitzgerald had this photograph and never reported it to any law enforcement agency?"

"That's right," replied the big man.

"God *damn it*!" the U. S. Attorney shouted. "When did this photo show up?"

"On Sunday morning," the big man said. "It was hand delivered to the GSG Tower security station."

"*Shit*!" said the U. S. Attorney. "If we'd been informed of this in a timely manner, we might've been able to get our own investigation rolling, instead of playing second fiddle to some hayseed Montana cop."

"Was he the one who went to Massachusetts?" the big man asked.

The others in the room remained silent, and the big man glanced from one face to the next. He knew he wasn't there to *ask* questions.

"Well," the big man said with a sigh, "it hardly matters now."

*   *   *   *

"Park County 9-1-1," Natalie answered the phone anxiously. She'd called Andy Freund, and he was seated at the console with her.

"Natalie, this is Gaddis," said the Springfield detective. "I'm right beside his bed, and I'm gonna hold the phone down to his ear. Wait just a second, and then you can start talkin'."

There was a moment of silence on the line, before Natalie exhaled and began to speak.

"Todd, it's me," she began, trying to imagine him incapacitated. "I know you can't talk, so just listen to me. I miss you, Todd, and I'm praying for you, too. I haven't prayed like that in a long time, because I didn't think prayer worked anymore, but it does. You being alive proved it to me, and I know you're gonna come back to me. I love you, Todd. I didn't get a chance to say it before you left here, but I really do love you, and I want you to keep that thought until you can get back on your feet. Now, Andy's right here, and he wants to talk to you, too, so I'll say goodbye for now."

"Hey, partner," Andy jumped right in. "I've been takin' calls from all over the country, and it sounds like you cleared up a pretty big mess back there. The folks at the hospital didn't want your name released, but Helena knows all about it, and Art Yost has locked horns with Boyle-on-my-ass, tryin' to keep your job open for you. I don't know how that's gonna turn out, but I think I can find a place for you in my budget—and I don't mean as the dogcatcher.

"There's also a lot a talk about a reward some guy's offered on a kidnapped kid who got found. I don't have any problem with you keepin' that money, but Al made a big to-do public announcement, sayin' CIB policy doesn't allow it. It's a lot a money, so you might just think about quittin' altogether. I think you and Natalie could live off of it, if that's what you two really want."

"Hey, hey," said Johnson, back on the line. "I think all this talk's got him confused. He's been shakin' his head, and he really wants to talk, but he still can't. I think you'd better let him get some rest, and I'll get the phone to him as soon as he can say somethin'."

"Okay, Gaddis," Natalie said, giving Andy a worried look.

"Yeah, Gaddis, that's probably a good idea. We don't want him to get frustrated with us," said Andy, gripping Natalie's shoulder for moral support. "Hey, partner, just as a way a showin' our appreciation, are you by any chance a fisherman?"

"What? I mean, I do a little spin castin'," Johnson replied.

"When you come out this way—and I *do* expect you to come out this way," Andy said firmly. "I'll line you up with the best fly fishin' you'll find anywhere. Deal?"

"You got it sheriff," said Johnson, ending the connection.

"Don't let this get to you," said Andy, his big hand covering her from neck to arm. "Burns are slow to heal, but he's gettin' the best of care. I'm sure the reward from this Axtell fella will pay any doctor bills he has, so you don't have to sweat that either.

"I wish I could send you back there, but I really do need you right here. And besides, you don't want to see him hurt like he is, and he wouldn't want to worry you, either."

Natalie nodded, and she gave Andy's big hand a squeeze. She would've held it, but the phone began to ring.

"Park County 9-1-1," she answered. There was a brief pause, and then she turned to Andy. "Somebody from the courthouse upstairs. They want to speak to you."

"Sheriff Freund," Andy said in his most official tone.

"Andy, this is Muriel Isaacs," said the county records clerk. "Have you got a gal workin' for you named Weinberg?"

"Yeah," said Andy, "you were just talkin' to her."

"Well, why in tarnation is she workin' for you?"

"Hell, Muriel, I don't have to ask anybody's permission to hire a dispatcher."

"Aw, that's not what I meant, Andy," Muriel snapped back. "She shouldn't *have* to be workin' for anybody at all."

"And why's that?" Andy asked impatiently.

"I just got a deed transfer by registered mail, and I need her to sign all the paperwork," Muriel replied. "As soon as her name's on the dotted line, she'll be the biggest landowner in the county."

"Bullshit," said Andy. "That can't be right. The place where we had the fire is the biggest single tract in the county."

"And that's the piece a land that now belongs to her," said Muriel.

Andy put the phone down, and he looked across at the woman who'd been his employee for only a matter of hours. Natalie sat wide-eyed, wondering what the problem of the moment might be.

"Remember when I asked you about getting permission to hunt up on the mountain?" he asked, not waiting for her reply. "Well, now it looks like *you're* the one who can give it to me."

For just an instant, Andy thought Natalie might fall out of her chair—and it was a bit of a drop for her, but then she put her hands over her eyes and began to cry. Rising awkwardly to his feet, Andy held out his handkerchief.

"You may *think* you've got yourself a place to live," he said lightly, "but don't plan on drivin' up and down that mountain road in the wintertime. It's a real bugger bear."

CHAPTER 8

▼

It took Todd three days of recovery before he could effectively drink from a straw, and another day for him to regain partial use of his tongue. After examining himself in a hand mirror, he found the edges of his tongue still raw and ragged from his electricity-induced case of lockjaw, but the swelling had gone down substantially. If he was careful, he could form words without gnawing on something important.

Gaddis Johnson was at his bedside daily, and Todd was thankful to see him on this sunny Tuesday morning.

"I...think...I can talk," he said gingerly, "but I...need to take it slow."

"You want me to call Natalie?" Johnson asked excitedly.

"No—"

"How about that Axtell guy? He's been callin' about you every day."

"Later," said Todd. "I need...to talk to *you*...right now."

Johnson nodded, and he took a seat beside Todd's bed. He took out his notepad, but Todd waved it away.

"This Tremain...or whoever...he is or *was*," said Todd. "He didn't kill...Draper."

Johnson shrugged, expecting more.

"Did you...hear what I...said, Gaddis?" Todd asked.

"Oh, yeah, I hear you. You're not makin' any sense, but I can hear you."

"But that's...important, Gaddis. Tremain...*didn't* kill him."

"This Tremain dude traveled just about anywhere he wanted and killed whoever he felt like killin', but you don't think he killed your Draper guy. How can you even say that? Is it the drugs?"

"Because…he didn't *know* how Draper died."

"What do you mean 'he didn't know'?"

"That's why he was torturing me," said Todd, pausing for another sip of water. "He wanted *me* to tell *him*. I didn't…understand him, at first, but he made me tell him. The burns on my left arm and right leg are…electrical burns. He had wires hooked up to me."

"Aw, this is crazy, man," said Johnson, glancing back at the door to see if they'd been overheard. "I didn't see anything like that when I found you."

"He had me strapped to a chair, Gaddis," said Todd. "I couldn't move. I couldn't see. I didn't have any idea where I was, but I could hear some noises above me and smell the gasoline just before the fire started."

"Well…why does all that matter?" Johnson said with a frown. "Who cares who really killed Draper? Tremain had more phony names than a telemarketer, and he probably killed more folks than Al Capone. If Draper was the one who bankrolled Tremain, who gives a flyin' dump if somebody else did the killin'?"

"But that's what I came here for," said Todd. "If Tremain didn't kill Draper, I've still got an open case."

"Hey, man," said Johnson, leaning close to Todd's bed. "The case you were workin' took down the biggest company in the world. It's almost too much to imagine, but think about it. The stuff in that file drawer is gonna put needles in people's arms. And the real shocker is, none a those folks are black—that's a joke, man."

"I'd really like to laugh, Gaddis, but the file drawer is whole other problem," said Todd, shaking his head as if to clear it. "I don't know anything about it. I don't even know how *I* got out of the house. The last thing I remember is the heat above my head, and then I woke up looking at you."

"The drawer was right next to you on the ground," said Johnson. "Maybe you don't remember carryin' it out, but you had it with you. I figured it was important, so I grabbed it before the brass got there. My lieutenant got pretty pissed at me when he heard I took it straight to the prosecutor's office, but he didn't have time to stay mad, since the State's Attorney made such a run with the stuff.

"Tremain, or whoever he turns out to be, kept some pretty good records himself. Maybe he just hired somebody else to kill your Draper dude. Maybe he was blackmailin' Draper. With both of 'em dead, we're never gonna know, and who really cares?"

Todd let out a long sigh, but he had to agree with Johnson's insight. The fires, the money trail, there were just too many similarities to ignore.

"So how 'bout some good news, for a change?" asked Johnson, retrieving Natalie's cellular telephone from his coat pocket. "Who're we gonna call first? Natalie or Axtell?"

"You better *know* the answer to that one," Todd replied.

"Got her on speed dial," Johnson said with a smile, handing Todd the phone.

"Park County 9-1-1," Vince Gilkey answered.

"Vince? This is Todd Milton," said Todd, giving Johnson a confused look. "I was trying to reach Natalie. Do you know where I can find her?"

"Gee, Todd," Vince replied. "I don't know what to tell you. Andy's gone to Helena, but I haven't heard from him all day. That ornery fella from CIB came down here last night, and he arrested Natalie. He didn't leave no note or nothin'. He just took her and left the 9-1-1 console unattended."

"Are you absolutely sure she got arrested, Vince?" asked Todd, which really brought Johnson to attention.

"Oh, yeah. I think this guy named Yost called Andy and told him about it this mornin', but he said the Attorney General was behind it all. Something about an internal investigation on *you*."

"Oh, man," said Todd. "This is a bunch of hooey, Vince. The case is pretty much over. Can't Rudy give it a rest?"

"Rudy," Vince echoed. "That was his name—the one who arrested Natalie."

"Just try to reach Andy, if you can, Vince," said Todd, angry at the thought of Natalie in a jail, "and have him give me a call on this cell number."

"I will, Todd. Are you doin' okay?"

"Yeah, Vince, and…thanks for asking. I'm able to talk, now, and the doctor said I can take short walks as long as I don't work the burn scars too hard. I need to get some more rest, though, so please try to get that message to Andy as quick as you can."

"Will do, Todd," said Vince, hanging up.

"What was that all about?" asked Johnson, as Todd closed the folding phone.

"Aw, I've got a head-butting match going with another agent back in Montana," said Todd, "and he was the acting bureau chief when this case first got started."

"Wait a minute," said Johnson. "I thought you were a deputy. What's all this about Montana agents?"

"Up until last Tuesday morning—the day before I met you," Todd replied, wincing at some of the memories, "I was an agent for the Montana Criminal Investigation Bureau. If you check my Park County deputy ID, you'll see it was issued last Tuesday.

"Anyway, Natalie was a material witness in the case. She used to work for Draper, and she's the one who got me the lead that brought me this far. Before I left Montana, though, Natalie and I had a couple of tough days and nights together. I took her up to the crime scene to identify the body, then we got snowed in up there overnight."

"Snowed in? In June?" Johnson asked in surprise.

"In Montana, Gaddis, it snows every month," said Todd, "June snowstorms are as common as a rain shower around here.

"But back to the details. When we got snowed in, I spent quite a bit of time alone with Natalie, since there wasn't anything else to do but talk—mostly about the case. At first, I thought she might've been behind Draper's death, somehow. I thought she had a motive as a...disgruntled employee, but she convinced me otherwise.

"When we were finally able to leave the crime scene, we ran into somebody's hired gun—literally. I don't know who he really worked for or where he came from, but he had GSG credentials. He shot up my truck and was trying pretty hard to shoot us up, too. I got grazed on the arm, but Natalie was able to get down on the floor. The truck quit on me, and we had to make a run for it. Now, I haven't really talked to you about her, but Natalie's no bigger than a minute, so, in the middle of all the shooting, I scooped her up off the floorboard of the truck and carried her to cover.

"Upon reflection, I think she liked being in a man's arms, and, after the shooting was over and I had a chance to think about it, I realized I kinda liked carrying her, too. She's a very pretty girl. I mean *really* pretty. Like *unapproachably* pretty—"

"I get the message, Todd," Johnson said, nodding. "She's a fox."

"Moving right along," Todd continued with a shrug. "From that point on, the two of us got a lot closer. In all the excitement of the shootout—even before we were sure the place was secure, she managed to distract me long enough to kiss me, and...well, there was no looking back.

"Up until I met Natalie, I'd been going solo for quite a spell, so it was nice to have a woman who was interested in me. I don't know if this is just wishful thinking, though. I mean, if GSG didn't steal her blind, she's got a lot of money in the bank, and there's a nagging feeling in the back of my mind that she might come to her senses and realize there are better men than me out there."

"Listen here, buddy," said Johnson. "When I talked to her, she didn't ask about anybody else, and she'd be a fool to pass on a hot-shot cop like you. I don't think you got a thing to worry about, and you just answered a question I've been meanin' to ask. Now I know how she could afford that fine ride."

"Yeah, well, after the one-sided gunfight on Monday," said Todd, finally getting to the point of his explanation, "Andy—that is, Sheriff Freund—put us up in a spare cabin, with me upstairs and Natalie downstairs. Only it didn't stay that way.

"What can I say? We're adults, and we were attracted to each other. On Tuesday morning, this other agent I was tellin' you about, Rudy Rosser, found us in the same cabin, and Natalie was only wearing a T-shirt—one of *my* T-shirts. And that's pretty much how I came to lose my CIB badge. But Andy still wanted me to work the case, so he made me a deputy, and here I am."

"So this Rudy dude went and busted your girlfriend 'cause he's got his panties in a twist over *you*?" Johnson asked, still not sure if he understood the situation.

"Something like that," Todd replied. "Rudy goes way back with the Attorney General, and I guess that's why the AG wants some kind of internal investigation. I don't think I violated any CIB policies, but you never know."

"Don't you worry," said Johnson, picking up the cell phone. "I'll get old man Axtell down here, and he'll hire a lawyer for both of you."

"Not a bad idea," said Todd.

As Johnson was looking for Lonnie Axtell's hotel telephone number, the cellular telephone he was holding began to ring. The detective answered it quickly and passed it to Todd.

"You got me," Todd answered.

"Todd? This is Art Yost. Can you hear me?" asked Yost.

"Yes, sir," said Todd, frowning at Johnson's apprehensive expression. "I can hear you just fine."

"I'm glad to hear your voice, Todd. We'd heard you weren't able to talk."

"I'm getting better, sir."

"Very good. I hope you don't mind my calling you. I got the number from Deputy Gilkey in Park County. He called here trying to find Andy Freund."

"I talked to Vince just a little while ago, sir. He told me Andy was headed to Helena this morning, and he said Rudy had arrested Natalie Weinberg last night."

"Yes, that's...that's all true, Todd. I first learned about the arrest this morning, when the AG called. I wasn't happy about it, but you know how the AG favors Rudy."

"I do, sir, but I'm more concerned about Natalie. Is she all right?"

"Oh, yes. That's what I'm calling about, actually. She left here about an hour ago…with Andy Freund. Somehow, Rudy had a polygraph test set up for her this morning. I think Rudy convinced the AG to let him do a misconduct investigation on you, and Miss Weinberg was sort of a captive witness. The legality of it all is still a little muddled. I didn't know about the polygraph until it was already over. Rudy had the test run by the Helena Police Department. I don't know what questions were asked, Todd, and I'm very sorry about all the innuendo, but I think everything can be put to rest, now, since Natalie passed the test with flying colors."

The last bit of information caught Todd by surprise, and he looked up at Johnson with raised eyebrows.

"Can you still hear me, Todd?" Yost asked.

"Yes, sir. I heard all that. I…appreciate you letting me know."

"In light of this," Yost continued, "I'm sure the AG will reconsider this…termination business, and, I don't know if Andy Freund told you or not, but I gave him your CIB badge and credentials. I would be very pleased if you'd pick those up when you're able to return, and I sincerely hope you'll continue to work for the bureau."

"Thanks for your support, Mr. Yost," said Todd, "but I'm going to have to give it some serious thought. I'll let you know what I decide."

"I understand," said Yost, his disappointment obvious.

Todd closed the phone once again, and Johnson took it from him.

"I guess things are gettin' a little bit better," said the detective. "You don't have the long face, anymore."

"I still think we should call Mr. Axtell," said Todd. "Just in case."

*   *   *   *

"You know what you oughta do?" asked Andy, his hands tightly gripping the steering wheel of his Crown Victoria. He and Natalie had just gotten onto I-90, headed east. "You oughta hire some total asshole attorney and sue those bastards."

"Asshole attorney? Isn't that redundant?" Natalie asked, bringing a smile to Andy's face. "I just wanted the whole business about me and Todd to be over and done with, and the look on Rosser's face was enough to make my day. I know you're a proud Montanan, Andy, and this is the most beautiful country I've ever seen, but I won't be too disappointed if I never see the Helena city limits again."

"I know just how you feel. Too many sheep-screwin' politicians up there."

"So, who had to fill in for me while I was in the slammer?" Natalie asked, bringing a cringe to Andy.

"Damn that chaps my ass—not that I had to fill in for you; the idea a that little prick puttin' you in jail," Andy growled.

"Actually, the officers at the jail were very nice about it, but I don't think they care too much for Rosser, either, judging from the way they talked about him after he'd left. They gave me my own private cell, and I was only in there for about ten hours."

"Well, Vince took the console, once we figured out you'd been *abducted*," said Andy, driving like the interstate number was the speed limit. "I still feel funny about you workin' the radio for me, though. It sounds like you don't need a paycheck."

"It'll keep me busy until Todd gets back," said Natalie, "and I like seeing the people at the courthouse, too."

"Since you type so good," Andy said, rubbing his chin stubble, "I might get you to straighten out some a the civil process papers we've got backlogged."

"Anything to stay busy."

"You *are* gonna stay with me and Jeanie tonight, aren't you?" asked Andy, feeling especially protective in light of the last twenty-four hours.

"You bet, Andy. I'm not planning to spend another night alone for a long time, although I hope you'll forgive me when I abandon your wonderful company for some...more intimate companionship."

"Yeaaaah," said Andy, his forehead wrinkled with confusion. "I don't get it—and don't think I'm tryin' to pry, either, but how did you pass that lie-detector test?"

"It was easy," Natalie said with a shrug. "I told the truth."

"You told the *truth*. Does that mean Todd's gonna be in deep cow chips?"

"No way," Natalie replied with a laugh. "Why do you think Rosser was so disappointed? He was so sure he had Todd—and *me*—caught in the act."

"I'm...not sure I'm hearin' you right," said Andy. "I mean...in the cabin...and after, when you both were in the shower. Catchin' you two in the act, like you said. Isn't that exactly what Rudy *did*?"

"I'm not denying anything, sheriff," Natalie said lightly. "It's just that when they made up the questions for the polygraph test, they asked me about...the wrong act."

Andy gave her as brief a sideward glance as his near-triple-digit speed would allow, but he didn't appear to be any more enlightened than he'd been when the conversation had started.

$$*\quad *\quad *\quad *$$

"I don't know what to say, Mr. Milton," said Lonnie Axtell. He'd taken a seat at Todd's bedside, and Todd had felt strong enough to sit up for the visit. "I've been making practice speeches in my hotel bathroom mirror since I got here, but no words can begin to express how I feel.

"I realize the other crimes this man committed may make my grandson's kidnapping seem like a parking ticket, but the years of uncertainty…the constant fear…the stress on my whole family…"

"I'm just very pleased there could be at least one happy ending out of all of this, Mr. Axtell," said Todd.

"Indeed," said the old man, looking down at his shaking hands. "Even the fraud perpetrated on this unfortunate family in Mexico. They thought they'd obtained a legitimate adoption. I've spoken with them, too. They're very nice people, and they treated the boy so well. I'm planning to have them visit us in Dallas."

"Then it sounds like much of your fear was unjustified," said Todd, "but, still, that doesn't make up for what you and your family must've felt for all those years. If there is any comfort to be had in all this, it's that no lasting harm came to your grandson."

"Yes, you're absolutely right, and, uh, about the reward," Axtell started to say.

"I really don't deserve it, Mr. Axtell," said Todd. "I'm a cop. I was just doing my job, and I wasn't even working on the kidnapping. Like a lot of cases, the kidnapping got solved by accident, while I was looking for something entirely different."

"To an old man like me, who thought he'd lost a part of his heart," said Axtell, "*how* the boy was found is much less important. That he *was* found is what matters to me and my family, and I'm a man of my word.

"The kidnapper—or kidnappers—hit me up for ten *million* dollars. I paid it, too, but I've never gone public with that bit of information, and I'll trust you to keep it to yourself. My lawyers tell me I can collect many times that amount from the soon-to-be remnants of GSG, and I expect to regain the business I lost to them, as well.

"When I posted the reward, I had it advertised in every law enforcement publication in the country. I thought two million dollars might make a cop try a little harder, but I fully expected to pay the reward for the recovery of some remains, nothing more. I made myself a promise, though. I said I'd double the reward if the boy was found alive.

"As the years went by with no news, I did my best to get on with life, but the sight of my daughter and her husband—in almost constant mourning—left me empty inside. After the GSG buyout, I dallied in the courier business, but I couldn't devote myself to it like I'd done with the truck line. Fortunately, the business did well without me.

"What I'm telling you, Mr. Milton, is that I've got a cashier's check made out to you in the amount of four million dollars. It may not be as much as a winning lottery ticket, but I sure do feel good about the way you earned it. And I want you to feel good about it, too."

Todd extended his right hand, still scarred from second degree burns, and the old man held it lightly. The look in Axtell's eyes was enough to make the reward seem insignificant. For the first time in quite a while, Todd felt like his job had meaning—even if he couldn't remember what he'd done.

*   *   *   *

"We can still polygraph *him*," Rudy Rosser said hopefully, as he stood in front of the Attorney General's desk. "If his termination hasn't gone through yet, he's still technically a state employee, and he has to take the test, or he'll be fired."

"Now there's some real incentive. You're not quite fired, Milton, but you will be fired if you don't take a polygraph test. What's the point, Rudy?" said Boyle, his hands on his throbbing temples. "She *passed*. You were so damn sure on this, but she still beat the box and passed."

"Well...*he* might not pass it," Rudy said hopefully.

"Are you telling me that Todd Milton had sexual intercourse with a woman who *didn't* have sexual intercourse with him?" Boyle asked incredulously. "What? Was she asleep? Or maybe she just doesn't remember it, is that it? As tiny as she is, she probably couldn't take *your* needle dick. It's time for you to go bark somewhere else, Rudy. You're just lucky Freund didn't get his hands on you. You think you're short now, huh? He said he'd pound you into the ground like a tent peg, the next time he sees you."

"What are we gonna do, then?"

"We're going to forget about the whole thing, Rudy. I'm tired of trying to explain Milton's status to the press—"

"I told 'em he was fired—"

"I *know* you did!" Boyle shouted. "That's the problem. That and *you*! Go back to your office, Rudy. Pretend like Andy Freund is looking for you and hide there until I've forgotten *I* even know you."

"My investigation…is it…done?" Rudy asked weakly.

"Your power of perception still amazes me," Boyle replied with a sigh.

✳   ✳   ✳   ✳

"You got me," said Todd, as he unfolded the ringing cellular phone.

"Are you alone?" Natalie asked seductively.

"Well…not really. They've still got the door guarded, but they're a good bunch of cops, and I don't think they'll try to eavesdrop," Todd replied, lowering his voice. "The question is, are *you* okay?"

"Yeah. I am now. Andy and I just got back from Helena-hand-basket, as he likes to call it. It was a little scary last night. Rosser tried the same handcuffing trick Vince did, but I didn't tell him the secret, so he couldn't get 'em to stay on me. He did make me ride up front beside him, though. I guess he thought I'd try to strangle him from behind or something."

"You should have," Todd said cheerfully.

"The stay in jail wasn't so bad," Natalie went on. "It was a first for me, and the officers there were very understanding. I got a good night's sleep in a cell all by myself, and the breakfast wasn't bad, either.

"This morning, Rosser took me out of the jail and over to an office in the same building. I talked to a detective there—a pleasant older man, and he asked me some preliminary questions before they gave me a polygraph test."

"I heard about that," said Todd. "Art Yost, the DOJ division administrator, called me earlier, while I was trying to reach Andy, and he said you'd passed the polygraph."

"That's right—"

"But how?"

"Like I told Andy," Natalie said with a giggle. "I told the truth—or maybe I should just say I didn't tell any lies."

"But…*how*?"

"That idiot Rosser had them ask the wrong questions—and somebody needs to tell him that the word 'fuck' is not an acceptable replacement for the term sexual intercourse."

"But we…haven't done that," Todd said slowly.

"*He* thought we had, though," said Natalie, "and that's the only thing they asked about. See? *You* can pass a polygraph, too."

"I don't think that'll be necessary," said Todd. "When I get back to Montana, I'm not going back to work for CIB."

"Now that I know what you're *not* gonna do," said Natalie, "why don't you tell me what you *are* gonna do?"

"I'm going to devote a lot of time to a woman I met about a week ago," Todd said evenly. "It seems like a lifetime since I last saw her, but hearing her voice when I was down and hurting made me want to get better that much sooner."

"When are you gonna be back?" Natalie asked anxiously.

"A couple of more days, maybe. I can walk, but I won't be running around with you in my arms for just a little while longer."

"I love you, Todd," Natalie said softly. "I never thought I'd say that to *any* man—not after the way Math treated me, but I do mean every word of it. I've had a lot of time to reflect—especially while I was in jail. If they'd asked me on the polygraph if I loved you, rather than if I'd *made* love to you, I would've said yes and passed. If you think you can overcome a constant stiff neck from looking down at me all the time, I'd like spend a real lifetime getting to know you better."

"You know something," Todd said lightly. "I'm feeling a *lot* better, already. I'll check with the doctor, and maybe he can get me released early."

Natalie felt the tears coming, but she couldn't suppress her laughter, either. Todd was warmed by the cheerful sound.

"Don't try to make the return trip with the same airline," she said, catching her breath. "GSG is in a turmoil right now. You'd better get yourself a ticket on a regular passenger flight."

"What about your car?" Todd asked.

"I've already taken care of that," said Natalie.

*   *   *   *

"He said he's never killed anybody," said the United States Attorney, seated in his Atlanta office, "and he's managed to account for his whereabouts during all the cases we've been able to identify."

"I suppose that's comforting, considering the deal you've offered him," said the United States Marshal for the State of Georgia, "but his size is going to create special problems for the Witness Protection Program."

"That's one of those 'cross that bridge' issues we'll address after the trials," the U. S. Attorney said. "With big boy's knowledge of the company practices—and the overwhelming evidence recovered in Massachusetts, there's no way I'll be offering any deals to the GSG defendants. I don't think the public would stand for it.

"On the other hand, there's a good chance I'll retire before the last case goes to court, but at least I don't have to worry about making any *other* plans for the next few years."

"He made a minor request to me," said the U. S. Marshal. "I told him I'd clear it with you first."

"What does he want?"

"Nothing much. He just wanted to check on the status of a former GSG employee. I think he said her name was Weinberg."

"Is she some kind of witness?"

"I don't know. The name didn't ring a bell, but he just wanted to make sure she was all right. Sounded like a…personal thing, to me."

"I…don't see any harm in it."

CHAPTER 9

▼

After making a half-hearted apology to his lieutenant, Gaddis Johnson was rewarded with a promotion to detective second grade—an advancement step that normally took five years and a lot of butt kissing. When the congratulatory handshakes from the chief and mayor were concluded, Gaddis stopped by his desk to finish up some paperwork that had been languishing since he'd met Todd Milton.

On top of the stack of reports, Gaddis found an envelope mailed from Montana, and he forced himself to set it aside, as he went about the more custodial tasks of a detective. It took two hours to clear away the mess, however, and he found himself clock-watching during the last few minutes of his work.

A telephone call caught him at the copying machine, and he dashed back to his desk.

"Johnson," said Gaddis, balancing the receiver on his shoulder.

"Hey, Gaddis," said Todd. "How's the life of a working man?"

"I was just gonna call you," Gaddis replied. "I put together copies of all that crap you said you didn't recover. I thought you'd want it for your Montana report. It fills *five* three-inch three-ring binders."

"I guess I'd better buy another suitcase," said Todd.

"Nah, I'll stuff 'em in a tote bag for you. I think we got some that say SPD."

"I talked to the doctor—" Todd started to say.

"When you gettin' out?" Gaddis asked excitedly.

"A couple of hours—"

"I'll be down there to get you," Gaddis said firmly.

"Thanks, buddy," Todd said warmly. "I'll be waiting."

Gaddis hung up the phone, and he started to turn away from his desk, but the Montana envelope caught his eye. The clock told him he had the time, so he sat down and rummaged through his desk for a letter-opener.

At first, Gaddis didn't recognize the contents. As the sixth of eight children, Gaddis didn't come from a wealthy family, and he'd never paid enough on an automobile to actually *own* one. But there was his name—spelled right and everything—on a Georgia motor vehicle title for a 1996 Porsche 993, signed over to him by Natalie Weinberg.

Not bad for a man who still had eight more payments due on a '92 Ford Escort.

*   *   *   *

Natalie's fingers were busy, and Andy was enjoying every minute of it. From his desk on the ground floor of the courthouse, the sheriff couldn't see the tiny woman who was seated behind the stack of ledger books resting atop the civil desk, but he could sure hear her progress. Natalie was attacking the civil backlog with the same enthusiasm she'd embraced on the firing range.

Andy had started Natalie off with a .357 Magnum, but he'd loaded it with .38 Specials so she wouldn't develop a flinch. The service revolver was just too big for her hands, though, and he'd worked his way down to his backup snub-nose. But even the little 5-shot .38 was more than Natalie could handle. In the end, he'd resorted to a .22 Ruger Bearcat—a kid-sized revolver that was way too small for his burly mitts. In other words, it was perfect for Natalie.

Remembering the accuracy of her early attempts at shooting, Andy just hoped Natalie's speedy fingers were hitting the *right* keys.

"What time's he due to be released from the hospital?" Andy asked from his office doorway.

"Sometime this afternoon," Natalie replied without looking away from the screen. "He said he'd call me, once he knew the flight schedule."

"Are you gonna want to meet him at the airport?"

"Yeaaah," said Natalie, giving him a stern look, "and you're gonna drive me, since I don't have wheels."

"I thought Clarence was workin' on that for you," said Andy.

"He is, but he's having to build another seat bracket, and he took some measurements, too. I think there are a couple of other modifications he needs to make."

"Why didn't you just get yourself another one of those Porsches?" Andy asked. "Clarence already had the stuff he took outa your old one."

"I didn't think a Porsche would be too practical around here—"

"Like hell!" Andy said with a laugh. "We don't have a goddamn speed limit. The Porsche was perfect."

"There's no way it'd make it up that mountain road," said Natalie.

"I guess you got a point there," Andy said, scratching his head, "but I still don't see how you're gonna be able to get up into that Wrangler Clarence's workin' on for you. The tires gotta be three feet tall."

"Clarence said he'd take care of that, too. Now are you gonna drive me or do I have to call a cab?"

"I'll drive. I'll drive," Andy replied with a sigh. "Just tell me where and when."

"The way the flights are set up," said Natalie, "I don't think we'll have to do anything until tomorrow morning. He might make it to Salt Lake or Minneapolis, but I don't think he can get anything into Billings or Bozeman until tomorrow. He said he'd call if it looked like he could catch a late flight into Missoula, and, if that's the way things work out, you can drive me over to his house and drop me off."

"Sounds like you got this all figured out," said Andy, walking up and putting his hand on her shoulder.

"Don't kid yourself," she said, a look of worry in her eyes. "I've never done this in my life, and I'm trying hard not to shiver."

*   *   *   *

"I bet they're gonna charge me an extra baggage fee for those darn notebooks you were so nice to give me," said Todd, as he lifted the heavy gym bag out of Gaddis's new Porsche.

"You can afford it, and don't mention it," Gaddis said with a smile.

Todd offered the young detective his hand, and Gaddis held it tight with both hands.

"Thanks...for everything," said Todd, the uncertainty of the experience still weighing on his mind.

"I'm glad I met you, Montana man," said Gaddis, unwilling to release his grasp. "You be sure to tell that woman a yours how much I like this car. I called her, too, but I think you can thank her a little better than me, if you know what I mean."

"You should've waited until you see what your license plate is going to cost," Todd said with a laugh, "and the darn thing gets worse fuel mileage than my Powerstroke. You might be calling Natalie to beg her to take it back."

"No way, man. It's a keeper."

Reluctantly, Gaddis released Todd's hand, and he took a step back on the airport sidewalk. They stood in silence for a moment, perhaps thinking about the week that had forever changed their lives.

"Don't be a stranger," said Todd, gathering up his luggage.

"I'll be out to do some fishin' as soon as I can get some leave time approved," said Gaddis. "Tell Andy he's gonna have to gut 'em for me. I'm from the city, you know."

"You drive carefully," said Todd, taking a last look at the shiny black sports car.

"Nooooo way," said Gaddis, as he opened the door and dropped into the leather bucket seat. "I'm takin' a trip outa town, just to see what this baby'll do."

Todd watched him drive away, and he could still hear the growl of the turbo-chargers long after Gaddis was out of sight. Todd turned toward the airport entrance doors.

The lines inside the terminal were long, due to the heavy summer travel. It seemed like every kid in Massachusetts and Connecticut was waiting for a flight, and the ones who weren't crying were yelling. Todd decided to take a seat across from the ticket counters to wait for the congestion to clear. Since he didn't even know what flights were available, he wasn't too worried about trying to catch a particular plane.

Not wanting to lug his bags all over the airport, Todd fidgeted for a few minutes, watching the pedestrian traffic. Then he remembered the notebooks, and the copies of the documents he'd never seen. Unzipping the nylon bag, he found the binders, numbered one through five. He pulled out notebook number one.

There were section dividers in notebook number one, separating one case from the next. The top page was an orphan, however, with a note from Gaddis attached. It read:

Todd—

Could not tie this page to anything else–I found it on the ground, so it must have come out of the drawer when you got it out of the house–it is a printout from a Vermont State Police dispatch log, dated September 5,

1994–I called VSP, but they say there is nothing on the page related to GSG–I checked with the dispatcher on duty and she said the calls listed are all routine–sorry, best I could do.

Gaddis

Todd gave the page a careful scan, taking note of the lack of activity. Although there were almost three hours of records on the single page, they all appeared to be related to a one-man patrol unit in the Bennington County area of southwestern Vermont. None of the calls required more than fifteen minutes to resolve, and most of them were concluded with less than five minutes of out-of-service time, but the codes used by the Vermont State Police were not immediately clear to Todd.

Todd returned the notebook to the gym bag, and he checked the directory signs hanging from the terminal ceiling. The rental car agencies were all located in one section of the building, and he carried his luggage in that direction.

*   *   *   *

It was unusual for Art Yost to travel too far from Helena without the excuse of a conference or seminar, but his appearance in Livingston, at the Park County Courthouse, had to be a first. He was making an unprecedented personal visit.

Andy Freund saw Yost walking down the hallway just outside the sheriff's office, and he waited in the doorway for the DOJ division administrator. Andy wasn't about to let his guard down, though, and he made sure Yost was alone before greeting him.

"Hope you're down here to tell me your office is on fire, Art," said Andy, offering his hand.

Yost took it with a pained smile, and he followed Andy into the outer room of the sheriff's office. Andy was quick to close the door behind them. Once inside, Yost was taken aback by the sight of such a tiny woman. At first, he thought Natalie was the daughter of one of Andy's employees, but then he remembered the more detailed description provided by Rudy Rosser.

"Miss Weinberg, isn't it?" said Yost, extending his soft hand.

"Yes," said Natalie, rising to take the stranger's hand—although Yost couldn't tell much difference in her height either sitting or standing. "And you are?"

"Oh, I'm sorry. I'm Art Yost, with the Montana Department of Justice," Yost replied awkwardly. "Uh, at the time he met you, Todd Milton was one of our employees, although his status is still pretty much up in the air right now. Did Todd say anything to you about getting his old job back?"

"I talked to him early this morning," said Natalie, "but *he* should be the one to talk to you about that."

"Yeah," said Andy, watching to see if Yost might break a sweat. "They were too busy talkin' about suin' the AG and DOJ for false arrest. Natalie just hasn't found the right mouthpiece yet."

"I hope that's a joke, Andy," Yost said with a sigh, "but even if it isn't, it doesn't involve me, thank God. I've spoken to the AG, and he's in a particularly receptive mood at the moment. Mr. Boyle has confined Agent Rosser to his office indefinitely, and *I* would like to see Todd return to CIB before Mr. Boyle's mood changes.

"As for me, Miss Weinberg, I want to offer my apologies for any inconvenience the Criminal Investigation Bureau may have caused you. I'm not here to mediate a lawsuit, but I do know when an agency has made a mistake, and I'd like to offer my personal apology, as well. Todd is well regarded by the other agents in the bureau, and I'm sure I'll be expressing their sentiments, as well, when I ask him to continue as our resident agent in Missoula."

"We're going to live here in Park County, Mr. Yost," said Natalie. "I've already met with a contractor, and construction on our new house will begin in mid-July. It won't be as big as The Manor, but it'll be located on the same site."

"When...you say 'we,'" said Yost, "I suppose you're referring to you and Todd."

"That's right, Mr. Yost," Natalie replied. "As soon as Todd returns to Montana, *we* are going make wedding plans."

"But the job market here," said Yost, almost pleading. "It's nothing compared to a growing commercial center like Missoula. I'm sure you could find a much more suitable job over there."

"Who said anything about a job?" Natalie asked.

"Well, you're not really thinking about suing DOJ, are you?" asked Yost. "The State of Montana doesn't have much money."

"No, that was the sheriff talkin', not me," Natalie replied. "Immediately prior to the on-going break up of GSG, I learned I'd inherited a...significant sum, from my previous employer. I've got property right here in Park County, an escrow account set up to pay the taxes on it, and a substantial severance settlement from the company. If you see me doing anything that even looks like work, Mr. Yost, I'll be doing it for fun, not a paycheck."

"Tell me somethin', Art," said Andy, taking a seat on the edge of Natalie's desk. "Who's the richest person you know?"

"Uh, let me see," said Yost, his brow furrowed in both concentration and concern. "I suppose it's that dark-haired actress. Oh, I can't think of her name, right offhand."

"Is it that damn carpet-muncher who protests everything from loggin' to pistol packin'?" asked Andy.

"No, but she's got some kind of animal cause, I believe," Yost said absently. "I think she's trying to preserve the western ground squirrel population."

"Oh, yeah," Andy said with a laugh. "The Gopher Goddess. I forgot about her, but you're right. She does like to throw her dough around."

"And I suppose there was a point to this little exchange," said Yost, looking from Andy to Natalie.

"Sure was, Art," said Andy, putting his arm around Natalie's shoulders. "I'd like you to meet the richest person I know."

*   *   *   *

"Like I told Detective Johnson," said the Bennington Post dispatcher for the Vermont State Police. "There aren't any calls on that page related to the stuff we've been seeing on the television or reading about in the paper.

"This is just a routine bunch of calls—mostly traffic tickets. None of these are felony cases, and the only violators on the list there were released with citations."

"I was just wondering about the codes," said Todd. "Are they all traffic related?"

"Let's see," she said, running her finger down the printout. "Yeah, they're all…no wait. Here's one that's a call for service, but the code is an animal complaint. Like a barking dog or something. But that's the only one."

"Do you know how it was resolved?" asked Todd.

"There *is* a case number," the woman said slowly. "That means a report was written. I can get you a copy, if you want it."

"That would be great," Todd said with a smile.

The dispatcher was a homely girl, but Todd's still-wounded smile seemed to make her move a little quicker. She made a hasty inquiry at a computer terminal, and then she crossed the small reception area to a printer. The report came out as a single page, but she took a moment to read through it, before bringing it to Todd.

"The code doesn't always tell the whole story," she said, passing the report across the counter. "You know who that is, don't you?"

"Yeah," said Todd, taking a deep breath. "How do I get to Pownal?"

*   *   *   *

"Art's not such a bad guy," Andy said, as his eyes followed Yost down the courthouse hallway. "He's about the only one at DOJ I can talk to man-to-man."

"I hated to disappoint him," said Natalie, "but I thought he should know the score. Todd almost got himself killed twice in three days, and for what? Thirty-five grand a year? For that kind of dedication, I'd expect a lot more money. They don't pay you guys nearly enough for what you have to do."

"That reminds me of somethin'," said Andy, walking into his private office. He came out with a paper grocery bag. "I've gotta destroy some evidence in an old case, and I need somebody to witness it. How's about takin' a little stroll down to the basement with me? There's an incinerator down there."

"This isn't like…dope, is it? I don't want to smell the stuff when it burns."

"Nah. You won't get high on this."

Natalie followed Andy down two short flights of stairs, and they entered the boiler room area beneath the main courthouse building. Even in the summertime, there was a fire going. Andy opened the bag, and he reached inside.

"Why don't you give these a toss?" said Andy, passing some familiar VCR tapes to Natalie. She held them with trembling fingers, unable to speak. "Todd told me you'd feel a lot better once these were disposed of. What do you say?"

"So…nobody's seen them?" Natalie asked almost breathlessly.

"Nope," Andy said abruptly. "They've been locked up tight in my office safe since last Tuesday, and I'm the only one with the combination."

Natalie took a deep breath, and she shuffled the four tapes like thick playing cards. They still had the labels Todd had attached to them. Vague labels that gave no real indication of the suffering, the humiliation, and the degradation that were once her life's work. Many times in the past, Matheson Draper had referred to the tapes as works of art, but Natalie didn't feel any pangs of remorse as she tossed them into the flames.

"Todd was right," she said, wiping a tear away.

＊　　＊　　＊　　＊

The driveway was long and a little dusty, but there was still enough daylight for Todd to find his way. There was a pole barn with garage bays, and Todd found a Jeep and a Camaro parked there. The house was a modest affair, mostly one level, with a large upstairs room graced with wall-to-wall windows facing south.

Todd walked up the two stairs to the covered porch, and he rang the bell. He heard movement inside, and then there was a man at the door.

"Come in," said the stranger, turning his back on Todd. "I hope you don't mind, but I wasn't expecting you."

Todd followed the man into a dimly lit living room, and he was offered a seat in an overstuffed chair. The man stood at the mantel of the fireplace for a moment, before taking a seat across from Todd.

"I suppose it's silly to make introductions," said the man, leaning back into a shadow. "I knew you weren't Tony Danzig, and I'm sure you now know I'm not Hank Cotterman. It was a silly ploy, Mr. Milton, and I'm sorry I had to do it."

"You've been out of the public eye for quite a while, sir," said Todd, "but I thought you looked familiar, even then."

"I'm sure it was the work clothes—and the days I'd gone without the benefit of a razor—that helped with the ruse."

"Still, sir, I do want to say it's a pleasure to meet you," said Todd. "I've read about you. I even saw the movie they made about you—"

"Pure drivel," the man scoffed from the shadows.

"After Desert Storm, sir, you were called 'Lightning Bob' by the press," said Todd, glancing about the gloomy room, "but I can't remember your full name."

"It's Robert...Alexander...Latham," he replied almost too softly.

Todd rose from his chair, and he crossed the room at a steady pace, admiring the many frames that covered every available space on the walls. He stood before Latham and offered his hand. The seated man grasped it briefly, allowing Todd to feel a strength he'd only suspected. With a respectful nod, Todd returned to his chair.

"Would it be too much for *me* to ask a question?" asked Latham. "I'm sure you have many questions, and I'll do my best to answer them all, but I have only one question for you."

"Sure, Colonel Latham," Todd said easily, removing the VSP printout page from his inside coat pocket, "but I think this is the answer you're looking for."

Todd crossed the room once again, and he handed the page to Latham. Todd could see the colonel nodding in the shadows.

"As you can well imagine," Latham said with a sigh, "things were a little hectic at that particular moment, and I must've dropped it in my haste. Very clever of you to finish the puzzle."

Latham started to pass the page back to Todd, but the Montanan turned and walked back to his chair. Latham held the sheet up for Todd to see.

"That's yours to keep, sir," said Todd. "Like you said, you must've dropped it."

"I'm…afraid I don't understand."

"I'm not a cop anymore, Colonel Latham," Todd explained. "I mailed off my resignation to the Montana Department of Justice this morning, and my temporary deputy status with Park County came to an end yesterday, when their newest deputy graduated from the academy. You see, I was carrying the badge meant for him, and the Park County budget is a little too tight to afford us both."

"Then…why are you here?"

"Like you said, sir. I still have questions. Maybe not as many as you think."

Latham rose from his chair, and he returned to the fireplace mantel. His years of military deportment were still obvious in his erect posture and squared shoulders. He turned to face Todd, leaning his back against the heavy mantel crossbeam.

"The first thing that came to mind when I saw you, Mr. Milton," said Latham, spreading his arms toward the framed decorations and citations, "is that all this was…for nothing. Only two days ago, I was selecting a burial site in Arlington National Cemetery, and I thought my efforts toward that end were fruitless, upon your unexpected arrival.

"I'm sure grave shopping sounds silly in light of more recent developments, but I was always impressed by the way Audie Murphy's stone was situated. It's no different than the others in the row, except he's at the end of a row. In my mind, he was perhaps the greatest soldier this country has ever produced, yet seeing his simple stone is more humbling to me than visiting the Lincoln Memorial—or even The Wall. He makes me wonder if glory has any value at all.

"I, too, had been given a plot at the end of a row. I don't know if I'll be able to keep it, now, but it was nice to think about for a while."

"Forgive me for interrupting, sir," said Todd, "but now I'm the one who doesn't understand. Why are you so concerned about a spot in Arlington? You're not even…fifty yet."

"And I won't ever reach fifty, Mr. Milton," said Latham. "I have an incurable case of lung cancer. I was never a smoker, but I was married to one for a few years. Secondhand smoke. After all the bullets that seemed to have my name on them as they whizzed so closely by, it looks like I'll ultimately be done in by some foliage from North Carolina."

Todd let his eyes wander about the room, now illuminated by the setting sun. There were photographs of soldiers; some from Vietnam, Kuwait, Somalia, and places Todd didn't recognize. Decorations framed with accompanying citations were too numerous to count.

"I'm truly sorry, sir," said Todd, turning back to Latham.

"Don't be," the colonel said lightly. "I've been fortunate enough to have led a soldier's life. It was all I could've ever asked for. I've fought beside brave men who never grew old. I've lost more friends than any man I know. When I *do* die, there'll be no family there to mourn for me, and that's probably appropriate, all things considered."

"I'm not on a schedule, Colonel Latham," said Todd, "and I've only got two questions, but I think it might take a while for you to answer them. Do you mind?"

"Not at all. I guess…you want to know how I did it, and, of course, why I did it."

Todd nodded slowly, but he made no effort to take notes. He was content to listen.

"GSG is—or *was*—a huge corporation," Latham began. "With over four million employees and a two-to-three percent annual attrition rate, it was easy for me to obtain employment with them under a false name. Once I was working for them, I learned their systems. GSG employees have better travel benefits than commercial airline workers, since GSG flights move more frequently, and I was able to travel easily by having myself shipped from place to place. It's a widespread company practice. With GSG, you're just one of so many seven-digit numbers.

"Tracking Draper wasn't too difficult, either, since he did the same thing. In a way, GSG made it almost too easy for me. Draper had his own private transport aircraft, converted to haul his Mercedes in a special cargo area. Whenever he'd travel, his own employee number would be logged into the system. I suppose it was a way to establish a cost center, but it also left a trail like a slug. Anyone who had access to a company computer terminal could tell when the boss was on the move. He could've easily afforded first class accommodations on a commercial passenger jet to anywhere in the world, but he didn't think twice about the enormous expense of maintaining a private airliner. That kind of wealth can be stag-gering to an ordinary man.

"Learning about Draper's aberrant behavior took me a little longer. He's a man who doesn't write, doesn't read. It would be one thing to say he was an uneducated man, but even the uneducated can be smart. Draper wasn't smart in any normal sense, however, and that's what made my task all the more daunting. That's where you came in.

"But I'm getting ahead of myself. You see I've worked for GSG as Hank Cot-terman for over two years. Employee number 4872511. I didn't plan to work there so long, but the young woman who owns the Porsche you were driving spoiled my plans last summer. I now regard the time I spent last year as a dress rehearsal. It did allow me to perfect my entry and exit, after all."

"You mean you could've killed Draper last summer?" asked Todd.

"Oh, yes, Mr. Milton. I spent two days watching him; watching the degener-ate with the tiny woman he so likes to degrade. I should've killed him then, just to save her the humiliation, but I wanted to be…tidy.

"This summer was much easier. I could tell from the shipping manifests that she wouldn't be joining him at the mountain hideaway for almost two full days. He arrived on Friday in the early afternoon, and her arrival was scheduled for Sunday morning. I actually flew out ahead of him, by way of St. Louis. My only concern was that the fool might recognize me, if we happened to cross paths in Billings. Since I knew where he was going, anyway, I managed to leave before his arrival, in a rented SUV.

"Before he'd even reached Livingston, to pick up Highway 89, I was four-wheeling through the Gallatin National Forest, down to Hick's Park. It took me a little longer than expected to hike cross-country—my health isn't what it was last year, but I found him alone, watching pornographic videotapes. It was still Friday night, a couple of hours before midnight.

"As you can well imagine, I didn't stay long. The hike out was much easier, being more of a descent, and I made a quick call to the Park County Sheriff's Office, before leaving the area for good. Then I was back in Atlanta by Sunday morning, delivering an item to the GSG home office.

"Since I knew that Draper couldn't be personally responsible for *my* loss, I had to see how their corporate officers would react. I had hopes they'd lead me to the person who had 'trespassed against me,' so to speak, but I was disappointed by them.

"That's where you came in—just as you've done today—unexpectedly. I don't know what lead you were following, but it brought *me* to the right door, and I thank you for it. The man's real name was Otto Bach, but he'd been living as Tremain for many years, now. I'd met him once before, in '72. Saigon. Needless to say, he wasn't too pleased to see me again."

"How did you know I was in Springfield?" asked Todd, leaning forward in his chair.

"The tracking numbers on Natalie Weinberg's car," Latham replied. "I listed the number as a 'lost item,' and the mindless automatons of GSG notified me when it was on the move again. At first, I thought it was her, especially when the shipment was given priority over all others, but I picked you up as you drove out of Bradley, and I didn't let you out of my sight until…I guess you'd say *exigent circumstances*…made continued surveillance impossible."

"You're the one who got me out of the house," said Todd, falling back against the cushion. "*You* recovered the file drawer."

"When Bach—or Tremain, as he's now being called—started making his hasty departure plans, he seemed to take a special interest in those files. *He* was the one who removed the file drawer from the cabinet, and he might've planned to burn it with the rest of the house. I didn't wait to ask.

"After I was…finished with him, I took a closer look at the drawer, just to confirm my suspicions. The missing page you found was only a part of *my* puzzle, and I saw the other documents when I made my brief perusal.

"Yes, *I* carried the drawer out of the house, and I went back for you when I heard your cries for help. When I'd first made entry, I didn't see any sign of either of you, and my first thought was that he'd killed you on sight, but I was glad then—and I'm glad, now—to see you're still alive. I would've remained with you a little longer, but the police siren…"

"I understand, sir," Todd said, rubbing his hands together. "I owe you my life, Colonel Latham."

"Nonsense," said Latham. "I should've done more, but I ran like a coward. When I think of how much you did to help me…

"But I'm still a little confused, Mr. Milton. How could you be so certain, from this single piece of paper?"

"The Vermont State Police patrolman wrote a report, sir," Todd replied. "Your dog was poisoned…with antifreeze."

Latham smiled, and he turned back to the mantel. He removed a photograph and carried it over to Todd's chair. Todd held it in the fading light. In the picture, Latham didn't look much younger, as he knelt on the turret of an Abrams tank with his hand on the neck of a handsome German Shepard dog.

"His name was Hans—an easy name to say in a hurry," said Latham. "He was with me in Kuwait, Iraq, and, later, in Somalia. He was the last of a family of good dogs, and I'd always meant to breed him so I could continue to own a pet with his bloodline. But it wasn't to be, and now we're answering the last question: why?

"Back in '94, Draper and I found ourselves on the same late night talk show. I don't know if you caught it, but, apparently, the market share was pretty good.

"Draper behaved like a real cad. There were other guests on the show—an animal trainer, an old character actor, and a young actress who'd made the transition from soft porn to mainstream. We made quite an eclectic bunch, I'm sure.

"Draper was full of himself, and he goaded the others into endorsing GSG. Let's face it, until a few days ago there was no way you could do business without them, and the animal trainer, the young woman, the old man, and even the show's host had nothing but good things to say about the company.

"Then Draper got around to me. That's when I first learned he was a little slow in the cranial vault. I'm a *lieutenant* colonel, and he kept calling me lieutenant, as he pressed me for another free testimonial. But I didn't have one. As a matter of fact, I even had a complaint. I told him—and, as it turned out, a large viewing audience—that GSG had damaged an antique piano I'd had shipped earlier that year. It was the only thing I'd gotten from my mother's estate, and somewhere within the great GSG family—who knows if it was a loading dock worker at one of their truck terminals or someone working for the GSG rail line—the piano was dropped, shattering two legs on a three-legged baby grand.

"My revelation took Draper by surprise, and he offered to pay me off right there on network television. As a result, I was forced to explain the concept of family heirlooms to him, and his reaction didn't make a very good impression on the folks watching at home.

"I learned later that GSG had experienced a seven percent decline in domestic business for the quarter following the show. I'm sure we're talking *billions* of dollars. Who would've thought a few words from a simple soldier could have made such an impact?

"The segment was rebroadcast a few months later, though, and I finally got to see what those former GSG customers had seen. While Draper was bandying with me, the cameraman had zoomed in on the ribbons on my chest. There aren't any other living soldiers who have a Medal of Honor and *two* Distinguished Service Crosses, and the close-up made those little white stars clearly visible on the blue field.

"I guess between that show and the kind people who'd read *One Day From Baghdad*, I'd managed to gain quite a following, and my simple words of complaint were enough to cast a shadow upon perhaps the world's most powerful man.

"There was a rumor that Draper had convinced Saddam Hussein to delay his invasion of Kuwait for six months, until GSG could better insure its oil interests. While the Kuwaiti oil fields burned, Draper was pocketing boatloads of cash, so the rumor could very well be true. Talk about your insider trading...

"It's just a shame Draper didn't have the guts to settle with me like a man, but, just like his hired lackey, he won't be missed. He was so used to stepping on whatever and whomever he pleased, but he never had the good sense to know which of those steps might be a step too far.

"For the record, though, the antifreeze I'd planned to use didn't kill him."

"I beg your pardon, sir," said Todd, placing the picture flat on his lap.

"Oh, I'd had every intention of drowning him in the stuff," Latham went on freely, "but I wanted him to tell me the name of the man who'd carried out his wishes. He never got the chance, though. His heart must've given out. I'm sorry to disappoint you, Mr. Milton, but I'm sure the autopsy will show that a man of almost unlimited power and resources was...*scared* to death."

"Well, I'll be..." Todd said, just above a whisper.

Latham lifted the photograph from Todd's lap, and he returned it to the mantel. He stood there for a moment, before turning back to face the Montanan.

"Do you know what Audie Murphy said of the act that earned him his Medal of Honor?" asked Latham, not waiting for Todd to reply. "He faced a hundred German soldiers and fought them to a standstill single-handedly, killing more men than Murder Incorporated, in a single day of battle. When asked why, he simply said, 'They were killing my friends.'

"Well, Mr. Milton...this dog was my friend."

Todd rose from his chair, and he walked over to the picture on the mantel. He could see from the smudged fingerprints on the glass that the image represented so much more than a fading memory. Todd turned toward the door.

"What will you do now?" Latham asked, giving Todd reason to pause.

"I'm going home, Colonel Latham," Todd said without turning around. "I've been away too long, and I've got other things to do in Montana."

"What about me?"

"What about you?" Todd asked, finally turning to face Latham.

"I didn't kill Draper or Bach for those people on that airplane—or for any of the other people wronged by GSG. I saw some of the things in the file drawer, but I didn't know the full extent of GSG's treachery until it was broadcast on the news," Latham replied. "My reasons were much more simple—more personal."

"Colonel Latham, sir," said Todd, turning to leave, "your reasons are good enough for me."

CHAPTER 10

▼

Andy Freund straightened his tie in the mirror of the airport men's room. He'd arrived with Natalie an hour before Todd's flight was scheduled to land in Billings, and the two of them had dined on the egg salad sandwiches Jeanie had made for their trip.

Natalie gave Andy an approving nod, as he emerged from the restroom, and she walked with him to the gate. Other people were starting to gather there, and Natalie was glad to have Andy as a lookout. She knew she'd be lost in the crowd.

The shrill whine of jet engines signaled the plane's arrival, and those waiting began to mill about in anticipation. Andy pulled Natalie close, and he stood behind her with his hands on her shoulders. If anyone got too close, Andy's sneer would send them on their way.

Thanks to a first class ticket, Todd was the second person off the plane, and he could see Andy waving above the throng. Andy guided Natalie to the edge of the crowd, and she ran up to meet Todd at the gate. They stood a foot apart, their eyes locked.

"I'm so sorry for what he did to you," said Natalie, her eyes welling with tears. "Will it hurt your lips if I kiss you?"

"Let's find out," he replied with a shy smile.

Todd knelt to hold her, and they embraced as the other passengers flowed around them like a midstream rock.

"I've got so much to tell you," said Todd, lifting Natalie easily, "but I hope 'I love you' will do for now."

"I love you, too, cowboy," said Natalie, as their lips came together again.

Oblivious to the milling crowd, Todd and Natalie finally took a much-needed breath when Andy tapped him on the shoulder. Andy canted his head toward the baggage claim area, and Todd nodded in agreement.

"I guess you've had enough of the East Coast," said Andy, giving Todd's scarred hands a closer look.

"I might make one more trip," said Todd, slowing his pace. "There's a funeral I'll need to attend."

Andy's brow furrowed in confusion, but Todd moved on without elaborating.

*   *   *   *

Art Yost let out a long sign, as he slipped Todd's resignation letter into the agent's CIB personnel file. Yost had saved the clippings from the eastern press, and those alone made the file a bit bulky.

The sun was still high in the summer sky, as Yost rose from his desk to leave for the afternoon. He left a note for himself to remind him of the next day's agenda.

For one thing, he needed to find another state agent.

*   *   *   *

Todd sat in the front passenger seat of Natalie's new high-rise Wrangler, and he had to cover his grin as he watched her swap cogs. There was just something about a tiny woman—dressed in tight shorts and a skimpy halter-top—wrestling with a five-speed and a padded steering wheel, while pressing the pedals in bare feet. The sight had an almost musical quality to it.

"We don't need to worry about money," Natalie said, as she led Andy's Crown Victoria out of the airport parking lot. "I got a big severance settlement from GSG, and I also inherited all the GSG property in Park County. I think every cent of my salary went into the bank, and it's been earning interest, and there's even an escrow account set up to pay the property taxes. What I'm trying to say is, I'm rich, Todd."

Todd gave her a knowing nod, and he reached into his coat pocket. He unfolded the check from Lonnie Axtell, and he held it out for her to read.

"Welcome to the club," he said, giving her a pat on the thigh.

*   *   *   *

The unmarked United States Marshal's van sped west on Interstate 20, as if it was trying to catch up with the setting sun. Inside, the broad-shouldered man stared blankly at the three deputy marshals assigned to guard him.

"Where are we headed?" one of the deputy marshals asked the driver.

"*He* doesn't need to know," the driver replied, watching his passenger in the rearview mirror.

*   *   *   *

Natalie's Wrangler had no trouble negotiating the long road up to the lodge, and she and Todd arrived while there was still sunlight on the slopes around them. After Natalie parked the 4X4, Todd carried her up the front stairs to the deck, and he lightly lowered her to the polished hardwood.

"Let's watch the sunset," he whispered. "I'll go get us a blanket."

Natalie leaned on the rail, waiting for his return, as a bald eagle caught an updraft far below. In the distant valley to the west, the Yellowstone River appeared as a vein of silver in the gray shadows.

There were footsteps behind her, and Natalie turned to see Todd dragging a reclining chair out onto the deck.

"I thought we'd be more comfortable," he said, covering the chair with the blanket.

Natalie joined him, and he pulled the blanket over them. It took her only seconds to wiggle out of her shorts, while he busied himself with the clasp on her halter. He held her close, as the shadows climbed up to meet them.

Between long kisses, Todd told Natalie the real story of Draper's death. He'd thought about telling Andy, but he first wanted to see how Natalie might react. He couldn't be sure she'd heard it all, though, since her main interest seemed to be amorous.

Wrapped in the blanket—nestled in Todd's arms, Natalie felt the excitement of their reunion subside, as her needs were satisfied by his kisses and tender touch. The outside air grew cold with the departure of the sun, and the warmth beneath the blanket made sleep beckon.

But then Natalie grew tense under the covers, as a sudden question came to her mind. She pulled the blanket down, so Todd could look her in the eyes. Todd waited patiently for the query he knew would come.

"You mean this was all over a dog?"

THE END

ABOUT THE AUTHOR

Will Cordes was born in Springfield, Massachusetts, and raised in Decatur, Georgia. He began his law enforcement career in the suburbs of Atlanta, where he worked as a police officer and deputy sheriff for twenty years. Will retired as a captain with the DeKalb County Sheriff's Office in 1996, and he then moved to Missoula, Montana to begin working as a resident agent with the Montana Department of Justice. He retired from the Montana DOJ in May of 2001.

During his law enforcement career, Will managed to fulfill almost every goal he'd ever imagined. He was an investigator with the sheriff's fugitive squad, and a sniper on the sheriff's office SWAT team. He was certified as an instructor in several law enforcement disciplines. Will achieved command rank in 1991, and he was able to attend the 170th Session of the FBI National Academy the following summer. While at Quantico, Will was also fortunate enough to fire a perfect score on the tactical revolver course, and he added his name to those of the other few members of the National Academy "Possible Club."

Will has been a member of the Police Writer's Club for many years, and he has written articles for *The Police Times*, the publication of the National Association of Chiefs of Police, and *Tactical Shooter* magazine. He is also a frequent contributor to *The Single Shot Exchange*, a monthly magazine catering to the interests of antique and classic rifle enthusiasts. His first novel, *A Man Adrift*, was published in the summer of 2002.

Will makes his home in Missoula, Montana, where he and his wife, Miriam, enjoy the varied Montana seasons. They share their home with Ty, a feisty French bulldog, and two cats—one named Phoebe Jane and the other undeserving of mention.

0-595-27871-X

Made in the USA
Thornton, CO
03/08/24 17:12:23

368a0754-0b95-476b-a1b0-32ae10e8eddaR01